THE MISSING PORTRAIT

THE MISSING PORTRAIT

a novel

BY

GERALDINE GLODEK

Dartmouth, Nova Scotia

Published by
ECHOLOCATION PRESS
3-644 Portland St.
Suite 143
Dartmouth, Nova Scotia B2W 2M3
Canada

echolocation@eastlink.ca

This is a work of fiction. All names, characters, places, and incidents are either products of the author's imagination or are used fictitiously.

Library and Archives Canada Cataloguing in Publication

Glodek, Geraldine
The missing portrait : a novel / by Geraldine Glodek.

ISBN 978-0-9877565-0-3 (bound).--ISBN 978-0-9877565-1-0 (pbk.)

I. Title.

PS3557.L63M58 2011 813'.54 C2011-907235-1

For

Jeremiah B. Dixon

There is a spirit which I feel that delights to do no evil, nor to revenge any wrong, but delights to endure all things in hope to enjoy its own in the end. Its hope is to outlive all wrath and contention, and to weary out all exaltation and cruelty, or whatever is of a nature contrary to itself. . . . I found it alone, being forsaken. I have fellowship therein with them who lived in dens and desolate places in the earth.

—— James Naylor, 1616 - 1660

THE MISSING PORTRAIT

1

Up da Mine

I'M A RAT. I get to tell the Pennsylvania parts of this tale. Any rat in this town could tell you how Mary Frances McDonald, a Mount of Olives Catlick High School girl, conceived her child in December, 1962.

First, a little about rats. The actual furry, run-around-in-your-cellar kind, like me. The kind that ran around the coal mines, too. From the very beginning of the mines here, back in the 1800s, every rat who valued his life learnt at least one word in many languages—FIRE! Fire's the first word a greenie miner learnt to holler in English. He yelled it into the gangway after setting a charge to blow in a breast, and it got passed along in English, Italian, Hungarian, Serbo-Croatian, Polish, Lithuanian, German, Russian, and a zillion other tongues. As for the rest of the English language, the people here eventually came to speak it with a mix of Irish brogue and Slavic intonations, raising the pitch of one word way up high when asking a question. Most can't pronounce their t-hayches, by the way, since a lot of their mother tongues had no such sound.

Miners were fond of the rats, even shared their lunches with them. Never mind bosses who told them to whack the rats with a pick. Rats, as any miner can tell you, are the most truthful and trustworthy creatures in the world, which is why you can take me at my word when I tell you the story of Mary Frances McDonald and her baby. Miners trusted rats with their very lives, you see, for rats had a nose for deadly gasses and an ear for the slightest shift in the earth. Rats could sense when the teeniest crack in a timber support was about to yawn and the whole post give way. All new miners got the same good advice from the old-timers: "When the rats scram, you scram."

Like the mules, mine rats went blind for lack of light. Some quit the mine while they could still see. Oh, they came back to visit, especially in winter, when the mine temperature was a lot warmer than the world outside. They liked swimming with their kuzzints in the rusty water in the ditches alongside the narrow rails where the mine cars ran. Some rats couldn't stand the drip drip drip from every crevice. That's another reason they got out besides for the sake of their eyes.

Some moved to Butternut Creek which runs through the small town of Mount of Olives and extends out to the western coal patch of Coneysville. It isn't a real crick, but a dug-out stream with a boulder wall on each side. It was once an open sewer system but, thankfully, as far as the rats are concerned, despite all efforts to make it just another pretty Pennsylvania trout stream, it will probably smell like sewage forever. It's always had little brass plaques on some stones, saying "Butternut Creek." But the local people aren't dumb. They may not be too adept at pronouncing their t-hayches, but they know a shit crick when they smell one. And so that's what they call it, the Shit Crick. "Butternut, my eye," they say.

By the 1950s, some kids had .22's, and the crick rats, of course, were their targets. Their tell-tale tails, dragging as they scrambled to hide between the stones, always gave them away. Some who survived the bullets high-tailed it over to the next patch, Otterdale, where our Mary Frances lived. There's a real crick down behind the long back yards of that one-street patch, just at the foot of the slagpiles, which are great hills of black rocks discarded from the mines. But, sad to say for the rats, that crick just isn't home. It smells like columbine and sweet fern. A good thing about Otterdale, though, was the leftover outhouses, so it's not like there was no relief.

Now, back to Mary Frances McDonald and her baby. She conceived the child in the former United Mine Workers building on Bloke Street in Mount of Olives. "Da Mine," as the locals called the place, was a three-story brick structure turned dance hall for teens. To get to the top floor, her and datdare Dolan's boy crossed the long dance floor to the stairs, walking on opposite sides of the room, pretending not to be going upstairs together. On the second floor they had to sneak behind the back of Jack Nash. Nash was a commuter sophomore at Bloomsburg State College. He was spinning forty-fives on a record player wired to speakers down below. His only light was a bendy-neck lamp atop a stack of flipped-over beer crates. He was sitting on a metal stool at a card table. Oh, he knew that duo was tiptoeing by, all right, but he didn't let on. They wouldn't be the first, wouldn't be the last.

Hand in hand, they worked their way to a tiny, windowless room, where a pull-down stairs was waiting. Once they reached the attic floor, where all the lights were out, Dolan's boy slid a piece of sheet metal over the floor opening so nobody would accidentally fall down the steps in the dark. The floodlights at Tom Collar's gas station across the street lit up the white ceiling and cast a faint, milky light in the front part of the room.

"Watch you don't trip over the barbells," Dolan's boy warned.

The barbells and other training paraphernalia belonged to a kid from Black Hollow. The kid had been training for the Olympics. From the rhythmic clanking of metal and the strained breathing, you could tell that someone in the shadows was helping himself to the kid's equipment.

Dolan's boy went over to the window and stood with his hands in his pockets, looking out.

Mary Frances stood in the center of the room. "Where?" she said. Her tone was meek, her voice soft, like she was talking in church. "Where do you want me?"

A boy came to her from behind and slid his arms around her. He squeezed her tiny little tits and kissed the back of her neck. "Right here's good," he whispered, backing her up and easing her down onto the kid's push-up mat.

Mary Frances turned her face away from the window. She closed her eyes and pretended she was only ten years old and in the House of Mirrors at Willow Grove Park near Philadelphia. She relived the night she skipped ahead of her grandmother and lured the poor woman smack into a clean glass panel that didn't lead to a passage after all. So immersed was Mary Frances in that memory that she almost giggled at the sight of Gram's nose squooshed against the glass, her curly gray bangs flattened and bunched like a steel scrubby. But that did not spare her from noticing there were four boys giving it to her up there on the kid's mat. Not like what Dolan's boy had told her. He said there'd be three, himself included, no names for the others. But there were four, one after another, done within two Elvis songs, one by the Shirelles, one by Stevie Wonder, and one by Mary Wells. Seconds afterwards, the boys were zipping up and predicting a win for Mount of Olives High by two touchdowns as they headed back down to the dance.

Dolan's boy turned back and poked his head up once through the trap-door hole. "Watch you don't trip over the barbells," he said. Then he went downstairs.

So, what the hell. Who's to say who the father was? And what could Mary Frances do but hide out in "wunna demdare Homes," as they called them with a wink, during the showing months, and give the child up?

The Home her mother drove her to, far away, and far into the night, was only for girls who signed in advance to give their babies up. The one mirror in the place was so tiny and positioned so high on the wall that all a girl could see of herself was her neck and her head. The intent was to keep the little fools from pondering their big bellies. Less to forget later. As you can imagine, a girl never got to see her child either. Mary Frances never even got to see the little slimy, purplish foot kick straight up the second the child was pulled loose from her body. The doctor, a broad-shouldered man bent below the blue sheet draped over her knees, did a handoff to a nurse, her hair teased and sprayed into a helmet, who pivoted and ran the squirming bundle three yards through the square arch at the end of the birthing room.

2

Filthy Rumors, That's All

After twenty-five years in the navy, our Mary Frances is back in the Coal Region, hoping to find out what became of her child. She's got plenty of questions, but her mother, Joyce McDonald, isn't doing any talking.

Joyce still lives in Otterdale. This is the mining patch with the nice-smelling crick down behind the long yards. There's only a single string of houses separated from the two-lane by a narrow street and a green. A dirt alley splits the patch into equal halves. On the lower end are ten small coal company duplexes—"halfa-doubles," the locals call them. On the upper side of the alley are four single homes once occupied by families that ran the huge colliery beyond the workers' houses. The colliery, reduced to one crusty concrete building and foundations packed with weeds, shut down around 1955.

It's winter now and Mary Frances is cruising along the two-lane, observing her mother's house, a humble halfa-double next to the center alley. The snowplow has made a swipe down the front street but the alley is drifted near up to the top of the fence pickets. Joyce's old blue Chevy has been cleared of snow. Mary Frances, instead of making a right turn into Otterdale, turns left into the cemetery on the hillside. She takes the horseshoe drive around the life-sized statue of an executed Jesus in his mother's arms, exits the cemetery, and pulls into the lot at the Otterdale Fire Company. Looking down across the snowy green, she's annoyed at the sight of her mother's cleared-off car. It's plain that her mother's been up and around, has even driven someplace and back. Just isn't answering her phone—that's the game.

Mary Frances walks to her old home, knocks on the front door, and sticks her head in. "Mom? Mom, it's me." She's smacked by the smell of plastic as she stamps snow onto the brown carpet sample and removes her boots. A clear plastic runner covers the burgundy carpet all the way through to the dining room. New clear plastic coverings, stitched onto the flowered chair and sofa, have replaced a set of brittle, yellowed ones.

"Mom?"

"I'm upstairs, Mary Fran. I'll be right down."

On the wall shared with the neighbor are twelve eight-by-ten school portraits of Jack, Mary Frances's older brother, who died in a drag race back in the 60s. These portraits from Grade One to Grade Twelve are arrayed in rigid rows like military graves. The other walls have dozens of photos of him in all sizes. There's Jack in black and white, napping on a baby blanket on the floor, Jack pulling a toy duck by a string, Jack riding a tricycle, Jack bouncing a ball. There are color photos of Jack flashing his first driver's license from the seat of a white Studebaker, Jack hosing down the car, Jack at the Bloomsburg Fair, handing little Mary Frances, seen from the back, the kewpie doll he had won for her at the cork shoot. His green eyes are full of mischief.

There are no pictures of Mary Frances on the walls. Portrait photos of her are crowded together on the maple coffee table. The one of her as a new Navy recruit towers over her eleven school portraits, one short of the usual dozen. There is none for eleventh grade, which would have been taken in September of 1963 had she started the school year on time. But no, she was having a baby. The absence of the portrait is cunningly downplayed by the random placement of the others.

The eyes on the girl up to Grade 10 are a child's eyes, full of curiosity, trust, and a sensible dose of doubt. In those, Mary Frances wears a Catlick-school uniform, a white blouse and plaid vest. The senior portrait is a girl all fancied up, her hair teased and sprayed into a stiff beehive. For that, students did not gather assembly-line style in school and get plunked down in front of a plaster wall. No, for these final portraits, individual appointments were made at a professional photography studio. Mary Frances remembers going behind a privacy screen to strip from the waist up to don one of the six strapless bras laid out. The photographer's assistant, Mrs. Gromyko, came in holding a blue chiffon wrap, chattering indecipherably with open safety pins between her front teeth as she draped the wrap onto the customer and tugged it into place, leaving Mary Frances's skin bare from the neck to the edge of her shoulders.

It isn't just the chiffon drape that makes Mary Frances's senior portrait stand out on the coffee table. No, it's more in the eyes. They are eyes that have seen things not seen by the eyes of the girls in the plaid uniform. They have a tinge of bitterness and despair. Looking at this collection of school pictures now, Mary Frances wonders if her mother still rattles off the same excuse to anybody who notices, despite the mish-mosh arrangement, that there are only eleven. The whole county can recite the excuse for the missing portrait: the poor girl broke her leg at her aunt's house in Vermont on the last day of August and couldn't get back to Pennsylvania by the day the school pictures were taken.

"Mom?" Mary Frances calls out again.

Joyce McDonald, holding a wicker basket with crumpled white sheets, appears in the archway. A sturdy woman with a square build, she has a jolly face and green eyes like both her children, only with the brazen mischief seen in so many of her son's photographs. Her gray hair, short and tightly curled, stinks of a new permanent wave. She grins. "Well, I'll be. Our Mary Fran, back in town." She sets the basket at her feet and spreads her arms.

Mary Frances, leaning over the basket, gives her mother a hug. "Happy New Year, Mom. A week late, but, cheers!"

Joyce, swinging her out to arm's length, looks sideways at the boots by the front door. "You came in through the parlor door," she says, wagging her finger. "Didn't you, you rascal?"

"I couldn't get to the kitchen door. The side yard was full of snow all the way through to the kitchen porch. How 'bout a shovel? I'll clear the walkway for you."

"No, no, I have a boy coming to shovel it. Come sit down," she says, gesturing toward the dining room.

"Still no sitting in the parlor."

"Never. You know that. Don't tease, now. So tell me, are you out of the Navy, Mary Fran, or just home on leave?"

"Out. Retired after twenty-five years." Mary Frances recalls telling her mother all about that when she returned home in early December. She does not remind her.

"And did you just fly in? Where was it, Philly? Harrisburg? Over here, sit." Joyce pats the arm of the tan sofa in the dining room, catching her imitation ruby birthstone ring in the tatted doily. Her fingers tremble and tangle with her daughter's when both women try to free the ring. The doily drops to the floor. Joyce, elbowing her daughter aside to pick it up, shakes her head. "I don't know what's the matter with me. I'd drop my own head if it wasn't attached. So which was it, Mary Fran, Philadelphia or Harrisburg where you flew in?"

"Philadelphia. December 7th." Mary Frances sits down on the couch, facing the profile of her mother in the brown vinyl recliner, which faces the television. "Mom, I have to ask you something. I know it's not your favorite topic, but— But can we talk about my baby?"

Joyce says, "December 7th you flew in. Pearl Harbor Day. You know, your father was near sent to Hawaii on datdare *Arizona,* the ship that took the worst pounding."

"Yes, I heard."

"You'da never been born if they hadda sent him to Pearl Harbor. I was just pregnant with our Jackie then, when your father was sent to the Mediterranean instead. Or was it Japan? Let me think. And then I had those two miscarriages between our Jackie and you. Five years apart that put you and him."

"Mom, I checked the state registry in Vermont. There's no record of me there. No record of me or my baby. It wasn't in Vermont, was it? I had my baby somewhere else, didn't I?"

"Of course, it was Vermont. Say, let me run down the cellar and throw these bedclothes in the washer."

"Couldn't that wait a few minutes?"

"No, I need to get them started. I won't be long." Joyce takes the basket down to the cellar.

"Patience, patience, patience," Mary Frances chants. She sits looking about the dining room, noting that the furnishings have not changed since her high school days. Like most Coal Region homes, the dining room has no eating table. It's a sitting room. In the corner, just past the other end of the couch, is the triangular china cabinet that holds "the good dishes," the ones that get used only on Thanksgiving, Christmas, and birthdays. It holds pieces of china collected from the days when the State Movie Theater existed in Mount of Olives. Movie goers got a rose-patterned plate, cup or saucer with each admission in 1957. Mary Frances notices that the butter dish and two cups, saucers, and dessert plates are missing. Recalling the doily falling onto the floor, she wonders if her mother has dropped and broken them.

Joyce returns from the basement, grunting as she settles into the recliner. She pushes down the side handle that raises the leg rest with a hardy thrust. "Where's my glasses?" Joyce says. "It's getting so I forget everything these days. Can't find my glasses. Can't find my teeth. What next?"

"Maybe you left them in the kitchen. I'll go look," Mary Frances says, leaning forward, starting to get up.

A look of panic flares up in Joyce's eyes. "No, no, don't! I don't need them unless I'm reading or watching a show. Sit, sit."

Mary Frances frowns and sits back.

Joyce puts on a bright smile. "Like my new perm?" She tugs on the bangs. They spring back into little corkscrews.

"Nice. Just have it done?"

"This morning. There's a girl down the next patch just opened a beauty shop. She's very good. Holly, her name is. The names they give kids these days. Why, in the old days, you wouldn't dare approach the baptismal font without a saint's name. The priest'd throw you out on your ear."

"Maybe I'll try Holly. I'm back here a month and haven't gotten around to finding a hairdresser yet. A whole month I'm back in the Coal Region, Mom."

"And look at your hair. Still straight as a poker. Red as a robin's breast. No gray yet. And you're still such a tiny little thing."

"They keep you pretty fit in the Navy. But I'm out a whole month already. A whole month I've been around, Mom."

"Is that right? Well, I'll be!"

"On Christmas I told you about the corner house I rented, remember? Over in Black Hollow? Same block we used to live on. A halfa-double. The Howards still live on the other side of the wall. I told you all this on Christmas. Don't you remember?"

"Was it Christmas you were here?"

"I was here on Christmas. And a little before. I helped you bring the decorations down from the attic. Remember I said I'd help you haul them back up? I've kept trying to call to see when you wanted it done. I see you got it done." Mary Frances lets out a sigh. "Mom, don't you ever answer your phone?"

"Yes, that nice boy, Rick Trounov, carted all the boxes up for me. He helps me a lot. So how long till you're out of the Navy?"

"I'm done. Retired. I got out on December 7th."

Joyce smacks herself on the forehead. "That's right. December 7th. Pearl Harbor Day. You know, your father was near sent to Hawaii in 1941."

"Yes, on the *Arizona,* the ship that took the worst pounding by the Japanese. Mom, please, can we talk about my baby?"

"You were in the Navy a long time."

"Twenty-five years."

"And now you're out and moving next door to the Howards. How are they these days?"

"Fine. They're fine. Mom, don't you ever answer your phone?"

"When I can get to it. I'm near seventy. Not as fast as I used to be."

"No, I guess not. Mom, do you ever listen to the messages on your answering machine?"

"When I remember. And if I can figure out how to work the darn thing."

"Whose voice is on the answering machine?"

"Rick Trounov's. You know that nice boy that does odd jobs for me?"

"I saw him once or twice when I'd come home on leave. That nice boy must be thirty by now."

"Hmm, I suppose he is near thirty. But wait till you see him." She turns to the front door, beaming. "He's coming by this morning to shovel snow and put a new clothesline up for me in the cellar. He still looks like a teenager." Joyce sighs through a wistful grin. "You know, that boy puts me in mind of our Jack. So lively he is. A real talker. And comical, too. Just like your brother was."

"Mom, Mom, Mom."

A flash of anger drives the merry spark from Joyce's eyes. "Don't mom me! If our poor Jack wasn't in the car with that good-for-nothin' Dolan's boy! Drag racing down that sinking Centralia highway, coal mines under it everywhere. Road rising and sinking like a, a—Where were that Mickey Dolan's brains? I mean before they were spread all over that highway like cottage cheese. That's what everyone said. Like cottage—"

"Stop! Please!"

"That Dolan's boy wasn't worth the room he took up. Outa high school and still drag racing."

"Our Jack was too, Mom. He was even a few years older than Mickey. And he got in Mickey's car of his own free will."

"Our Jack'd be rolling over in his grave if he heard you blaming him for the whole thing. Your father, too. You'd have the two of them rolling over in their graves."

"I'm not blaming Jack."

"Indeed you are. And you stick up for that good-for-nothin' Dolan's boy after— You of all people! Why, he's the one led you up those stairs, I heard."

"What stairs?"

"No stairs. Filthy rumors, that's all."

"There were stairs. Way at the back end of the dance floor up the Mine. Mickey and I went up those stairs together and—"

"*Went* up? He *forced* you up those stairs, you mean."

"No, Mom."

"Oh, honey, you've listened to so much dirty gossip it's twisted your own memory. Let's drop it right now. Like I told you on Christmas, why stir things up? That was over twenty-five years ago. You were just a girl. Let bygones be bygones."

Mary Frances notices that her mother does remember the Christmas visit after all. "My baby's not a bygone. My baby's still alive somewhere. I hope so, anyway. I'd like to meet my child. Was it a girl or a boy? I don't even know that much. Do you know?"

"No." Joyce grips the arms of the recliner as if she expects to be electrocuted.

"Why did you tell me I had the baby in Vermont? Why did you lie?"

"I didn't lie. I drove you there myself. You remember."

"In the night. And you brought me home in the night. I laid down in the back seat, blindfolded, the whole way. You had construction paper taped over the windows. I couldn't see a thing."

"You agreed to that. We both agreed it was better not to be reminded of the child you gave up every time you drove along those highways. That was the best way. It was better to see as little as possible. Less to forget later."

"I can't forget. And it wasn't Vermont. I checked the state registry, I told you. I contacted every unwed mother's—"

"Can't you just call it a Home?"

"I contacted every Home that existed in Vermont in 1963."

Joyce, lowering the leg rest on the recliner, says, "Let me run down the cellar, make sure the washer hasn't stalled. Ricky will have that new clothesline up and there'll be nothing to hang on it."

"Stalled?"

"If it went off balance."

Mary Frances wraps her hand around her mother's fingertips. She closes her eyes and speaks softly, "Please, Mom. Stay up here and talk to me."

Joyce flicks her daughter's hand away. "And have that nice boy walk in on this dirty talk?"

"I'll stop my dirty talk the second he knocks on the door."

"That's the thing. I told him not to bother knocking when he's got some little job for me. Just come right in." Joyce twists around and looks at the parlor door apprehensively.

"The parlor door? You let him come in the parlor door?"

"He's doing me a favor. I can't ask him to traipse through the yard to the kitchen."

"Let's talk in the kitchen, then." Mary Frances stands up.

Joyce grabs her sleeve. "No, don't! I'll call you later."

Mary Frances remains standing. "Okay. I won't talk about the stairs I went up with Mickey Dolan, about what went on at the Mine. Just tell me what I need to know to find my baby. You're the only one who knows, the only one who can help me. Let's go where Rick won't hear us." She crosses the dining room and stops abruptly under the archway leading to the kitchen. "Holy cow!" she exclaims. The table is set with the good china—two dessert plates, two cups, two saucers. There are jars of different jams. On the china butter dish is a stick of real butter, the waxed-paper wrapping nudged slightly open. Sitting on a cutting board is a loaf of fresh bread covered with a tea towel. Mary Frances goes over and presses her hand on the towel. The bread is warm.

"The bread's from that new bakery up town," Joyce says. "I've always liked Barker's. And the Hollywood's, too. But they had a coupon for this new place in yesterday's paper. So I thought I'd try it."

Mary Frances picks up a cup. "The special china. Somebody's birthday?"

"No, just a little treat for Ricky. I'll pay him for the clothesline. But he won't take a penny for the work. That's how he is. Ricky's such a lively boy! Like our Jack was. A real talker! And comical, too."

"Don't you think he might have some other jobs to go to when he's done here?"

"That's enough outa you, little girl! Why begrudge me a little company? With your father dead going on forty years. Our poor Jack killed so long ago by that good-for-nothin' Dolan's boy. You, off to the Navy—what did you say—twenty-five years? Did you expect me to sit on my thumbs all by myself for twenty-five years, waiting for you? After you left me here to fend with the filthy rumors?"

"I thought I was sparing you. I thought the talk would die down soon after I left and you could show your face again."

"Well, it didn't. For years people whispered. In the supermarket. In church. In the unemployment line. There wasn't a street in Pennsylvania where I could show my face. I tried not to let on I heard. But I heard. I heard the whole story. And I don't mean just you and Dolan's boy up on that top floor of that old United Mine Workers building. They shoulda never sold that place for a dance hall after the union left. I heard, don't worry. About you. About Dolan's boy. About the herd of other boys was up there with— It was like— Never mind."

"Like what? Tell me."

"I won't repeat it."

"Like the father could have been anybody? Like I was up there with so many boys that night that the father could have been anybody?"

Joyce looks at the parlor door again. "I don't want that poor boy walking in on this filthy—"

"Okay, okay. I'll stop back tomorrow."

"So you'll go then? That's a good girl." Joyce gets Mary Frances's coat from the chair in the dining room and shoves Mary Frances's fist through one armhole. "You can go out through the parlor this time. The snow, you know. The back porch and yard are full of snow. Don't worry. Ricky'll have it shoveled out in no time. I'll call you. Don't be upset with me. I just don't want to be all upset myself when Ricky comes."

So much for the Pennsylvania parts of this tale for now. I'll be back, don't worry. I'll be back.

3

A View into the M-WIT

THE MAINE HOTEL FOR WOMEN IN TRANSITION had once offered a lively view of the harbor at the bottom of the steep street—wharves with stacks of lobster traps, dockside fish-processing plants, the green and red lights on all the little lobster boats and big trawlers easing out at dawn and returning to port pursued by clouds of clamoring gulls. Now the three-story hotel, called the M-WIT by the locals, was continually mooned by the backside of the twelve-story Harborview Inn, a popular place for conventions and trade shows.

The T-shaped lounge of the M-WIT stuck out over the sidewalk. The west wing, looking out at the stately portico of the Colonial School of Art, had a kitchen so tiny that a woman stirring a pot at the stove could be whacked by the door of the fridge behind her. The east wing still offered a remnant view of the waterfront, but to get to the window, a resident had to kick a path through boxes of discarded clothing free for the taking. From that window, a woman got to see slivers of water between old warehouses, which had been vamped into offices and fancy boutiques. She'd see a little of the Maine Iron Works eight blocks away, its red light blinking day and night atop the crane, and an old Navy destroyer bobbing alongside the dry dock.

Stripped of their former view, the women at the M-WIT got ogled by guests at the Harborview Inn. The only protection from the eyes across the street was a row of fat, white window slats hanging vertically. So skimpy was the privacy they afforded that the women seldom bothered to close them. Some slats were missing. Some, snapped short, left big spaces above the sill. Yellowed with years of kitchen grease, they hung like a mouthful of broken, dirty teeth.

Now and then the residents were treated to a view of a naked male posing for them at his suite window at the Harborview Inn. After a few futile calls to the police, the women kept a big flashlight handy. While one woman shined it on the exhibitionist, everyone made a show of pointing and doubling over with laughter till the man shrank back. A nasty mood would then creep up in the lounge. Sometimes a hard silence would reign, sometimes impatience and snappy remarks, like, "How much longer you gonna hog that stove?"

In Suite 419 of the Harborview Inn, Ray Moleski, a trade-show participant from Mount of Olives, Pennsylvania, was setting up for a party in his spare room. Formerly a track star who had moved like lightning, Ray shuffled about gingerly at the age of forty-five, fussing with high school mementos on a table by the window—photographs, ticket stubs from football games, prom tickets, yearbooks from the early 60s. When he tired of rearranging them, he stared into the M-WIT lounge.

The lights over there looked brighter as the winter daylight faded. Ray could see women from late teens to seventies on the U-shaped array of blue couches, watching television with plates on their laps. Others were eating at tables stuck end-to-end along the windows. Ray tried to pick out the young redhead that had caught his eye during last year's trade show. He was sorry he'd told his old high-school buddies that she was a Mary Frances McDonald look-alike, only a lot bigger, a whole lot bigger, and twenty-some years younger than Mary Frances. In his mind it was a passing remark. To them it was the one attraction that could convince them to join him for a party in an icebox like Maine. A few glasses of wine, Ray figured, and they'd waste the first evening going on about Mary Frances, reminiscing about the big bang upstairs at the Mine. Maybe waste the whole visit trying to get at her look-alike across the street.

Ray's door burst open and Ned Miller, followed by two buddies, made airplane noises as he zoomed a two-foot plastic lobster around the room and brought it to a landing on the table with the mementos. He let out a big whistle. "Check this out! Ray went all out for us. Look at this stuff! Four years at Mount of Olives High right before our very eyes!" Ned, five-foot-four, spent long hours in the gym. When he was fourteen, failing to recognize the grace of a true wrestler, he built up his body and prepared himself for team tryouts by practicing a menacing gorilla-like walk and making fierce, darting eyes. In three years of tryouts, he never made the wrestling team, but the ape-like ways remained with him.

He picked up a framed photo. "Here's all five of us, that time we painted the window of the Barker Bakery for the Halloween art contest. We came in second place, h'aint no?" Ned thumbed through a yearbook. "Hey, looka. September, 1960. All five of us mixed in with four rows of other freshmen in front of that oak tree in the town park. Looka. There's me. There's you, Ray, and you, Tim, and you, Shitfoot. And there's Bruce the Moose on the Loose. Now looka this next yearbook. Sophomore year, same scene, all five of us in with our class in front of the same oak tree. Junior year? No Bruce. Where's Bruce?"

"Redshirted," Shitfoot said. "You know damned well he was redshirted The coach never passed along a rising star like Bruce. Kept him three years in tenth grade. Best fullback Mount of Olives ever had. Where is Bruce anyway? I thought he flew in with you, Ray."

"Napping next door," Ray said, pointing a thumb at the wall to his right.

Ned pounded on the wall with both fists. "Not for long, he won't be. Yo! Bruce! Get up!"

Bruce came through the door with tousled hair and dark circles under his eyes. Ned's greeting was a shove in the chest. "Hey! Bruce the Moose on the Loose! How ya doin'?"

Bruce, a huge man with a shy, childlike grin, shrugged. "Still kicking. Managing my dad's old box factory back in Mount of Olives. Married with five kids. How 'bout you?"

"Oh, I got a desk job in the big city. I'm not crazy about it, but I'm making big bucks. Got three kids who have to have the latest everything."

While the others bestowed back-slapping greetings on Bruce, Ned looked through some more yearbooks. "Hey, take a look at our senior portraits. Jesus, Tim, look at you, same hair. Don't you ever change it?"

Tim Giovannini's blond hair topped his narrow skull like a shoe brush. "I had a long ponytail in the late sixties. Remember? Oh, that's right. You were in Vietnam. You didn't see it." Tim glanced at the roll-in bar. "Got anything to drink, Ray?"

"Drinks. Right. What's the matter with me?" He set several kinds of wine on the bar. "Pick your poison."

Ned looked across the street into the lounge of the M-WIT. "Hey, Ray, where's this Mary Frances McDonald look-alike you promised? That is the place, datdare hotel, right?"

"I didn't promise. I said I happened to see a girl who looked like Mary Frances when I was here for last year's trade show, that's all. I don't even know if she still lives there."

"You don't even know if she— Thanks a lot!"

A look of irritation crossed Ray's face. He poured himself more wine and sat down.

"Do you think it's Mary Frances?" Shitfoot asked.

Ray exchanged a look with Bruce, the only other one of the five old buddies living back in Mount of Olives these days. The look signaled a quick joint decision not to mention that Mary Frances had just moved back to the Coal Region. Ray shook his head. "No, too big. I told you she was two heads over Mary Frances, and a lot heavier. Couldn't be more than twenty-five or so, not our age."

"Besides," Ned said, "our Blessed Virgin Mary Frances is back in town, asking around about the little bambino she had. That's what my mom told me. So she can't be living here in Maine."

Tim Giovannini sat up with a start. He wanted to shake every detail out of Ned. Where? What street in Mount of Olives? What does she look like now? He got up and paced in silence, stopping at the bar to refill his glass. He tried to make himself sit back down, but couldn't. He tried to think of an excuse to go back to his room and phone his sister Betsy. Find a way to slip some questions into the conversation without sounding overly interested.

"Maybe that young look-alike is Mary Frances's kid," Shitfoot mused. "Wouldn't that be something!"

"All the way up here in Maine?" Ned challenged.

"Why not?" Shitfoot, finally taking off his imitation Russian *shlyahpa,* revealed a balding head. The inside of the hat was caked with the tan powder used to avoid a shine on a theatre stage. "They say the kid was born in Vermont, practically next door to Maine. That's the story her mother gave when Mary Frances sat out the first few weeks of her junior year, remember? Only she said Mary Frances was up there at her aunt's farm in Vermont, mending a broken leg."

"Hey," Ned said. "Wanna hear something funny? My mom goes to the same church as the Avon lady now that the town is down to two Catlick churches. Anyway, after Mass one Sunday—you know how the parishioners all gather on the sidewalk and shoot the shit?"

"Yeah," Ray said. "Gossip time."

"Well, the Avon lady tells my mom she stops at Joyce McDonald's one day in Otterdale, wanders into the parlor, and sees the famous coffee table. All of Mary Frances's school pictures crowded together and mixed up with one Navy picture. Just for fun, she counts the school pictures out loud. 'Seven, eight, nine, ten, eleven.' Now, of course she knows why there's only eleven, not twelve. Everybody in Northumberland County knows why the McDonald household is short one school picture of their Blessed Virgin Mary Frances. Before the Avon lady goes out to the kitchen and spreads her lipstick samples out, she says, 'Gee, there's only eleven school pictures of Mary Frances there.'

"And Joyce falls for it. She goes on and on about Mary Frances's summer vacation at her aunt's in Vermont and the broken leg. Same story she's told since the sixties. Next time the Avon lady comes back, Joyce steers her right to the kitchen table. But the Avon lady wanders into the parlor again anyhow. And she acts like she just discovers the eleven school pictures on the coffee table for the first time. And guess what. Joyce gives the same spiel about the broken leg. The Avon lady gets the same rise out of Joyce McDonald every time she comes to the house."

"Nice Avon lady," Ray said, topping off everyone's glass. "Surprised Mary Frances's mother still lets her in. Maybe the town's down to one Avon lady, too."

Ned scowled at Ray. "Aw, it's just a joke, for Christ's sake. She's just having a little fun. If Joyce McDonald can't take a joke, tough shit for her."

Ray answered in a flat voice. "Somebody ought to report her to the home office."

"It's a joke, I told ya! Jesus, Ray! What, you turning into a fussy old man already? Lighten up! So, about this baby. It was born right here in New England. Vermont. Close enough. Could be that Mary Frances's kid grew up here in Maine. Ends up in a place like datdare Heartbreak Hotel, or whatever it's supposed to be across the street over there. Oh, well, an illegitimate kid. Whaddaya expect?" Ned laughed. "And so now the Virgin Mother is back in town. Lookin' to see if anyone can help her find her kid. Not even the least bit concerned about how she's embarrassing her mother. Evidently, she plans to stick around. My mom says she moved into a house in Black Hollow."

"Get the hell out," Shitfoot said.

"It's true. They say she's still a little bombshell. Hey, Shitfoot, you're a lawyer. Do a little legal digging. Help her find her kid. You might get some little rewards along the way. Wonder if she'd go for a baldy like you. Or you, Tim. She's bound to be impressed when she sees you haven't lost one bristle from that golden flattop of yours. Maybe you can lure her to, what is it, Nowhere, Illinois? Sell her one of your classic cars. Get her in the back seat. Got any Edsels in the lot? You can take her on a sentimental journey."

"As a matter of fact, I've got two Edsels. But I'll pass on your idea. Shitfoot can catch up with Mary Frances. I'm not interested."

Ned chuckled. "Not interested. Right, right." Ned went to the window and peered into the women's hotel again. "Holeeeeee shit! Looka, looka, looka! Two lezzies on the couch over there. Two little chubby one's watchin' TV. The blondie sneaks a lick of the other one's ear. Hey, anybody got binoculars? I gotta see this!"

Tim took a pair of opera glasses from his pocket and handed them to Ned. "Woooo-weeeee!" Ned squealed. "Looka. That dark little stringy-head likes it, too. Looka how she grins when the blondie does it. Hey, there's a few good-looking ones wandering around over there. Hope they're not all lezzies. Anybody else want a look?" Ned held the opera glasses out, suddenly noticing what they looked like. "Jesus, Tim, where'd you get these dainty little binoculars? You steal them from Tinkerbell?" He bounced them in his hand.

Tim ran his hand across the bristles atop his head. "Careful with those. They're opera glasses. That's real ivory and gold. Just—just be careful, okay?"

"Okay, okay. Cripes, who'da thought one of us would turn into an opera fan?"

"I hate opera," Tim says. "Those little beauties are only woman testers. I don't leave home without them." He took the opera glasses from Ned and put them into a white leather case.

"Woman testers?"

"That's right. Here's how they work. I see a good-lookin' girl, twenty-one, twenty-two. I'm a little older, but good-lookin' and loaded with money, so she's game for me, too. I'd like to take her out. To a nice place, I mean. Not some dump. She's dressed to kill. But how do I know she's not some pretty little lowlife with one classy dress to sucker in some sugar daddy like me?"

"Okay, so where do the opera glasses come in?"

"Patience, Ned. Stand right there and pretend you're the girl. Hello, there. How are you today?"

"Fine."

Tim stroked the white leather case. "Nice weather." Slipping the opera glasses out, he wiped the lenses with a handkerchief, passing them before Ned's eyes several times. "It's going to be a lovely evening. Would you like to go to the opera with me? Now, see, Ned, if your eyes are bulging at the sight of the opera glasses, I know you got no class, never been anywhere nice. Don't even know what these things are. But if you say casually, 'Sure,' like operas are old hat to you, then you're in my league. I sit through another godforsaken opera. Then I take you to some classy place where I can show you off. And then, late in the night, I get you alone and—bang!"

"Better you than me. Sit through an opera just to get a piece? I'd sooner a roll-in-the-hay with wunna demdare down-and-outers across the street in exchange for a burger at a drive-through." Ned grabbed the opera glasses from Tim's hand and scanned the lounge at the M-WIT some more. "Actually, there's a few over there in decent clothes and decent haircuts. What kind of place is that anyway? Can't be a battered women's shelter. Too public." Ned saw a tall, heavy red-haired woman turn the corner from the hall into the lounge. "Wo! I think that's her, that Mary Frances look-alike you promised, Ray. Whoooo-weeee! Look at her, big as a fridge! She could swallow Mary Frances whole! Well, that rules me out as the father."

Tim, unable to contain himself, took the opera glasses. "I'll be damned. Almost a carbon copy. Damned good-looking, if you could shrink her down to size. Some broken leg. Looks to me like it keeps on swelling."

Ray said, "You guys laugh. She may be huge, but notice how she moves. Like a dancer. Pretty graceful, if you ask me."

Ned snatched the opera glasses back. "True, true." Tim gasped as Ned tossed the opera glasses to Shitfoot. "Here, Shitfoot, don't you want a look?"

"Sure." He watched in silence for a while. "Yep, a carbon copy. And, yeah, she does move like a dancer. Carries that bulk like it's a feather. I'd say that rules me out as the father. Cripes, I'm so clumsy I tripped over my own luggage this morning."

Ned laughed. "You? You're ruled out anyway, Shitfoot. You weren't even there that night up the Mine. It was just me, Bruce, Ray, and that idiot Mickey Dolan. You and Timmyboy here both missed out."

"Granted. I can dream, can't I?"

Shitfoot held the opera glasses out to Bruce, who was sitting at the bar with his back to the window. "Here, Bruce, want a look?"

“No, thanks.” Bruce’s shy, boyish smile was gone. His big frame was hunched over the bar, and he jiggled his glass, whirling the wine in a circle.

“Sheeze,” Shitfoot said. “What’s the matter with him?”

Tim took the opera glasses and watched the red-haired woman leave the lounge and disappear into a corridor on the left. A light went on in the last room on the same floor of the M-WIT. “I could use a shower,” Tim said. “I’ll be back in a bit.” He walked down to the stairwell at the end of the hall and looked across the street through a window on the landing. He watched the woman grab a colander, a box of rigatoni, and a jar of sauce. Then she turned her light out. Tim went down to the hotel lobby and asked to have his room changed to the last one down the hall. He hurried to the center stairwell and stared into the M-WIT lounge, where he could see the young woman re-emerge from the west wing, holding a large metal spoon and watching TV from behind the blue couch.

“Hey, Sharon,” one of the women said to the woman Tim was observing. “I hear this is your last night here.”

The stove timer buzzed and Sharon drained her rigatoni. “Yep. Another two-year stay gone by already. But remember, six weeks out and I get to come back in for another two years.”

“That’s right. We’ll leave the light on for you.”

“Thanks!” Sharon took her plate over to the enamel-topped tables along the big windows. “I’ll definitely be back.”

A woman around fifty came shuffling into the lounge from around the corner. Sharon immediately pegged her as a newcomer who arrived in the middle of the night and hates where she’s ended up. She was dressed in one of the half-dozen loaner outfits, this one the size-six tan slacks and loud orange blouse printed with coins from around the world. The woman turned her face toward the lounge wall as she crept between the sofas and the bookcases behind them. Her left cheek had the yellow-green tinge of a fading bruise. Her left eyelid, half swollen shut, was the color of red wine. She was hugging a can of clam chowder and a pot.

Sharon, sensing that the woman did not want to be noticed, made a point of turning toward the window. Tim ducked to the side. Sharon looked down to the ground floor of the Harborview Inn and watched the banquet staff clean up the appetizer table. Guests, mostly older men in business suits, many accompanied by young women in shape-hugging dresses, began sitting down at tables covered in red cloth and decorated with vases of yellow roses. As the final remains of the appetizers were carted away, plates with colorful meals were set down before the guests.

A few minutes later, the M-WIT's resident assistant, Kate, an energetic woman of thirty, came into the lounge with a black plastic tray as big as a super-size pizza. "Surprise!" she sang out. "From the banquet manager at the Harborview Inn!" No one was surprised to see the tray of leftover appetizers. "Julie and Trish, how 'bout running downstairs to the front desk. There's more. Say, Sharon, since this is your last night here, let's call this a going-away party."

Sharon blushed. "Yeah, but you know I'll be back. Six weeks out, then I can come back for another two years. You know I'll be back. I came back last time, and the time before that, and the time before that."

"Maybe you'll find your own place this time," someone called from one of the couches.

"Naw, nothing I can afford. Anyway, all my friends are here. I'll be back."

Kate set the tray down in front of Sharon. In the center, drying pink dip was curling away from the sides of a plastic bowl. Stumps of celery looked seared on the ends. Baby carrots, covered in green crumbs, were skitter-scattered like a log jam among shrubs of broccoli.

Kate beckoned with a big, rolling motion of her arm, "Okay, everybody, dig in!"

Tired, sock-footed women rose from the couches and dug in. Men watched from suites and stairwells across the street.

4

The Vigil

SHARON SLAPPED THE BUTTON DOWN on her wind-up alarm clock and propped herself up on her elbows. She smirked at the array of junk she'd have to pack or pitch—empty soda cans, used tissues, cosmetics—things everywhere, on the tile floor, on the nightstand, on the counter that ran wall-to-wall along the windows. The sleeve of an orange sweater hung out of a drawer under one end of the counter. A white sock and a huge bra dangled from a drawer under the other end.

She sneered at the familiar smell of urine reeking in the hot, dry air. Her pissy nightgown was sticking to her like tape. Sliding her feet to the floor, she peeled the wet flannel from her calves, stood up, jerked the nightgown over her head in one swift tug, and flung it onto the floor. "Big, fat, piss ass," she muttered at her image in the long mirror on the closet door. She covered herself up with her blue terrycloth robe and thrust her nightgown and wet bedclothes into a black plastic bag, the urine smell belching out as she strangled the bag shut. "Big, fat piss ass."

Gathering her soap, towel, shampoo, and toothbrush, Sharon walked briskly down the narrow hall toward the bathroom, her black flip-flops slapping her heels. The wall to her right was discontinued at the lounge and picked up again twenty feet later. Sharon slowed down so she didn't leave a wake of piss smell. "Good morning," she called out as she walked along the edge of the lounge, where a series of windows looked down into a courtyard with stone benches, a small tree and a few bushes. Sharon, noting the ice gripping bare branches like sheaths of glass, reminded herself to dress warm. The smoke of burnt toast found its way up her nostrils from the kitchen. She turned and saw that the new woman, now dressed in the loaner robe of pink terrycloth, was shooing the smell of burnt toast out of a small jalousie window pane with a dishtowel.

"Sharon!" hollered Eileen, who was doing yoga on a mat along with a television instructor, "what time do you have to be out by this morning?"

"Ten."

"Where you going?"

Sharon shrugged. "I'll figure something out."

"When you coming back to visit? You can stay in my room. Two bucks a night for a spare rental cot for up to three nights."

"No visits allowed."

"You're kidding."

"Nope. So no use bothering with a visitor's cot for me."

Jeanette, crouching on a couch with Tolstoy's *War and Peace,* said, "There's no such rule. They told Sharon that because they don't have an army cot that will hold a cow with ten-ton teats." Jeanette's blond curls jiggled as she laughed at her own wit. "Yeah, she'll be back the very second her six weeks out is up. She's got her very own hourglass stamped on her left hand there to tell her exactly when she can come barreling back here."

Sharon blushed and shoved the strawberry birthmark into the pocket of her robe.

Eileen, propping herself up on her elbows, said, "Go piss up a rope, Jeanette."

Jeanette stretched out, holding her book high in the air. "Tsk, tsk, tsk. Truth is something the women in this scruffy place do not like to ponder. Actually, they do not, for the most part, have the brains to do so. The M-Witless."

"I see *you're* in this scruffy place," Eileen said.

"In transition. I take the name seriously, the Maine Hotel for Women in Transition. I'll be out as soon as my new apartment's painted. It's up on the east end beach, by the way, with a full view of Skull Bay. Meanwhile, I'm not watching sitcoms and reading trashy magazines like the rest of you bottom feeders. Now take that newcomer over there in our beloved one-size-fits-all pink terrycloth robe. I'm the only size-six in here who has not worn that ratty thing.

You can see by her manicure she won't be long for this place. And the rings. She'll be moving on quickly like me." Jeanette closed her book and said to the woman in the pink robe. "Honey, I advise you to get the hell out of here as soon as you can, somewhere other than home, from the looks of that shiner you got there. Furthermore, if I were you—"

"Well, you're not me, so fuck off!" The woman threw salt on her eggs and took her plate to her room.

"Yes," Jeannette continued, "the new woman will be out of here in no time. Now, as for Miss Sharon there, I predict she'll be here through the next fifty blue moons with her little six weeks out every two years."

Sharon backed out of the lounge and went to take a shower. Afterwards, taking a yogurt cup filled with water to her room, she made a paste of baking soda, which she smeared all over the vinyl mattress cover before removing it and stuffing it into a plastic bag. She raised the blinds and pushed open the jalousie panes at the bottom of the four tall windows. Then she put her roll-along black suitcase on the bare mattress and began packing her clothes.

This activity was not lost on Tim Giovannini, who was watching through his opera glasses from his room at the Harborview Inn. He watched Sharon take down seashore posters till the cinderblock walls, their pores crusted over with sand-colored paint, were as bare as badlands, save for a small mirror near the counter. Tim panicked when he saw her flip the bottom half of the mattress toward the head of the bed, leaving it doubled. "Act fast!" he exclaimed. "She's moving out!"

The flip of the mattress, like a signature on a document, released Sharon from struggling with having to leave. She was done here. She shrugged and pulled the jalousie panes shut. Then she hauled the garbage bag of wet things down to the basement laundry. By ten o'clock, she was out the front door in her lime green coat and yellow tammy. Her green-and-yellow plaid backpack hung from her right arm. She set her suitcase near the door, walked under the steel canopy to the curb, and made a visor of her hand like a scout. Then she pawed the insides of her backpack till she pulled up a pack of cigarettes. She smoked two, taking long, slow drags.

Tim took the elevator downstairs and watched Sharon from the lobby. He stepped outside when he saw her work her arms through the straps of her backpack and step out from under the canopy. She stood at the curb, looking perplexed. She smiled up at the dazzling sight of tree branches covered in ice and began her departure from the M-WIT, her suitcase following like a loyal mutt.

A woman poked her head out of the M-WIT and shouted, "Good luck, Sharon!"

"Thanks! I'll need it."

"Sharon," Tim whispered. "So her name is Sharon."

Ahead of Sharon was a man who looked like he was bowling, a street worker tossing blue grains of ice melt from a plastic five-gallon bucket hanging from his left arm. The grains crunched under Sharon's boots. Tim gave her a half-block lead, staying across the street, matching her pace. The worker with the ice melt turned the corner. Sharon continued down Spring Street, shuffling along the icy sidewalk.

She fondled the snowberries on a leafless bush alongside a parking lot. She petted a calico cat on a car roof. She pulled out some brittle brown weeds from under the guard rail between the parking lot and the sidewalk. Then she moved on. An old woman grabbed Sharon's arm during a near fall on the icy handicap incline at a street corner. The two walked arm-in-arm, talking about the weather, till they reached the cobblestone streets of the Old Port. The brick buildings, trimmed with carved wood of colonial patterns, housed expensive boutiques and souvenir shops. Across the street from where Sharon and the woman stood, a small crowd had gathered on the corner in front of a bronze statue of a man stooping down and putting bands on the claws of a lobster. A herring gull was perched on the statue's head. The group of women, men, and three children stood in silence, their eyes fixed on the ground.

The old woman squinted at the sign they had propped against the bronze lobsterman. "What's that say? War—war does, does not—does not what?"

“Bring peace,” Sharon said.

The woman waved the back of her hand at the silent group. “Hey, how ’bout you walk me across to the Green Mountain Coffee Roasters, and then we’re done, eh?”

“Shoo-uh,” Sharon said, dropping the “r” like the home-grown New Englander she was. She guided the woman across a small plaza where three benches and a few trees stood behind the lobsterman statue. Sharon cupped the woman’s elbow at the coffee shop door, easing her inside and stepping back. When the door closed with a whoosh, Sharon felt abandoned at the threshold. She sat down on a bench till she began to shiver.

A woman in a puffy green parka came out of the coffee shop and walked toward the silent protesters, stopping to ponder their sign. Then she slipped in among them and stared silently at the ground like them. No one from the group looked at her, nor at the three teenage boys who joined in a few minutes later. Sharon, blushing when passersby glanced at her shivering alone on the bench, went and stood at the back of the group of protesters. Tim came from across the street and stood beside her. The vigil soon ended with handshakes. A woman from the group stepped out and faced the others. “Good morning, everyone. I’m Linda, clerk of the Vine Street Friends Meeting. ‘Quaker’ may be a more familiar name to some of you. We have unprogrammed worship every Sunday at ten at our meetinghouse on Sixth and Vine. You’re all welcome. While the war on Iraq continues, we also have silent worship on Wednesday evenings at 7:30, and we’ll be holding a vigil here on this corner every Saturday from 9:30 to 10:30. Right now, some of us will be going for coffee at Green Mountain Coffee Roasters just behind the lobsterman statue here. Feel free to join in. By the way, as most of you know, Vice-President Quayle will be in Portsmouth, New Hampshire, on Monday evening, hoping to stir up support for the war. We have two vans of protesters going. Let us know if you need a ride.”

Tim stepped forward to face Sharon. “You going for coffee?”

"Me?" Sharon pointed to herself while looking over each shoulder to see if the man meant someone else.

Tim smiled in an especially kindly way. "Yes, you. Everyone's welcome. Come and join us."

"So you're one of these Quakers?"

"Yes," he said. "Well, I'm just visiting Maine, so I'm not part of this group, but yes, I'm a Quaker." He was able to tell that lie while looking into Sharon's eyes with steady admiration.

Sharon had to look away. Not until she thought of something to say could she look at him again. "Oh, so you can tell me about this unprogrammed worship then."

"I can, but first I have to tell you, I couldn't believe my good luck when I saw you standing here. I recognized you instantly."

"Me?"

"You. Sharon. Oh, yes, you're Sharon, the picture of your mother."

Sharon chuckled, shaking her head fast. "Ho! Nah, nah, not *my* mother. My mother's this, this—" Sharon thrust out her hands and made the outline of a slim, shapely female. "Yeah, she's tall, but more like—well, she's not a giant, like me. Buddy, you got the wrong Sharon."

"No, I don't think so. The red hair, eyes the color of catnip like your mother's."

"My mother's hair don't stop traffic. It's dark brown and, well, for all I know it could be gray by now. Maybe not. I don't think she's even forty-five yet. It's straight, too. When she walks the beach, it doesn't frizz in the salt breeze, like mine. And her eyes are brown, not some weird shade of seaweed washed up on a mucky beach, like mine. Boy, do you ever have the wrong Sharon!"

"No, Sharon, you have the wrong mother. Your mom's a wonderful person from Pennsylvania. Red hair, green eyes like yours. Kind and thoughtful."

"Kind and— Don't you think I know my own mother? Get this straight. My mom is a bitch, and she grew up in Lewiston-Auburn, right here in Maine. Look, I gotta go."

“Sharon, wait, please. Didn’t you ever wonder if you were adopted?”

“Sure. Half the women where I live wonder that. Seems our real moms and dads would have treated us a lot better.”

“In your case, I’m sure that’s true. You couldn’t find a nicer person than Mary Frances McDonald.”

“I think I’ll pass on the breakfast. Thanks anyway. I gotta go.”

As she started to walk away, Tim followed. “Please, you said you wanted to know more about Quakers. If there’s one thing anyone can tell you about Quakers, it’s that they don’t lie. I’m telling you, Sharon, your real mother is a woman named Mary Frances McDonald from a little coal town in Pennsylvania. She’d give anything to find you.” Tim Giovannini backed away, toward the coffee shop. “Take some time to think it over. I’ll be at the Quaker worship tomorrow at ten o’clock. Sixth and Vine. If the worship’s not your thing, you can meet me outside on the porch afterwards, at eleven-fifteen. We can talk more about your mom. Only if you want to, of course. My name’s Howard, by the way. Howard Parker. Maybe I’ll see you tomorrow. Have a nice day.”

5

Purple Triangles for the Night

THE GUY'S A CRACKPOT, Sharon thought. Me, the picture of some beautiful mother in some Pennsylvania coal town. He's probably an escapee from P-6 at Maine Med.

Still, the idea of a real mother who'd give anything to find her grabbed her fancy, a mother who would have loved her no matter what, who would love her from the moment they met if they were to meet now. "Oh, don't be an idiot," she chided herself. "Big, fat piss ass." She walked to Colonial Street and stood outside the library, debating whether to kill the morning or the afternoon in there. She saw a very small person with a greasy gray coat, head thrust deep in a trash can, hand holding up the hinged dome cover. Bits of trash were flying up over the rim and onto the sidewalk. A head bound in a black woolen scarf popped up. It was a man with a whisker-stubbled face, windburned and bright with pleasure at something just fished out. "Ho, there, Sharon," the man said, "look what I found. A camera. The film's not even used up. It says there's twenty-four shots. It's on nineteen only. And here's a purse. And a wallet. Nothing in the wallet but a driver's license and some other junk. No money. Here's some prescription pills, same name as the driver's license, Jane Williams. No credit cards. Whoever snatched the purse already got those."

"Lucky you, Bill. You can take it to her house and get a reward."

"Not me! Last time I tried that I ended up in the clink for stealing it. I got an idea, though. Let's finish off the film. Then I'll get it developed, keep my pictures, stick her share and the camera in the purse with the pills. Throw the whole shebang in the library book drop. Let them get the purse back to her. Okay, take my picture, will you? Over there by the Victory statue. I'll pretend I'm a proud Civil War soldier."

"Sure." Sharon waited for Bill to cross to the Victory statue on the triangular brick plaza in the broadened area of Colonial Street. Victory, seen at a profile from where Sharon was standing, was a massive, robed, female figure holding a shield in her left hand, a sword in her right, its tip on the stone pedestal. Pigeons, no respecters of honor and posterity, strutted across the big bronze feet. On the sides of the pedestal were life-sized figures of sailors and soldiers. The heads and shoulders of all were piled with stiff snow. A herring gull perched on the head of Victory looked down upon the frozen city. Bill, taking his place among the Civil War heroes, held an imaginary rifle.

"Ready, Bill?"

"Yeah. Shoot!"

Sharon snapped a picture. "Hey, let's take another one someplace over here." She looked about and saw the man from the Quaker vigil approaching. She waved him on. "Hey, Mr. Quaker, would you do us a favor?"

"Certainly."

"Take a picture of me and Bill."

"Certainly. Where?"

Bill crossed over from the plaza. "How 'bout here by this treasure chest," he suggested, patting the trash can where he'd found the camera. "Or better yet, in here behind the iron bars." Bill walked through the gateway leading to a small sitting area between a high wrought-iron fence and the stone building housing the library. In that area was a stone bench, a white birch tree, and a bronze figure of a little girl with a basket of apples. "Come on, Sharon, let's pretend we're in jail," Bill said, gripping the bars.

Sharon came around and gripped the bars, suggesting, "Let's look mean and tough."

They put on tough faces. Tim snapped their picture.

Bill winked. "And now, a picture of me and you stealing apples." The bronze little girl stood high on a pedestal. Bill and Sharon, donning sneaky expressions, stood on each side of her. Bill had to stand on his toes. Even then his fingertips barely touched an apple in the little girl's basket.

"Hey, Bill," Sharon, said, "know a good place to take pictures? I do! Let's go in that Unitarian Church down the street. There's a cannonball stuck in a chandelier in there from the Revolutionary War. You can climb up on my shoulders and point to it. And Mr. Parker here could take our picture."

Bill scratched his head, confounded. "A cannonball! In the light fixture? You don't say!"

"Cross my heart and hope to die," Sharon said, carving an X across her chest. "First time I had to do a time-out from the M-WIT, it was still tourist season. I took the city tour of old churches. I saw that cannonball with my own eyes."

Tim wondered what a time-out from the M-WIT was.

"Woo!" Bill said. "That must be one hell of a strong chandelier!"

Sharon punched his arm. "No, you dope! The cannonball didn't hit the chandelier. It hit the building. When they fixed the building, they put the cannonball in the chandelier in memory of that battle."

"Oh. Well, don't waste your time going there. Or any church. They're all locked. I tried them all this morning. Me, I'm gonna hang out in the stores, get warm. I'll take a little siesta in the library later. The shelter don't open till eight tonight. Whatever I do, I gotta be on my good behavior. Stay on my meds. I just got out of P-6 again."

"Yeah?"

"Yeah, and they said next time I went off my meds I was in for a long, long stay in some inland joint. Sons-a-whores. They know I'd sooner be dead than live away from the sea. And stupid me, I was dumb enough to tell that to one of their shrinks. Now they got me by the balls." Bill gave the camera a loving pat. "Well, thanks to this little baby I'll have proof I'm living a normal life, proof I'm staying out of trouble. I'll have pictures!"

Sharon threw her arm around Bill. "That's right, Bill. You tell 'em!" She took out her wallet. "Hey, I want to be part of your defense team. Let me spring for the cost of developing the film." She offered him a five.

"Great! Thanks! What about you? I see you got your suitcase. Another time-out from the M-WIT, huh?"

"Yeah. Six weeks. Then I get to go back. I hope I get my old room back."

Bill raised an imaginary beer mug. "Here's to getting your old room back."

Sharon met his toast. "Cheers."

Bill stuffed the five into his pocket. "Maybe I'll see you later. My toes are numb."

"I have some extra cash, Bill. I've been sorting donations at the Salvation Army for eight years now. Let's cross over to the Victory Deli. I'll treat you to a muffin and coffee."

"Naw, no thanks. I just had a pack of crackers. Catch you later."

Sharon watched Bill walk past Longfellow's childhood home, a plain brick house with narrow, tall windows and shutters and a plain lawn. He skirted around the new bank next to it, a big building of shiny blue squares that protruded to the very inner edge of the sidewalk, casting a sharp, angular shadow over Sharon and the poet's little lawn. Jabbed by loneliness at Bill's departure, she crisscrossed her arms over her chest and squeezed her upper arms.

"Excuse me, Sharon," Tim said, gesturing with an open address book, as though he intended to call someone listed in it. "Is there a telephone nearby?"

"In the library. Take the elevator downstairs. The phones are in the hall between the periodicals room and the children's library."

"Thanks."

"You're welcome. Oh, and thanks for taking our pictures."

"Any time." Tim went into the library and found a good spot to watch Sharon from.

Sharon towed her suitcase across the street to a convenience store. She slapped a buck on the counter. "One tic-tac-toe lottery ticket." Using a dime, she rubbed off only one of the silvery coatings, revealing an X in the upper right corner. Then she put the scratch ticket into her coat pocket.

Tim watched her go into the Victory Deli next door and sit at a window table. He took out his opera glasses, chuckling at the thought of trying those little woman testers on Sharon, sure she'd never owned anything worth more than ten bucks. He pictured her passing flat out at the sight of the opera glasses, creating a crater that would put the moon to shame. Yet he looked through all the fat, disregarded the big-boned frame, and he drooled over the beautifully chiseled profile of little Mary Frances McDonald. This Sharon McNobody, he thought. She's not going to get up from that table and just walk away. She's going to talk to me. If not today, tomorrow.

Tim went outside, walked around the block, then crossed to Sharon's side of the street and ducked into the Surplus Store two doors up from the Victory Deli. He came back outside in an army camouflage jacket, brown knit cap, and a pair of sunglasses. He stood on the street, pressing the store bag, which held his black overcoat, against his chest. He kept stamping his feet to keep from freezing.

Sharon took her time eating a muffin and drinking coffee as she read the help-wanted ads. She decided she could manage on what she made at the Salvation Army store twenty-five hours a week. She pulled the scratch ticket from her coat pocket, but put it right back, deciding to make herself walk six blocks between each scratch to stretch out the game. Something to do till lunch time.

She went out, pulling her suitcase. Tim followed. Keeping a block's distance and ducking into a doorway here, an alley there, he took out his opera glasses, which he cloaked with a handkerchief he coughed quietly into now and then. At first, he gazed with curiosity as Sharon paused to drink in sights. She even stroked things—bare, brittle bushes, drooping tree branches. She stopped and smiled at the sunlight shining through the veins of a composting leaf impaled on the point of a wrought-iron fence. She stooped down, took off her left-hand glove, and let the shadow of the leaf fall upon the back of her hand, watching the pattern with a look of fascination. The light fluttered on her strawberry hourglass. Sharon turned her face upward and smiled a childlike smile, as though some kind person had just put a bandage over a wound. She moved on, petting every stray cat. She whistled to little birds in trees, cawed back at crows.

She was starting to get on Tim's nerves. Maybe the freezing air didn't faze her, but the wind was stinging his face. Why the hell didn't she stop dawdling and get the hell wherever she was going? Tim noticed that she stopped every so often and took something from her pocket, a notebook, he imagined. She always did this at an intersection. Writing the street names down, he figured. He did the same, noting the street names in his address book. The duo walked up and down and around the streets of Harbor City, switching directions at random corners.

By noon the temperature had risen to nineteen. The wind had died down to two knots. Sharon had circled back to the business district and walked through the Old Port, pulling her suitcase along the brick sidewalks leading to Long Wharf. A small white ticket booth stood padlocked at the beginning of the dock. Behind the booth was a brown dumpster. A woman with purple sweatpants and a black jacket was climbing out of it. "Hi, Sharon," she said.

"Find anything good, Tina?"

"Not like in the tourist season. Man, when those tourists come down the gangway from that tour boat in the summer, it's can after can after can. Look at this." Tina stretched open a black plastic bag. "Only three deposit cans and one bottle."

About halfway up the dock was a supply shack the size of a refrigerator. Its white boards were bright and warm-looking in the early afternoon sun. Mist rose from the wet dock planks. Sharon pointed to the shack. "I was just about to sit up there and have my lunch. I have lots. Appetizer stuff left over from the Harborview Inn last night. Want some?"

"Oh, man! I'm hungry as hell. Cold as a son-of-a-bitch, too."

Sharon pulled two plastic garbage bags from her backpack and spread them out on the dock. "Let's sit on these. Keep dry. I have one of those little car blankets, too. We can cover our legs." The two women leaned against the shack. Sharon ate slowly, stretching out the day. Tina, a woman with a thin, pointy face and quick, squirrel-like motions, tried to slow herself down. "Why do you eat so damned slow, Sharon? God!"

"Nothing better to do. Might as well take my time."

"You make me feel greedy."

"You're not greedy. I'm just slow. And you're wicked hungry. Eat. Eat as fast as you want. As much as you want. I'm not that hungry. I just had a muffin. I'm thirsty, though. Got anything to drink? Beer, wine? Gin, anything! I shoulda bought some last night, but if they catch you with booze at the M-WIT, you're thrown out for a year. So *do* you?"

"What?"

"Have anything to drink?"

Tim circled around some cars in the neighboring parking lot and positioned himself behind the shack. He listened to everything, hoping to hear where Sharon was headed.

"A little brandy," Tina said. "It makes me feel toasty. Here." She pulled a bottle from her pocket and passed it to Sharon, who took a swig and sighed. "Now that's what I call a friend. Thanks."

Tina shook Sharon's suitcase "Where you off to?"

Tim got his address book ready.

"I'm on another time-out from the M-WIT."

"Oh. Think you'll get your old room back?"

"I hope so."

The women ate in silence, till Tina said, "Don't you hate those damned, fancy-ass condos on those wharves over there?"

"Yeah. Speaking of greedy, now that's what I call greedy. A bunch of rich jerks bored with their fancy neighborhoods, pushing out the lobstermen, ruining the whole look of the waterfront."

"Yeah," Tina seconded, "and they don't even live in the damned things in the winter. I heard the owners are mostly from Massachusetts. Mass-holes. And some hotsy-totsies from New York. When they are here, they crab to City Hall about the noise of the lobster boats going out at five in the morning. It's a working waterfront, for God's sake!"

Sharon giggled. "Don't worry. I get back at them in the summertime."

"How's that?"

"Well, the captain of that little wooden tour boat, the *Longfellow,* he lets me ride the last ride of the night for free 'cause sometimes I help catch the ropes when the deckhands try to fling them over the pilings and miss. There's three old guys who play music on the last tour. Accordion, bass fiddle, and banjo. The condo people hate it when they come back playing at midnight. They crab to City Hall about that, too."

Tina hummed a sad, lethargic tune while pretending to play a violin.

"Anyway, Tina, the music on the last tour is the sing-along kind, stuff like my grandmother taught me. Boy, do I sing along, loud and clear. Just as we're pulling back into the slip at 11:55, we hit the condo creeps with 'The Pennsylvania Polka.' That really irks them!"

"Why would that song irk them?"

"The words, the words. Picture some poor little rich bitch sound asleep in her silk jammies. Suddenly she hears, 'Strike up—the music!'" Sharon belted out the first verse for Tina.

"Hey, Sharon, ever think of being a singer? You sound pretty good."

"I sure have. All my life. A dancer, too. My mom got it in her head that I was gonna be a dancer. That's the only thing I think we ever agreed on. She wanted me to be tops! Like she was before she took up with my dad. She even auditioned in New York and got in with a chorus line. Boy, did that turn out to be a disaster!"

"What happened to her?"

"Me. She got pregnant with me, and that was the end of her dancing career."

Tim wrote in the back of his address book, "Mother, dancer, pregnant, ended career. Sharon wanted to be singer and dancer."

"What happened to you, then? You said your mom was gonna make a dancer out of you."

"Let's just say my career ended at the age of nine. That was it for me and my mom, too. We were enemies after that. Maybe someday I'll tell you about it. Not now."

Tim wrote, "Sharon ends dancing career at age nine. Mother and daughter enemies after that."

"Speaking of Pennsylvania," Sharon said, "I met this guy from Pennsylvania this morning."

"Yeah?"

"Oh, stop! I don't mean a guy guy. Some fuddy-duddy business guy. Or maybe a lawyer. Who knows? Not like us, anyway. He says I'm the spitting image of some beautiful woman in some Pennsylvania coal town. And she's really my mother."

"No shit!"

"Cross my heart and hope to die."

"Well?"

"He said she's been searching for me, and he could get us together. I figured he's just some nut. I walked away."

"Sharon!"

"Look at me, Tina. The guy's gotta be nuts."

"No, you're beautiful. And you're nuts, too, walking away. What if she's rich? It would be like winning Megabucks."

"Speaking of Megabucks, I got a scratch ticket here. Not exactly Megabucks, but we can win up to two thousand. One more square to rub off." Sharon pulled the ticket from her pocket.

"To hell with the lousy scratch ticket. What about that lady that might be your real mom?"

"An X! Three on a diagonal. Hold on. I'll rub off the prize amount. Twenty-five bucks. Better than nothing. Come on, let's go back to the place I bought it. I'll give you half. I'm freezing my butt off here."

"Me, too. And where does he live, this guy who says he knows your real mother? Can you find him again?"

"Like I said, he's from Pennsylvania. But he told me a place I could meet him tomorrow morning if I want to know more."

"You're nuts if you don't meet him! Are you gonna?"

"I guess I should think about it."

Tim followed the women to Colonial Street. They split the lottery cash on the sidewalk and parted ways, Tina still wearing Sharon's car blanket over her shoulders. Tim followed Sharon to the library, where she dozed for two hours in the reference area after reading random encyclopedia entries. After that, she roamed among the library stacks until 4:30. Then she went to the Goodwill Store. Tim got his shoes shined across the street.

From the ten-cent-special table, Sharon slipped a scissors and a blue vinyl, flannel-backed tablecloth inside her coat. She took them into the restroom, cut six big triangles out of the tablecloth, and stuffed them into her backpack. She threw the vinyl scraps into the trash can and covered them with a wet paper towel. On the way out of the store, she bought a brown car blanket and threw money into the donation jar to cover the cost of the scissors and tablecloth.

It was dark outside. The sky was clear and full of stars that brought a smile to Sharon's face. She thought of how the stars were there for everyone, no matter who you were or where you lived, anywhere on Earth, even if you didn't live anywhere at all. She drew the air in deeply, all she could hold. No one could stop her. Even if the cops caught her with the vinyl triangles they'd think she had stolen, even if they dragged her down the street, handcuffed and squirming, she could still look up, still drink up the stars. And the moment she got sprung from the jail house, they'd be hers again.

She went to the Salvation Army dining hall for a free supper. Almost last in the long line outdoors, she looked over the crowd when she finally got inside. She was not surprised to see Alice and Lucy, the two schizophrenics who lived at the M-WIT. Both were in their sixties.

Alice was a short woman with more than a dozen barrettes in her short gray hair, who was forever spewing curses about men. At the M-WIT, her curses rose above the shower and toilet stalls, which she would forget to come out of if no one came by to extricate her. "Men! What the fuck do we need 'em for? Unless to have a baby. That's the only thing. If the world didn't need babies, nobody would need men. Fuck 'em! Fuck 'em all!"

Lucy was a tall, skinny woman who often forgot to eat and pay her rent. Everyone said she was once a high-school history teacher. She was never seen without a stack of textbooks, an attendance book, and a loose-leaf binder in the crook of her left arm. Except for taking a shower, she never put her books down, even to cook her breakfast and lunch, which she always ate in the M-WIT lounge. She always wore the white bib apron she used to wear in class to keep the chalk off of her clothes. At the rare times she addressed anyone, it was always with a question beginning with "Did you know that . . .?"

Sharon looked for a place to sit in the dining hall, a large room with eight rows of long tables end-to-end. Lucy walked up to her. "Did you know that I come from a very unusual family in Massachusetts? I'm the latest of seven generations of virgins. We're all virgins. Always were. Always will be. We're the oldest New England family on record. My great, great, great, great, great, grandparents, all four of them, came over on the Mayflower."

"I see," Sharon said, pulling off her scarf and gloves. "How interesting! Hey, Lucy, wanna sit with me?"

"No, thanks. I have to take attendance." Lucy wandered about the room with her armload of books, making little marks in her attendance book.

With more than two hours to go till the homeless shelter opened, Sharon took a crossword puzzle book from her backpack and worked on it as she ate small forkfuls of her New England boiled dinner—ham, cabbage, beets, potatoes, and green beans.

Tim Giovannini, figuring it would take Sharon an hour to eat, picked up a ham and spinach calzone at a pizza shop and went back to his hotel room to get rid of the coat he'd been carrying around in the Surplus Store bag. He returned with an extra sweater under his camouflage jacket and found himself pacing outside the Salvation Army dining hall till seven-forty-five, when the hangers-on like Sharon were finally shooed out the door. Tim noticed that they all seemed to be headed to the same place, down the hill, where dozens of scruffy people formed a line outside a sprawling building.

Tim got in line eight people behind Sharon. Soon he found himself in a large foyer with a broad inside door divided by a center post. At each end of the door was a woman handing out a washcloth, a towel, and a sample-size bar of soap. "Men to the left, women to the right," they kept repeating. Tim went to the woman on the left and said, "Where am I?"

"You don't even know where you are?" She pointed to the outside door. "Come back when you're sober."

"Sober!"

"Shelter rules. No drinking in the shelter. No drunks keeping everybody else awake all night. You can come back at ten-thirty. That's if you don't have another drink between now and then."

"And when's check-out time?"

"Check-out time!" The woman grinned. "You got till eight in the morning to fold your blanket, roll your sheets up and toss 'em in the laundry cart on your way out the door. You don't check out. This ain't the Harborview Inn, you know."

Tim left without answering and went back to his hotel.

Sharon went into the shower room and changed into a flannel nightgown in the handicap toilet stall, which had its own sink. She slipped a menstrual pad into her underpants and covered them with one of the waterproof purple triangles she had cut out at the Goodwill Store. She put another pair of underwear over the triangle. Then she brushed her teeth and went out to find an empty cot. The sliding panels between the men's and women's sides had been drawn closed. Quiet descended quickly over people who had spent much of their day fighting with the bitter air.

6

The House of Giovannini

It's me, the rat again. Told you I'd be back. Now for a little Timmy genealogy. Years before our Tim was born, his grandfather, Giovanni Giovannini, sailed in the steerage to America. He came from the Italian Tyrol around 1900 when he was twenty or so. Back in the old Tyrol, his family was hurting for work because the silkworm industry, where they all labored for as far back as anyone could remember, had gone kaput because of some silkworm disease.

The story around the barber shops in Mount of Olives, Pennsylvania, is that Giovanni Giovannini's mother and father sent him packing. He's told the story himself many a Saturday under many a layer of shaving lather. Just like lotsa parents in lotsa struggling European countries of the time, Giovanninis gave their kid the old line: "Go! Go to America. Go make a life for yourself and your children. There's nothing here no more."

"I don't have any children," Giovanni says. "I don't even have a wife yet."

"You will. You will."

"I can have a family here in Europe, make a life here. I can fix anything. Anything!"

"Do your fixing in America," they tell their son. "People there can pay for your work. You hear what our neighbors' children write back from America—the streets are paved with gold. You can feed your children."

"I don't have any children," he reminds them for the five-hundredth time.

"You will. You will."

"Won't it break your hearts if I go? You'll never see your grandchildren."

"What grandchildren? Giovanni, you don't even have children."

"I will, I will," he says back to them.

And his mother and father say, "Our hearts will break faster if you stay. Go! Write to us."

After the same go-around for months, Giovanni Giovannini sailed to America, to Mount of Olives, where lots of other Tyroleans were settling. He wrote terrible lies to his mother and father. He gave them the old line, "The streets are paved with gold."

He didn't let on the streets were caked with coal dust, black as the hole in the middle of your eye. If you were a single miner, like Giovanni, you most likely lived in a boarding house with plank floors and a johnny stove that was taken outside to a shed in the summer, where the cooking was done so's to keep the house cool. Usually people of one's own kind, Krauts with Krauts, Pollacks with Pollacks, Micks with Micks, lived in the same boardinghouse, though some were mixed. There was a washing shanty out back with tin tubs for miners to wash off the coal dirt, in case the colliery you worked at didn't have a washhouse. When the boardinghouse had more boarders than beds, some men had to share, sleeping in shifts.

Some married men got to live in one side of a double home, a clapboard structure, painted red, usually, that's if it was painted at all. Often, they shared the place with other relations or took in boarders.

The part about the streets being paved with gold was not a complete lie. It depended on who you were, where you came from, what your name was. If it was Blair or Whittington, there was, at least, some chance you sat in a wing-back chair at the end of the day, counting your cash. You pulled your gold watch from your pocket and told your rosy-skinned little ones it was time for bed, and their *au pair* would be coming to bathe them and tuck them in. In the morning, the tutors would be coming to give them lessons in history, geography, English, French, literature, science, and mathematics.

If you had some Hunkey, Mick, Dago, or Kraut name, you feared you might be struck dead for questioning the wisdom of the Almighty in giving you a houseful of little ones. You shooed them to bed early, for at five in the morning, when the mine whistle blew, your ashen boys, coal dirt hopelessly stuck under their fingernails, would be tagging along with Papa to the colliery. Boys as young as seven worked in the breaker above the coal hole, sorting rocks and wood from the coal that came tumbling down from the tipple at the top of the breaker. A few worked inside the mine as door boys. For ten hours, a door boy sat alone in a small, dark chamber, listening for a mule hauling a coal car on rails toward the door on either end of the chamber. The doors had to be kept shut for the proper air flow. The door boy would open them to let the mule driver, usually a boy around twelve, pass through with the car. Many a door boy, sitting on the ground and slipping into a few moments of shut-eye, his back against the door, got knocked senseless by busted planks, trampled by the mule, and finished off by the coal car.

Miners worked for long hours and a short pay that never caught up with their debt at the company store. They worked deep in the earth, blasting, digging, shoveling, loading coal cars under groaning timbers, often wondering if they'd live to walk their boys home from the breaker that night.

If you were a wife spared from the factories, you, your daughters, and your sons too young for the breaker would start out after breakfast, pushing a wheelbarrow with burlap bags to the slag-piles, where you would glean little bits of coal from among the rocks thrown out of the breaker. With a little luck, your children went to school long enough to learn to read and write and add and subtract. Girls and boys often went to garment or lace factories, or to silk mills or shoe factories.

That's how it really was. But Giovanni never wrote home to the Tyrol about that. Nope. Now, after living a few years in America, he married a friendly, hard-working girl from the silk factory. Her name was Lucia. They had a boy named Ricardo. Giovanni wrote home about that, having to tell no lies about the joy Lucia and Ricardo brought to his life. It was all true. Then again, Giovanni wrote how he fixed things for people, which he did for his neighbors in the mining patches. And when they could spare it, they paid him, but usually they sent over some cakes or homemade hooch, or they babysat Ricardo so that Giovanni and Lucia could go walking together in the evening. When Giovanni wrote home, he didn't mention that most people couldn't pay him, only that he found lots of work fixing things. Two decades in America and he never mentioned that he'd dug coal for fourteen of those years. He didn't mention that his boy Ricardo got on at the coal breaker at the age of seven after only one year of school. He certainly didn't mention that he took to sleeping on the parlor floor rather than create another child to toil in someone's factory or breaker.

His boy Ricardo spent only a year as a breaker boy. Then Lucia sent him back to school, and she went back to the factory. It was only long after Giovanni got on as an apprentice in a garage and Lucia was too old to bear another child that Giovanni hopped back into her bed. Ricardo, a fix-it whiz like his old man, became a mechanic too. Side by side father and son worked in the same shop. The parents lived with the least they could, saving for that day Ricardo would own his own garage.

Ricardo's reputation as a fine mechanic grew. In 1944, he was offered a chance to buy into the Ford dealership on Fifth Street in Mount of Olives with the understanding that he would run the maintenance shop while his partner, a man of fifty-two with no children, ran the showroom and sales end of the business. Ricardo's parents chipped in every penny they could spare. They were glad to fork the money over, but one thing made them squirm. They worried what easy money might do to their son. Their neighbor's kid was handed a shoemaker business built up from scratch by the generation before, a generation that had started out in the mines. The day that boy took over, he cut the wages and raised his prices. He splurged the receipts on dinners for fancy families who'd come to America with silver spoons in their mouths. He never mixed that company with his family. After a year in the business, he all but abandoned his family and the gritty friends he'd grown up with. Lucia had nightmares about her boy Ricardo. She'd dream he bought himself a Victorian mansion uptown and she and her husband would look in from the porch, never to enter. She'd wake up weeping, spilling the details between sobs. Giovanni began to have the same dream and they would console each other in the mornings.

"Don't forget where you came from, Ricardo," Giovanni would say in Italian. He always spoke Italian to his family. "When people work hard for you, pay them right. Remember, that magic you work with your hands, it is a gift from God, don't forget, a gift from God. You didn't make it yourself. This opportunity here in America, it is mostly your good fortune, too, not your own making, even though, yes, you work hard. The people in the mines and factories, they work hard too, remember. They work hard and they get nowhere. Be thankful, Ricardo. Give back to the world. Give to others not so lucky. Remember all that died in the mines or can't get to work in the light of day. You remember where you came from."

"I will, Papa."

And Ricardo remembered. He was not only a whiz with his hands, but he could see how to run a business. When his partner retired, he became the sole proprietor. He was fair to his workers, fair with his prices. In those days, it was a matter of great pride for a man to say his wife did not have to go to work, but Sophia, Ricardo's wife, had a head for numbers and her own vision to contribute to the business. She insisted, to his embarrassment, that she work in the office doing the books and planning the buying. The success of the dealership was as much hers as his, and he was secretly grateful to her, though he often pleaded with her to stay home. Together they made a great profit. They gave back to their community. When there was a charity drive, Giovannini Motors was the first to contribute and contributed the most.

Ricardo and Sophia had a daughter. Like many parents who were now at least two generations from the old country, they picked an American-sounding name for her, calling her Betsy. They prized her all the more when the doctor, barely able to save the life of mother or infant, said it was not likely that Sophia could bear another child. But five years later, in 1946, along came baby Tim. The Giovanninis impressed on their children the hardships in their family history, reminding them to be grateful for the grace of God and the strokes of luck that made them a little better off than most families in the Coal Region.

So now we're up to the 1950s. Betsy, you see, she mixes with everyone. Factory people's kids, coal-hole people's kids, everyone. Timmy, well, before he's even out of elementary school, he begins to think things out. Why go backwards? He gets notions about class. He sticks with what he considers the important kids.

He doesn't have to weed out breaker boys or sweat shop kids or anything like that. Little children no longer work in breakers or factories, or pick coal from the slagpiles. Well, a few kids still get sent off with wheelbarrows to glean coal off the slagpiles for their families, but Tim pays no attention to them. Throughout the region and the country, the demand for coal is way down. Quite a few collieries have gone kaput. And mines that still operate are often run by people with a heart, descendants of immigrants who labored in them in Giovanni Giovannini's day. Lotsa factories, too. Some miners have had to swap their coveralls for slacks and sport coats to commute to Harrisburg, the state capital eighty miles away, for clerical jobs. Most mothers work in garment factories or at the cigar factory, and their work weeks are often cut short. All in all, the Coal Region's an economically depressed area in the comfy days of Ike. (Ike is short for President Eisenhower. Even the rats know that.) Yet many families have gotten enough of a foothold to do away with the outhouses and spiff up the old company homes they've bought from owners of the larger collieries, who've moved on to more profitable enterprises, leaving behind stripped mountains and slagpiles.

Children, most of them, stay in school through high school. There's no longer a clearly divisible line between them that have and them that don't. But our Timmy Giovannini has a keen eye for that dividing line, blurry or not. All the townspeople know what it is, too. These days, you don't have to be a Blair or Whittington to be above the line. Now all kinds of eastern and southern European descendants have hung their names on store and shop shingles.

In Timmy's eyes most kids are below the line, meaning their parents still earn a living with their hands. A kid two or three generations above the dirty hands is higher above the line, and those whose families started out clean from the days of William Penn are tops. The whole town considers you way above the line if you're a doctor's kid, a dentist's kid, a lawyer's kid, a Bloke Street store owner's kid, a TV cable company owner's kid, a factory owner's kid, a mine owner's, a politician's, judge's, or car dealer's kid. Those are the kids Timmy accepts as friends, especially those whose families live in the big Victorian homes once occupied by the coal barons.

Many families below the line take for granted that the Timmys of the town are the only hope for their daughters. Friendships among some teenage girls from below the line get set aside with opportunities to pit their fresh blooming beauty against one another's in the hopes of being picked by a Timmy.

Our Tim has hopes, too. He hopes to be friends with Hal Jones. Hal Jones, a dark-haired, handsome son of an accountant, is almost three years older. Hal says his grandfather was a doctor, and every male ancestor as far back as Hal can trace was a professional of some sort. The women in Hal's family have never had to go out and find jobs. On Wednesday nights and Saturday nights, when there's a dance up da Mine, Hal likes to lie down on the floor, scooching around like a car mechanic on a creeper, treating his eyes to the view under the fanning skirts. With sufficient political connections and with a family who has enough cash to pay bribes under the table, Hal gets around all complaints. Some girls dance away from his big brown peepers. Some think granting him a gander is a foot in the door of his well-heeled heart. Our Tim wishes he were old enough to go to da Mine. If only he were, he'd creep right along the floor with Hal. True friends, for all to see. He wishes he could claim clean ancestry as far back as Hal. But the next best thing would be to be known as Hal's best friend and be considered just like him—smart, athletic, wealthy, which Timmy already is, and sought after by girls.

Hal, a ninth-grader, likes to prowl the streets, bobbing and swiveling his head, flaunting his availability. He really has no friends, only disciples, all of the wealthier sort, and even they drop off one by one when they get bored out of their pants with his self-absorption. So Hal is always in need of new disciples. On the first day of school in 1957, he waits at the door of the Mount of

Olives Junior High, damned near rubbing his hands at the sight of Tim Giovannini and Ray Moleski, newcomers about to start seventh grade. Ray attended the same Catlick elementary school as Tim. Hal knows whose kids they are, and he pegs them as easy recruits as he watches them saunter in all but wearing signs, Tim's saying, MY FAMILY OWNS THE BIGGEST FORD DEALERSHIP IN NORTHUMBERLAND COUNTY, and Ray's saying, MY DAD IS SUPERINTENDENT OF SCHOOLS.

Tim stutters at Hal's greeting, a casual, "Hi, guys." Ray takes Hal's greeting in stride. Within minutes the two seventh-graders, shoulder to shoulder, are moving through the corridors like a street sweeper with Hal at the wheel. Any boy whose family is not politicians or business owners gets swept aside at a glance. "Not what you want for a friend," Hal coaches. "A going-nowhere kid like that will be a liability when it comes time for tykes like you to go out looking for girls."

The come-follow-me selections are made with nods and with jerks of Hal's head in such a way as if tossing the rejects over his shoulder. Mickey Dolan, whose father is a mechanic at Giovannini Motors, runs after them, calling, "Wait up! Wait up!" Tim is mortified. Then, outright pissed. "Get rid of him," he hisses at Ray. Ray says no, him and Mickey Dolan's been best buddies since first grade. Tim beats it outa there, stalling in the boys' lavatory, before anybody sees him walking the halls with the likes of Mickey Dolan.

Hal keeps his acolytes on the hook by presenting them with opportunities that will seal their admiration and gratitude. This is especially necessary when he doesn't see them every day, after he has moved on to tenth grade in the senior high school building and Tim, Ray, Ned, Shitfoot, and Bruce are only in eighth grade. Hal turns sixteen in October of his sophomore year and gets his driver's license by Christmas. He gives the tykes a thrill, cruising with them uptown on Saturday nights, blowing the horn of his dad's year-old Ford Edsel, all of them whistling and calling out "Hey, baby!" while puckering up and making smooching sounds at girls on Bloke Street in can-can slips, full skirts with poodles and fancy embroidered scribbles, light-stepping girls parading on the sidewalks in bobby socks and saddle shoes.

Just after New Year's, Hal dangles before his groveling five a ticket to the Buddy Holly, Ritchie Valens, Big Bopper concert at the Surf Ballroom in Clear Lake, Iowa. Hal holds the concert ticket up in the air like a puppy treat, and the thirteen-year-olds yip and leap for it. Then he whisks the ticket behind his back and says, "My kuzzint from Dubuque, Iowa, is going to the concert. He sent me his two extra tickets. That means that I—and—

and—

and—

one friend from Pennsylvania—

the one I pick to go—

just one, mind you—

can all stay at their place on the way to and from the concert in Clear Lake. Clear Lake's another few hours from Dubuque. That means we'll have to spring for a motel room in Clear Lake one night. And probably one night between here and Iowa, on the way there and back, maybe around Toledo, Ohio. That's three motel nights altogether. Can any of you guys afford that?"

"My dad owns a goddamn lumber company, for Christ's sake," Shitfoot says.

"My family's owned that box factory for two generations," says Bruce the Moose on the Loose. "We got lotsa dough."

Ray Moleski, whose father is superintendent of schools, remember, says, "Are you kidding? My dad just about runs the eastern half of Pennsylvania!"

Ned, whose dad is the mayor and hopes to run for governor, says, "Come next November, my dad will be running the whole state."

Timmy Giovannini says, "Of course my old man can afford to spring for a lousy motel. We've got the biggest car dealership in the county."

"Ok," Hal says, "Money is no object. So that qualifies all of you. You, you, you, you, and you. But there's one other little detail.

How do we get there? That's the sixty-four-thousand-dollar question."

"You have your driver's license, Hal," Shitfoot says. "And two cars."

A sulky look drags Hal's face down. "Yeah, yeah, we have two cars. A lotta good they do me. Boy, would I like to whiz into that hick farmer town in Iowa with our brand new Edsel! Give those little farmer girls a thrill. But my dad's being a total prick. He says a few weeks on the road's not enough experience for a thousand-mile drive. Especially in winter." Hal's voice cracks as he whines, "Damn him, I can drive."

Tim Giovannini steps in front of Ray and Shitfoot and says, "Hey, I know. I'll ask my dad for one of our Edsels. A brand new one! We have a whole lotful of new cars, you know. Just name the model, Hal. I'll get it for you."

Hal says, "Now there's a thought. Tell you the truth, though, I don't know who to pick. I hate to leave anybody out. But one spare ticket is one spare ticket. It's all I have." Hal pauses and pretends to think, while the others argue among themselves about who deserves to go. "Wait!" Hal says. "I have an idea. Line up. Shortest to tallest."

Ned, Ray, Shitfoot, Tim, and Bruce all line up. Hal pokes Ned and Ray in the chest and says, "Tails, heads. On the first flip, tails will be out." He flips the coin with his right hand, slaps it onto the back of his left hand, and says, "Heads! Sorry, Ned, you're out of the running." He announces that tails also loses the next round, and that eliminates Ray. Hal puts his hands in his pockets and feels for his trick quarter with tails on both sides, distracting everyone with lugubrious consolations for the first two losers. Then he says, "Tim, you're tails. Heads loses. Shitfoot, you're heads." Tim beats out Shitfoot, and now it's between Tim and Bruce. "Tim, you're tails again. Heads loses."

"That's not fair!" Tim protests.

Hal holds up the tickets. "Who owns these tickets?"

"You do," our Timmy says. He lowers his head and bites off the curses trying to launch from his lips.

"Tails! You're out, Bruce. Sorry," says Hal, reaching up and giving him an affectionate pat on the shoulder. "Maybe next year, you guys. Timmyboy, it's me and you off to Iowa!"

Timmy, who does not feel fit to loose the shoelaces on Hal Jones's sneakers, can only gulp his gratitude and grin.

Hal tries not to roll his eyes at the thought of that skinny twerp with the prickly blond flattop tagging along, turning off every girl in Iowa. It would be great, Hal thinks, if he could keep Tim busy making a chart of how many barns he sees along the way, or how many silos, or have him do a paint-by-number of some stupid corn-field. He hopes he hasn't pissed off his other disciples so much that they'll turn him down next time he needs something. Trying to look sheepish and guilty, saying he wishes he had more than one ticket to hand out, he coughs as an excuse to cover his mouth. Picturing himself at the wheel of a brand new Edsel, he's all teeth, grinning like datdare Cheshire cat.

7

Holly

SO BEFORE HE SAYS A WORD TO HIS DAD about the concert ticket, up and down the sales lot goes Timmy Giovannini, rubbing his chin, looking over each Ford, kicking a tire on this one, grabbing a tail fin on that one, giving it a good shaking, shoving a few cars with his hip to test for sturdiness. Of the five rows of cars, the last has eight or so inches of snow on the vehicles, mostly pickup trucks. The plow's been between all the rows and behind the last. But in the snow between each vehicle in that last row, there's not even a footprint. Timmy sees Bum-Knee Fantini, the custodian and courtesy-car driver, limping through the lot, dragging the garbage cans out to the curb. Ted Fantini's walked with a limp for near twenty years. When he was fourteen he missed the turn on his sled, comin' down datdare big hill from Jumbo's coal breaker over in Black Hollow. He slammed into a shanty and that was it for his knee.

"Hey! Fantini!" yells Timmy. "What's with the snow on those cars and trucks in the back? We haven't had snow for three, four days. How 'bout getting a broom out here and taking care of it? And a shovel, too, for the ground in between."

"Well, well, well," says Bum-Knee. He lets go of the garbage can handles and stands with his big rubber boots spread, his arms folded. His lips are chapped and bleeding in the left corner, the tip of his large nose near frostbitten. His eyes are droopy with weariness. He's swept off cars and shoveled between them after two back-to-back storms. He looks Timmy up and down and says, "Who died and left you boss?"

"I'm sure my father would say the same thing."

"Oh, he would, would he? Dat's nice ta know."

"I mean it, Fantini. We gotta move these vehicles. People won't buy them if they can't see them, or they gotta walk knee-deep in snow to see the interiors. They can't be left go any longer."

Fantini says nothing, turns away, and resumes his trip to the curb with the cans. This brings the blood up to Timmy's face. "That's it! I'm gonna tell my father!" So he marches through the lot and into the showroom. Two steps inside and, "Where's my father?" he demands of Sylvia Androlevitch, the receptionist behind the semi-circular counter. The counter rises about two feet above her desk and you can barely see her brown eyes over it from across the room.

Sylvia's a senior at Mount of Olives High. She works at Giovannini Motors on Saturdays. She's got long, curly, brown hair and a habit of wrapping strands of it around her fingers. "Your dad's in the far-back office, looking over the books," she answers. "He asked not to be disturbed unless it's really important."

Timmy thinks neglecting to clean a whole row of vehicles and making customers tramp through three feet of snow to look in the side windows is pretty important. He also thinks the owner's son being ignored by a hired worker should definitely be brought to the owner's attention. And then he considers why he showed up in the first place, to pick out a car for the trip to Iowa in three weeks. He's not sure what to bring up first. His blood's still simmering from the brush-off he got from Fantini. He looks down the back hall to the closed office door and gets the feeling he better think things over.

"Is there anything I can help you with?" Sylvia says. Her smile is nervous, a bit twitchy. But all Timmy sees is a sexy, come-on smile. It takes the edge off the slight he just took from Fantini. He goes over and leans on the counter, disappointed to see Sylvia's wearing a turtleneck sweater. To tell you the truth, he's downright irritated. Last Saturday she had on a yellow V-neck, and Timmy got enough of a gander to report back to his buddies. Only he got a little carried away, telling what he had hoped would happen instead of what did. What was mere rubbernecking on his part while she kept blushing and pressing her hand flat against the V-neck, became her twirling her curls around a finger and placing a lock enticingly between her breasts. According to Timmy, she kept running the tip of her tongue along her top lip every time he happened to glance her way. Of course, Tim conceded, everyone knew she had a boyfriend, the Coal Township quarterback at that, so there was no getting near her. But it didn't stop her from playing that little game.

So now she sits there all covered up, the little bitch, Tim says to himself, like all of a sudden she's a lily-white saint. "How long do you think Dad'll be, Sylvia?"

"Till eleven, he told me."

"Twenty minutes, then. Tell him I'll be back."

Timmy takes a walk to the post office to buy stamps for the postcards he's planning to send back from Iowa. He buys a rolla fillum for his new camera at Rea & Derrick's Drug Store. At eleven-fifteen he's back. His father's just coming out from that back office.

After that bout of fresh air, Timmy's decided not to start in on Fantini's defiance. Getting that car's the thing, he's decided. "Hi, Dad," he says, "you look like you can use a coffee. How 'bout I get you one?" As he heads toward the electric Perk-a-Pot, he says to his father, "Which coffee mug will you have, Dad, the one with the Edsel Ranger Sedan on it, or the Edsel Villager Station Wagon? I'm gonna have the Edsel Cor—hey! Sylvia! What's with the dirty Corsair mug in the sink here? And the Thunderbird. That's dirty, too! Dad, you let her sit there at the desk when there's dirty coffee mugs in the sink here? And look at this sink, all gummed up!"

"Leave Sylvia alone. Gimme any old mug." Mr. Giovannini, taking out his wallet, says, "And what is it you want, Timmy, a five, a ten, or a twenty?"

Timmy puts on a pouty look as he pours the coffee. "Can't a kid offer his dad a lousy cup of coffee without being accused of wanting money?"

"Not this kid."

"Well, I didn't come here to ask for money."

"What, then?"

"Just a loan of something, that's all."

"Oh?"

Timmy, seeing Sylvia's interest perk up, says, "Can we talk in the back?"

They go into the back office. Timmy decides to come right out with it. "A car. I need a loan of a car."

"You're thirteen, Timmy. You don't have a license."

"I won't be driving."

"Oh?"

"Hal Jones. He'll be the driver."

"And where will Hal Jones be driving you?"

"Just to a concert. Dad, Dad, it's a big one! Buddy Holly, the Big Bopper, Ritchie Valens, Dion and the Bel—"

"And where is this concert?"

"A place called the Surf Ballroom."

"New Jersey, is it? Atlantic City, maybe? Or is it Ocean City, Maryland? One of those big shore places."

"Hal told me, but I forget. Geez, Dad, what kid dwells on the name of a town when all he can hear in his head is Buddy Holly, Buddy Holly? No kidding, Dad. Hal Jones invited me. Only me. Me and him are the only kids in the whole town with tickets—"

"Oh? And how does that happen to be?"

"Hal's got connections. He's got a kuzzint who lives not too far from the concert hall. He sent Hal two tickets."

"Since when are you Hal's best friend? He's a junior or senior, I believe. And how can these be the only two tickets? Half this town's got relations that migrated to New Jersey or Maryland to find work. Tickets should be easy to get."

"They're not exactly a dime a dozen, Dad. This is Buddy Holly, Ritchie Valens, the Big—"

"The Big Bopper, I know. But how come—"

"Dad, can we talk about the car?"

"I don't think so. We can see what your mother says."

"Oh, forget her. Can't this just be man to man?"

"Your mother's as much a part of this company as I am. She'll be in on this."

"O.K., but for now, can it be just us?"

"All right. But why is it you need to provide the car? What's the matter with the two cars the Joneses have? They bought them here brand new and they bring them in for maintenance right by the book. They're more than dependable."

"Hal's dad says no."

"And Timmy Giovannini's dad says no, too."

"Aw, come on, Dad. Geez, it's only a car, a stinkin', lousy car. We got a whole lot fulla cars."

"What about a bus, Greyhound or Trailways?"

"If you make me do that, I hope you're willing to pick me up at three in the morning. I can't show my face in broad daylight, stepping off a bus when my own family's got a whole lot fulla cars."

"All right. You can take the blue one, the courtesy car."

"But, Dad, that's two years old!"

"It'll get you there and back."

"Half the town's ridden in that thing. Anybody that leaves his car for a tune-up, he's carted off to work in that thing, picked up at the end of the day."

"Oh, so it's just not good enough."

"I want a new one, Dad."

"A particular new one, I suppose."

"The gold Edsel. Just think! The hottest new thing in Fords and I'll be advertising it for you!"

"If I meant you to advertise, I wouldn't send you off in an Edsel. Your mother predicts the Edsel's done for by next year."

"Aw, don't pay attention to her. Edsels are the hottest thing."

"No Edsel."

"Okay. The new red Thunderbird convertible, then."

"A convertible? When is this concert?"

"February. I know, I know, it'll be cold. Probably can't put the top down, but people can imagine how great it would be in the summertime."

"Sheeze!"

"And," Timmy says, "those hubcaps. They don't really go with the car. How 'bout a set of spinners?"

"Okay, okay, the car, the spinners. On one condition. The driver's over twenty-five."

"Be reasonable, Dad. Hal Jones has a license, six months already."

"No."

"What about his brother, John. He's twenty-one."

"No. Just how far is the concert, I want to know. Do you have this famous two-of-a-kind ticket on you?"

Now, Timmy, of course, has it right in his wallet. He's been flashing it all over town. He's tempted to pat his pockets and do a little digging, all for naught, and say he must've left it in his room. But he decides to bite the bullet and hand the ticket over. Ricardo Giovannini does a double take and jumps to his feet. "Clear Lake, Iowa! Halfway across the country! So this is why you wouldn't answer my question, where is this concert. And you letting on it's at the shore in New Jersey or Maryland." Pinching the ticket at each end, Ricardo says, "I have a mind to tear this thing up!"

"Dad, no! Please! I never said a word about New Jersey and Maryland. You named them. All I mentioned was the Surf Ballroom. You asked what city. I didn't remember the city."

"But you knew the state."

"You didn't ask about the—"

"All right, you already have the ticket, you can go. You can have the red Thunderbird, the spinners. If, and only if, your mother agrees. And one more thing. Ted Fantini will drive."

The father sits down and the son jumps up. "Bum-Knee Fantini! Dad, have you—"

"Mr. Fantini to you. To you and your buddies."

"Have you seen the parking lot? The whole back row! Snow everywhere! On the cars, between the cars. The man's obviously not responsible."

"I told Mr. Fantini to let that row go. Anybody wants to see a vehicle in that row, well, we can clear it on the spot. Ted's overworked already. A trip might do him good. I'll call Hal Jones and see if he can get a ticket for Ted, too."

So off they go to Iowa, Hal and Timmy in the back, Bum-Knee in the front. Three days early they leave to allow for bad weather. As they're pulling out, Ricardo tells Bum-Knee he's to stop the car immediately and turn back for home if either boy addresses him as anything but Mr. Fantini, or if he hears any foul language, even something as mild as shit or damn. Our Timmy's got his school books to study during the ride, along with advance assignments, like his parents insisted. Timmy doesn't dare take his school work out in front of Hal, of course.

To Timmy's irritation, Bum-Knee's polite as pie to him. Tim can't provoke him no how. It's like Bum-Knee's noggin's got a tunnel that lets words go in one ear and right out the other every time Timmy orders him about, saying things like, "Yo! Mr. Fantini! The light ain't gonna get any greener. Step on it!"

Timmy's pleased with any scrap of attention he gets from Hal, who mostly looks out the window. He racks his brain for some way to start a conversation with Hal. The brain obliges with a delightful image of the huge Lionel Train set up in his attic, a system he and his dad have been building since Tim was six. Tim loves remembering how they smiled at one another as they handed each other pieces of track, how they beamed together at the sight of all the curves and tunnels and loading platforms erected along the way. Tim starts out describing the size of this treasure and adds, "It's got some special edition cars you'll never see again. Worth a hunnert bucks apiece by now! And we're still adding the latest models." Suddenly Timmy catches the what-da-hell look on Hal's face and realizes he's made a big mistake. Hal's words are a nightmare come true. "You mean you still play with trains?"

"Um, well, not exactly," says Timmy. "It's my dad's collection, actually. Way back when I was a little kid, my dad figured every boy should have a train. I never cared much for them, but Dad was really— Mom made me play along with him, though, so I wouldn't hurt his feelings."

“Sure, Timmyboy,” Hal says. Hal’s got a stash of *Playboy* magazines tucked inside a spiral notebook he’s ripped the pages out of. Tim’s eyes bulge like planets at a nude. His rubbernecking is met with a flick of Hal’s elbow. “This isn’t for little tykes who play with trains,” Hal whispers. He squirms sideways, leaning his head against the window and hiding the picture from Tim.

Timmy pouts in silence.

With the off-and-on snow, they spend a night in Ohio and one in northeastern Illinois. Bum-Knee asks for an extra cot in the same room as the boys, since he’s their chaperone. The motels don’t want no trouble, so they’re glad to oblige.

After that train talk blunder, Timmy’s afraid to say much to Hal. His next big blunder comes when they’re about to cross a long bridge into Dubuque, Iowa. The setting sun is making big red and gold balloons of the puffy clouds. Timmy bolts straight up at the sight of the Mississippi River. “Holy sh— uh, cow!” he says, rolling down his window. He twists to the side and grips the door. He hardly feels the icy wind on his fingers. “The Mississippi River! Somebody pinch me and prove this isn’t a dream!”

Hal pinches the back of Timmy’s neck. “Shut the fffff– Shut the window already!” he says. “It’s ten degrees out!”

Timmy’s caught between his thrill at seeing the Mississippi and his dread of offending Hal. He gets brave and puts in a word for Old Man River. “Sorry about the cold,” he says, rolling up the window. “But look, Hal, look! This is the Mississippi! I must’ve read *Huckleberry Finn* ten times. Just last month, I read it again. And here it is. The Mississippi River, right before my eyes! Imagine floating down that thing on a raft.”

“You’re still reading *Huckleberry Finn?* I got through two pages of it when I was seven. That was enough for me. What a bore!” Hal flashes Timmy a look at the Playboy centerfold model from the December issue, a topless blond with a Santa hat, her ten-gallon tits resting on the rim of the chimney she’s sticking out of. “How ’bout ‘The Night before Christmas,’ Timmyboy? Are you still reading that, too?”

"My dad makes me read famous books between customers when I come in to help on Saturdays. 'An idle mind is the devil's workshop,' he says. He wants me to learn the business, so I come in, and that's the way it goes some Saturdays. I end up reading what he calls classic works. Anyway, Hal, you gotta admit, the Mississippi is a heh—a heck of a lot more impressive than the Susquehanna."

"My family has a cabin on the Susquehanna. No use inviting you there, I see."

"Whaddaya mean, no use! Tell me when, I'll be over."

Suddenly the tunnel between Bum-Knee's ears closes up. He says, "Forget it, Tim. You're not invited."

"Right on, Mr. Fantini," Hal says. "Little Timmyboy is not invited."

Bum-Knee sighs. "You never were invited, Tim. Only you just gave Hal an excuse to say so."

"Just 'cause I said the Mississippi's better than the Susquehanna? Okay, Hal, I take it back. I'm sorry I—"

"Yo! Mr. Giovannini!" Bum-Knee says. "The truth ain't gonna get any clearer. Quit makin' an ass outa yourself."

"Making an—" Hal slaps his hand over Timmy's mouth. "You heard what your dad said about foul language. Do you want to see Buddy Holly or don't you?"

"I don't know," says Timmy. "Maybe we should just go home."

Hal shakes Timmy's arm. "Of course, you're invited. I was just kidding, giving you a hard time. The place is closed up till spring. As soon as we open it, come up any time."

"There, Mr. Fantini," says Timmy.

Bum-Knee can't see siding with this teenage asshole from now on. He doesn't let on he heard the remark. "We're in Dubuque," he says. "Let's find a pay phone, Hal, and call your relations. Find out how to get to their house."

There's a booth on a corner just ahead. They park and get out. Hal looks up at the old houses on the steep streets before him and scratches his head. "What are these cliffs doing here? I thought the Midwest was supposed to be flat as a fuh—flat as a pancake."

Despite the delayed invitation to Hal's family cabin on the Susquehanna River in Pennsylvania, Timmy's been sufficiently insulted to stand up to Hal for the first time in his life. "These are bluffs," he says. "If you'da read more than two pages of *Huckleberry Finn,* you'd know to expect bluffs along Midwest rivers, especially a big one like the mighty Mississippi."

They stay a night in Dubuque, and then they're off to Clear Lake. Bum-Knee has observed Hal and Mike, Hal's kuzzint, rubbing their hands at the thought of prowling the streets of Clear Lake, checking out the chicks. Timmy echoes everything they say and rubs his hands, too. The other two exchange looks or just ignore him. If Tim wasn't such an asshole, Bum-Knee thinks, a person could almost feel sorry for the kid.

The talk of prowling doesn't surprise Bum-Knee. Having seen Hal in action on the streets of Mount of Olives, Bum-Knee has already made a point of reserving motel rooms between Mason City and Clear Lake, where there's nowhere to go but to bed or some snow-covered cornfield. The boys are pissed. Once they unload the car, they have to go four miles back into Mason City for supper. By then it's dark. All the boys get to check out is the diner they eat in. Mostly old farts in their forties and fifties, they complain. Later, they don't even get a look at the town of Clear Lake, except to find their way to the Surf Ballroom. Bum-Knee, who doesn't have a ticket, explains to the people at the door that he's chaperoning these boys from far away, and would it be all right if he comes in to check on them about every forty minutes? They agree to it.

The first time Bum-Knee goes through the big lobby into the ballroom, he sees all dissere slow dancing going on. He sees girls weeping into the chests of their dance partners as Ritchie Valens sings "Donna." The stage area is decorated with palm trees and an ocean backdrop. Bum-Knee looks about. It's impossible to pick out his three charges. On the other side of the dance floor, he sees a raised area with two rows of booths and tries his luck back there. He sees Timmy's managed to get a girl into a booth. They've got two bendy straws shoved into the same tall strawberry milkshake. Timmy cringes at the sight of Bum-Knee. Every muscle in Timmy's face is begging the chaperone not to come to the table and ruin everything. Bum-Knee stands back. Timmy goes over to him.

"So where's the prowling kuzzints?" Bum-Knee asks.

Timmy points them out on the dance floor. He thanks Bum-Knee for being a good sport and not coming to the booth.

Bum-Knee has found a bar he can walk to and from between his forty-minute checks. Since he's the driver, he drinks orange juice, though he's dying for a beer. He's standing right outside the Surf Ballroom door when the concert ends. After a few dozen teenagers pour out, Timmy, given the brush-off from the girl who drank half of his milkshake, comes out alone. The air is gusty and frigid. A light snow blows through the streets, catching the lamplight like stardust. Timmy stands shivering with Bum-Knee till the last group of teens exits, the lights go out, and a man starts locking the doors. Bum-Knee asks the man if he's sure everyone is out, and the man is sure everyone's out but the cleanup crew. About ten minutes later, Mike and Hal come walking up the street, holding hands with two girls in bobby socks and coats bulged out from the puffy skirts beneath. The boys look at Timmy and Bum-Knee, but walk right past, like they haven't seen a thing. "Hal! Mike!" says Bum-Knee. They keep walking. "Yo! Hal! Mike!" Bum-Knee walks up behind them and hooks his hands over their coat collars. "The car's back this way," he says. And to the females he says, "Goodnight, girls."

"Just a minute, please," one girl says. She takes a paper from her purse, writes something on it, and hands it to Hal, who beams at what he reads. "Write to me," she says. She kisses him on the cheek. The other girl kisses Mike on the mouth.

After crawling through the traffic out of Clear Lake, it's past midnight when they get to their motel. The plan was for Hal to share a room with Mike, and Timmy with Bum-Knee. But the chaperone decides to split the older boys up and share with Hal himself. Hal fumes and pouts and flings his clothes as he gets ready for bed. He doesn't answer when Bum-Knee says, "So how was the concert?"

No one can fall right to sleep. No one speaks. At 12:55 they all hear the small plane that has just left the Mason City airport.

Bum-Knee lies awake till nearly three. He's out cold when Hal wakes up at eight-thirty, dresses silently, sneaks the car keys from the drawer in the nightstand, and slips out with a toothbrush full of toothpaste. He takes a long overdue leak behind the motel. He brushes his teeth and rinses his mouth with snow. Then he gets into the car.

Timmy comes running out, his unbuckled belt flopping up and down under his unbuttoned jacket. He has no socks on and his left foot, not quite in the shoe, is mashing down the back of it. "Where do you think you're going with my dad's car?"

"Bum-Knee sent me on an errand."

"He did?"

"For aspirin. Says he has a hell of a hangover."

"Can I come?"

"Sure."

"Wait! My socks!"

"To hell with your socks. It's now or never."

"Okay. Now." Timmy gets in, all smiles and forgiveness.

At the end of the lot, Hal can't tell which way to go to get to Mason City, to the address the girl gave him. All around he sees farm fields with corn stubble sticking up through the snow. On both sides of the road the snow in the drainage ditches has been whipped into stiff peaks curling over like breaking waves. For as far as Hal can see, the roads are flat, flat, flat. A baby can drive through this state, he thinks.

He turns right and floors it on the clear road with no curve in sight. He's up to sixty-five and both boys are laughing when, suddenly, snow rises up from the fields and blows across the windshield. Hal slams on his brakes, and the car spins around in a snowdrift. When it comes to a stop, all the windows are covered with snow. Hal leans forward and peers through a tiny clear spot on the windshield. He's looking into a farm field, with part of a barbed wire fence visible. "Stay put," he says to Timmy, and gets out. The front wheel on the passenger side is partly suspended over a drainage ditch. Hal sees an abandoned gray pickup truck upright in the ditch and realizes he almost landed on top of it. "Holy shit!" he says. "What the hell kinda place is this?" He opens the driver's side door and motions for Timmy to slide across. "Tim, get out here and look at this."

Timmy, flattered by the invitation to help investigate, slides over and gets out. He hopes he doesn't say the wrong thing.

"Goddammit," says Hal. "What the hell's the matter with the people out here? Don't they know how to make a road? You call this a shoulder over here? There's no way you can fit a car on it. And look here," he says, crossing in front of the car. "Looka this ditch. Looka your wheel hanging over it. You're lucky I had such good control because you certainly can't count on the state of Iowa to save you. A road clear one minute, covered with drifts yay high the next. They must know the winter driving is treacherous. And do they provide guardrails? No! They trick you into cruising along on this, this, this—platform, this fifteen-foot-high catwalk, let you think it's safe just 'cause it's flat and straight. Looka that pickup in the ditch, Timmy. That coulda been us!"

"Thank God you had control, Hal."

"Don't thank God. I'm the one."

"I know. I only meant—"

"Let's go back."

"What about the aspirin for Bum-Knee?"

"To hell with him. If he doesn't have the sense not to drink when he's chaperoning, he deserves a hangover. Let's go."

Timmy looks up. "What's that plane doing up there? It keeps circling. Look! And here comes a helicopter!"

"Jesus!" says Hal, "I bet they're looking for us."

"Why would they be looking for us?"

"That friggin', lousy Bum-Knee probably woke up and saw the car was gone."

"I thought he sent you for—"

"Christ all friggin' mighty, Tim! Were you born yesterday? Huckleberry Tim! Grow up! You saw that chick give me her address. How dumb can you be?"

"You mean you were going to see her?"

A police car with flashing lights comes speeding toward them. Hal digs his wallet out of his back pocket. “Man, it’s a good thing I remembered to bring my driver’s license. Where’s the owner’s card? In the glove compartment?”

“I’ll check, but probably Bum-Knee has it.”

“Goddamn him!”

The patrol car speeds past, right through the snowdrift. Another passes, and another.

“They’re not interested in us,” says Timmy.

“Yeah? Let’s get outa here anyway before they change their minds.”

They scoop out snow from around the tires. Tim’s bare ankles are bright red and they ache like hell, but he doesn’t dare whine like a tot. Hal gets in the car, grabs the steering wheel, and works his left foot on the ground like he’s driving a scooter. Timmy pushes the car from the front, and then from the back. When they finally break free, they drive on at ten miles below the speed limit. Helicopters, cop cars, fire trucks, and ambulances keep coming. “Something’s going on here,” Timmy says, “something really bad.” He turns on the radio. “. . . of Ritchie Valens, Charles Buddy Holly, and Jiles P. Richardson, better known as the Big Bopper, were found in a cornfield five and a half miles north of Clear Lake. Their small plane had taken off from the Mason City Airport at 12:55 a.m. Also killed was the pilot, twenty-one-year-old Roger Arthur Peters of Clear Lake.”

8

Egged

AND NOW A LITTLE HISTORY ON TIM'S BUDDY, Ray Moleski, the guy who goes all out with the party suite at the Harborview Inn in Harbor City, Maine, when he's forty something. In November of 1963, not one supper at the Moleski house in Mount of Olives, Pennsylvania, gets eaten without interruptions by the phone—people pleading, threatening, swearing. Tom Moleski, Ray's dad, Superintendent of Schools, promises each caller he'll try like hell to keep every school open. He means it, too. He really does. But doubts about his success attack the poor bastard like fleas jumping up from a carpet as he shuffles back to the table. It was gonna be just a matter of time till school number one would be closed for good, and he wouldn't be able to wash his hands of it. For years he's tried to slow the exodus of families as mines and factories shut down. He's hounded the politicians for tax breaks for businesses to stay alive, keep people employed. Pleading the case outside the region, he's persuaded two firms to build factories along the highway just west of the Mount of Olives football stadium.

The only public high school in town will go on, sure, but there's little hope for the elementary schools. Too few pupils to justify the maintenance and big heat bills in so many buildings. Something has to go. Everyone thinks someone else's neighborhood school should be closed. The six Catlick elementary schools have already begun to double up, the orders handed down from the bishop way down in Harrisburg. Tom envies the bishop, a man who never has to look into the eyes of people whose children's schools he orders closed. On November 20, Tom Moleski, Superintendent of Schools, announces that the Washington Elementary School will be closing its doors when the school year ends in May.

On Thanksgiving morning, when almost every tree, every post on every porch banister, every telephone pole is decked proudly with shiny strips of red-and-white plastic for the year's biggest football game—Mount of Olives versus Coal Township—the Moleskis wake up to an awful sight. The plastic strips on their front porch are gummed over with egg drippings that have frozen in the night and stayed put like cataracts. Curses have been scribbled with soap on the windows of all three family cars. Ray Moleski, a senior in high school, urges his father to hunt the bastards down and prosecute them. But his father just stands still on the porch in the frosty air, quietly looking over the mess, his breath blowing from his nostrils in sporadic puffs. He goes inside and sits down on the easy chair, sits for a long time, staring up at the ceiling.

Ray's mother is standing stiff against the kitchen wall, staring at nothing with big brown eyes lined in black. Her blunt-cut hair and bangs are black as tar. She looks like you could open the front of her like a lid and find a mummy inside. She doesn't bat one mascara-caked eye when Ray pokes his head in and calls, "Mom!" Ray paces past his father's easy chair six times before hurling himself onto the leather couch so hard that the cushions hiss. Another two minutes of silence and Ray can't take it anymore. He jumps up and leans over his father, showing a fist. "You gotta fight back, Dad!"

"I've been fighting back, Ray."

"No, no, I mean make these people pay."

"They've been paying."

"You just gonna sit there?"

"Yes."

"Oh, great. Mr. Tom Moleski, Superintendent of Schools, lolling in a chair after some lowlifes egg up his house and—"

"That's enough, Ray."

"Yeah, well, I hope you get somebody to clean it up before my friends drop by."

"Now that you mention it, I think I'll just leave it for a few days."

"Dad!"

"Yes, I think I'll just leave it."

Ray glares at his father, but the man will not be moved. "I hate to tell you, Dad, but we're not driving around with soap curses all over our windows. I'm wiping them off!"

"All right."

The next morning, Tom invites his son for breakfast at Annie's restaurant, a long, narrow place with wobbly counter stools, worn linoleum, and booths with scratched-in graffiti going back to 1920. After a meal of scrambled eggs and home fries eaten mostly in silence, Tom says to his son, "Ray, I want to show you something." He leads him out to the sidewalk and points at a FOR-SALE sign in the front window of Allen's store. A mustached mannequin in a hard hat, dungarees, and a plaid flannel shirt gazes blandly into the street, a black lunch can next to his boots. "You're getting old enough to start paying attention," Tom says.

"To what?"

"It's your town, Ray, my town. You know, Sammy Allen's grandchildren, those twin girls, go to that grade school that's shutting down in May."

"That's the breaks."

"Let's go in and talk to him."

"And get eggs thrown in our faces?"

Tom chuckled. "That's the breaks, if you get the pun. Eggs aren't so bad. We just ate a few at Annie's."

"Very funny, Dad. What do you expect me to say to this guy? I know. I'll say, 'My dad's been going to bat for your lousy grandchildren for years. Trying to get new factories to take over where the mines left off. Put thousands to work again, so people can stay in the region and their kids will fill up the classrooms. So you can keep your lousy grandchildren's asses parked in the same schools they've been parked in. It's not Dad's fault, Sammy boy. Dad did everything he could for the schools, the town, you, everybody.' That's what I'll say."

"I see you *have* been paying attention. That's good, son, that's good. You've got some understanding of the history here in Pennsylvania, the facts. But you might try regarding that history with a little humility, Ray. You and your buddies."

"We've bettered ourselves, our families. What's wrong with being proud?" Ray points to Allen's store window. "And that lowlife in there. The bastard. Egging our house after all you tried to do."

"We don't know who egged our house."

"It had to be him. He must have rung our phone a hundred thousand times, trying to talk you into keeping his grandchildren's school open."

"Like I said, we don't know who egged our house. Probably not Sammy Allen."

"Why not? 'Cause he's a businessman? Wilsons built up that business decades ago. The Allens worked in the mines. The mines, the factories. Everybody knows Sammy Allen got that store for a song when the Wilsons saw the handwriting on the wall and got out before Mount of Olives turned into a ghost town. Half ghost town, half old-folks town with no use for steel-tipped boots anymore. That's when Sammy got this store. It doesn't make him a real businessman. Sure, he's standing behind a cash register, but he'll never get the coal dirt out from under his nails."

"Let's go in, Ray. He's just opening up. No customers yet." Tom ushers Ray up the concrete steps.

Sammy's thick gray hair, combed straight back, has let loose a lock that shudders over the cash drawer as he nods his head with each dollar bill passing from hand to hand, his lips silently forming the numbers. He glances at Tom and Ray, but keeps on counting. Tom and Ray turn away and look out at the street. When the cash drawer closes behind them, Tom turns and says, "Sam." His mouth opens again but he finds nothing to say.

Sam looks as sheepish as the man standing before him. "Don't worry, old Tom," he says. "I'm not gonna knock your block off. Anybody could see what was coming. America's booming everywhere else since World War II, but not the coal towns. Schools were bound to start closing. I don't know how you held out as long as you did."

Tom goes over and extends his hand, his face relaxing. "Thanks, Sammy. I'm glad somebody realizes I really did try."

Sam glances at Tom's hand but does not shake it. He reaches under the counter and takes out a checkbook, writes a check, folds it in half, and puts it in Tom's hand.

Tom unfolds the check. "Two hundred dollars! What's this for?"

"To get that egg mess scrubbed up offa your porch. The porch, the walls, the banisters. I did it. Me and, and, well, me and a few other people. I'd just as soon not say who."

Ray's face shoots out beams of righteous indignation. He opens his mouth, but his father silences him with a glare.

Sam slices open a long, narrow box and lifts leather belts out of it, a few at a time, hanging them on various hooks on a pegboard as he speaks. "Wednesday was the twins's birthday. Diane and Donna. Just started third grade this year. They really like their teacher, that Flannigan's girl from over't the Gap. You know, Emmett and Nancy's daughter."

"Barbara Flannigan. Yes, I know," Tom says. "A first-year teacher. She went all through school with our Suzie."

"We weren't gonna say nothin' to the twins. Not till after Christmas, at least. But, you know, with people stoppin' by at the birthday party— The party started at noon on Wednesday, seeing as there was only a halfa day with the next day being Thanksgiving. When parents came by after work for their kids, we got to talking. The children picked up on this school talk. Before you know it, this one was crying, that one was sulking. A few kids cheered, thinking they were done with homework for good."

"Yes," Tom says. "I can imagine."

"That birthday party turned mean. The twins were asking where Miss Flannigan's gonna teach next year so they can go there. Well, somebody says we don't know if she'll have a job at all, probably have to leave town. Our little Donna's wailing her heart out. Before you know it, the whole place is whipped up. It's getting dark out. I don't know what the devil possessed me, but— It's amazing what can come into a man's head, what he might think of doing, when he knows you can't see his face. Like those Ku Klux Klan with their hoods on, burning crosses in the night, heading out for work the next morning like nothing happened.

"I march over to the fridge, grab a box of eggs, and out the door I go. Everybody follows. Not the kids. My wife and daughter make them all stay. That little grocery store on Second Street was still open. We buy every single egg datdare Shinski's lady has left. We all hush up as we get near your house. Those red-and-white plastic strips flapping everywhere were making a hell of a racket. Couldn't hear one egg smack that porch.

"I hate to say it, Tom, but I felt so good after I threw my last egg. Like this big tangle of knots inside all gave way and— Well, I felt free and easy. I thought it over in the night, though. Thought about the mess. Thought about you. Had to admit that you held out as long as you could. I couldn't sleep worth a damn. I figured on cleaning the egg mess up in the morning. I showed up alone at sunrise with a bucket and rag, hoping to clean it before you saw it. But, man! Talk about hopeless! Must have been over a hunnert eggs splattered on that porch!"

"More like a thousand," Ray says. "And after all my dad did to save that school."

"Quiet, son."

"No," Sam says. "Ray's right. You didn't deserve that."

"No, I don't think I did. And Barbara Flannigan doesn't deserve to lose her job. That's the way of the times here in the Coal Region, like you said. I see you've put your store up for sale."

"On Thanksgiving Day. We're still making a profit, not much. But it's a living. Wilsons sold us the whole building cheap just to be done with it. The building's paid off. Low property tax. We get a little rent from the apartment upstairs."

"Why quit, then? You're not sixty-five yet, are you?"

"Sixty-one. Too young to collect Social Security, if that's what you're getting at."

"Yes."

"I put that sign up out of shame, after I saw that mess on your porch."

"Well, take it down, will you?"

"To be honest with you, Tom, I kinda got used to seeing it there. Wouldn't mind traveling a bit. Two of my daughters are down near Philly, Elaine and Janet. Our Linda's out in Wyoming. Our Chuck is in Memphis. Got grandchildren we hardly get to see. We'd keep our house here, though, next door to our John and the twins. It's something to think about, selling this store."

"Have you thought about how much you'd ask for it?"

"Thought about liquidating everything. You know, a big going-out-of-business sale. Donate what doesn't sell. Clear the whole place out. Maybe somebody would open a pinball arcade, something like that, a place for the teenagers to hang out. We'd be lucky to get thirty grand for the building alone, then."

"What about selling the business, stock and all? There's still a need for these things."

"Yes, well, there's that store in Shamokin. People can go there. Like I said, my store doesn't make that big a profit. Don't know as it'd be worth if for somebody who had to pay a mortgage and overhead."

"This store's been here since my dad was a kid. I'd hate to see it go." Tom walks down an aisle, looking over the merchandise as if he's strolling through a museum. He comes back to the check-out counter, chuckling. "Wilsons used to let us kids try on the big work boots while our dads were shopping. We'd clomp up and down the aisles with our giant feet. I bet my old buddies still shop here."

"Well, sure."

Tom places Sam's check on the counter. "Here. Don't worry about the cleanup. I'll take care of it."

Sam hands it back. "No, I need to. My parents are rollin' over in their graves on accounta what I did. That's not how they brought me up."

"Okay, then. Come on over. We'll both clean it up. Start a charcoal fire on the grill in the snow. Have beer and hot dogs."

"It's a deal!"

On Monday, Tom Moleski turns in his resignation and makes an offer on Sammy's store. By January, he's behind the cash register. He sits down to suppers with sighs of satisfaction, telling stories about people he encountered that day, childhood buddies he had once explored colliery shacks with, shot pool with, and rolled down hills with in the winter, making snow sausages of themselves. Ray meets those tales with a stony face.

9

Confessing

NED MILLER, SPRAWLED OUT ON THE SOFA in Ray's entertainment suite at the Harborview Inn, traced his fingertip on the rim of his wineglass and spoke through a yawn. "So where the hell's our Tim? Tim and his dainty little opera glasses?"

Shitfoot's voice rose from the wingback chair. "Exploring on his own today. That was his plan."

"His plan. It's going on nine o'clock already! It's been dark for hours. Serves him right if he gets frostbite. Running about with those fussy little woman testers up here in Uncle Sam's Icebox. 'Would you like to go to the opera with me?'"

Bruce, sitting at the bar and browsing through yearbooks, grinned. "Uncle Sam's Icebox was Alaska, not Maine. Also called Seward's Folly. After three years in tenth grade I got that one down good and firm."

Ray shuffled around, topping off everyone's wineglasses. "You guys haven't been back home for a while. Wait till you see the public library. The whole back wall's been converted into the local sports hall of fame. Rows of photos. And there's our Bruce's face, right up there with the best."

"I kinda wish it wasn't," Bruce murmured. "Feels funny, sitting there reading magazines with my old hulking teenage self looking down on me. Oh, well, I guess that's the way they do things." He finished off his wine in three gulps. "Man, I've been drinking like a fish. Must be something about Maine." He reached for the bottle and refilled his glass.

Tim came through the door, a dusting of snow sparkling on his shoes. Ned sat up. "Hey, Tim, where the hell ya been? The sun went down hours ago! Ray, pour Tim a glass of wine."

Tim shrugged. "Out and about. Checking out the young chicks." Tim tapped glasses with Ray. "Thanks. Hey, everybody, what's up? Any of you guys score today?"

"No luck," Shitfoot said. "The young chicks weren't exactly prancing on the beaches in bikinis, you know. Saw some lighthouses, though. Man, the ocean's wild up here! Crashing on the rocks, dragging back a million stones. Sounds like thunder. I gotta hand it to Ray. Maine really is something to see in the winter. And I thought all I'd get to do is be cooped up in some hotel room with you guys. You shoulda come with us, Tim."

"I got some great photographs around town, down on the waterfront. Lighthouses are nice, but there's lots of old nooks and crannies in an old New England town like this."

"Well, welcome back," Ray said. "God knows we won't be all together in one place till our next class reunion."

"That would leave me out, remember," Bruce said.

"No," Ray said, "it wouldn't. Just show up. Who cares what year you graduated? As far as we're concerned, you're part of our class."

"Thanks. So, Mr. Ray Moleski, proud owner of the finest little store for work clothes in Pennsylvania, this was the last day of the trade show. Come away with any good ideas? I see you got yourself some samples there."

Ray sat down next to a stack of boot boxes. "I am a proud owner. I really am." He lifted the lid from one box, pulled out a sample work boot, examined it inside and out, flexing the sole, and pressed the boot against his nose. "Man, the smell of genuine leather! My dad would have liked these. You know, I'm glad he bought the store."

"Glad!" Tim spouted with a sneer. "That's not what you said thirty years ago. Your dad was Superintendent of Schools, for Christ's sake! Now that's something to be proud of. And he gave it up to run that ragbag of a store. If it was a jewelry store or something, I could see it. But work clothes. Jesus! Hey, Shitfoot, 'member when we chipped in for that plaid flannel shirt from Ray's dad's store and pulled that swap?"

"Yeah, yeah. On prom night. We snuck up to Ray's closet and swapped it for the white shirt that came with the tuxedo he rented. 'Member that, Ray? You were fit to be tied. We're lucky you didn't kill us. You hated that store! You turned red as a beet whenever anybody even mentioned it."

"I remember. It was my dad I was ready to kill. I hauled after him with that plaid shirt in my fist. God, how I yelled at him! 'I'm the laughingstock of all my friends!'" Ray looked Tim in the eye. "Glad. Yes, glad my father bought that store, and I wish I'd've come back and joined him while he was still alive. I wanted to. I was too damned proud. I used to write Dad letters from my office in Florida, asking if I could move back and work alongside him in the store. I tore all those letters up. I hated Florida. I was a duck out of water down there."

"I don't get it," Shitfoot said. "But, what the hell, to each his own. Here's to Maine. Here's to old friends. Eat, drink, and be merry. Enjoy this chance to be together. One of us could be dead by the next class reunion."

Tim smirked. "We're only forty-five. I think we'll last another few years."

"You never know," Ray cautioned. "Look at poor Mickey Dolan. He didn't even make it to legal drinking age."

Ned rolled his eyes. "Drag racing on the Centralia highway. That was no surprise."

Ray knocked his knuckles on his chest. "It shocked the hell outa me."

"Me, too," Bruce said.

"Aw, c'mon," Ned said. "With the road sagging over those mine tunnels, it was a twisted ribbon. We all knew—and Mickey knew too—it was a matter of time till some drag racer's brains would be scattered all over that road like lumps of cottage cheese."

Ray took a swat at Ned from across the room. "Did you have to put it that way? I don't like thinking of Mickey with his—"

"I'm only repeating what the whole town said," Ned persisted. "My mom still talks about it. She says Mickey Dolan's brains were spread all over that highway like cottage cheese. Some was even flung up on the slagpiles alongside that road."

"I know, I know," Ray said. "Still, Mickey was our buddy, one of us. I'd rather remember him sitting next to us at the stadium, or—"

Tim Giovannini chuckled. "One of us. Mickey Dolan was never one of us. His dad was a damned grease monkey, for Christ's sake. He worked for my father, oiling and lubing, tinkering with engines. Hell, Mickey'd come into our dealership on a Saturday to ask his dad this or that. Nothing important. Just an excuse to get around me and give the impression he was a friend of mine, while I'm there trying to learn how the books are done with him breathing over my shoulder."

"Well, Mickey was a friend of mine," Ray insisted, "first grade through graduation day. I'd've flunked chemistry if it wasn't for him helping me with my homework. Mickey was one smart, bighearted kid. Too bad I didn't have the guts back then to stand up to the things you guys said behind his back. No, I was too glad to be among Hal's chosen people. I wasn't about to risk it."

"You're lucky we let Mickey tag along at all," Tim said. "We did it for your sake. So he ends up cottage cheese. The kid was going nowhere anyhow."

"I said knock it off about the cottage cheese!"

Tim let out a big breath of exasperation. "Calm down, Ray! Jesus! The fuss you make over Mickey Nobody meeting his end on some sunken old coal road! Look at me. I found Buddy Holly laid out in that frozen Iowa cornfield. Think about it, you guys, those were three talented young men. Buddy Holly, Ritchie Valens, the Big Bopper. Now, *their* lives were going somewhere."

Tim stood up and began to pace, pausing from time to time to shake his head and take in a long thoughtful breath. "I can still see strips of Buddy's yellow leather jacket flapping in the wind. All bloody. Fifteen feet away there's poor Ritchie Valens. Both of their heads busted open. Brains and blood slopped all over the snow. How do you think I liked seeing that, Ray? How 'bout it, Ray? Think I can forget it? And the pilot, still in the plane. His legs sticking straight up. We had to tramp forty feet through snow to find the Big Bopper. And there he was on the other side of a farm fence, clear—"

Ray sighed. "I know, I know. 'Clear into the next cornfield, laying across the stubble. Blood and guts everywhere!'"

Tim leaned over Ray's chair. "What, are you mocking me, trying to make a jerk out of me? Okay, so I told the story a few times too many. How could I help it? It's no picnic coming upon a scene like that. It's a horror show that stays with you for the rest of your life. Put yourself in my place, Ray. Only a kid. Thirteen! Imagine. Just you and your best friend, Hal Jones, minding your own business, happily cruising down some ho-hum Iowa two-lane, and suddenly—Christ Almighty—there they are dead, three of the biggest stars in the history of rock 'n' roll. You can't forget it, Ray! You have to tell it again and again, hoping the nightmares will stop.

"Yeah, you guys were so jealous when I won that concert ticket from Hal on a coin flip. Think about it. How lucky was I in the end? Just me and Hal, two scared teenagers with those dead bodies. No phone booth. No passing cars to flag down. We nearly froze to death ourselves waiting to get someone's attention. Finally, a small plane flies over. All we can do is wave our arms and hope the idiot looks down and sees us. If it wasn't for me and Hal, those three stars could have laid frozen in that cornfield till spring. Thanks to us there were emergency vehicles coming from everywhere in a matter of—"

"All right, already," Ned barked. "We all read all about you and Hal Jones and Buddy Holly, and so forth, in the *Mount of Olives Gazette.* My mom even put the clipping in one of our family albums. Let's get back to Maine here. Hey, look, I sprung for my very own pair of binoculars. A *man's* binoculars!" Ned went to the window and leered into the lounge of the M-WIT. "Anybody want a look?"

Bruce poured himself another drink. "No, thanks."

Shitfoot reached for the binoculars. "I'll have a look. Hey, I don't see that big clunky redhead." He swiveled his head. "Nope, not there. Tough shit for you, Timmyboy."

"What's it to me?"

They all groaned. Ned grinned. "'What's it to me,' the man asks. The first night we're here I say, 'Look, there's Mary Frances McDonald over there,' and Timmyboy comes bounding across the room, panting at the window. Somebody toss me a rag. Wipe the saliva offa the windowsill here."

"Yeah," Shitfoot seconded. "Then he spends half the night staring at that fatso, peeling off ten layers of flab with his eyes, knocking off a foot of height, till he pares her down to Mary Frances McDonald size. That's when the drool comes oozing out."

Ned nodded slowly. "Yeah, Timmyboy, fess up. You're still sulking over missing out on the big bang with Mary Frances up the top floor of the Mine."

Tim took a slow sip of wine. "What did I care about that? I got her cherry months before you guys even got close enough to get a whiff of her. Christ, was my dad ever pissed when he saw that blood stain on the back seat of that Thunderbird! Remember?"

"We know all about the blood stain," Bruce grumbled.

"I was grounded for a week. I wasn't left drive anything but that beat-up blue courtesy car—that damned, six-year-old junker Bum-Knee used—for the rest of the school year. Christ! Okay, so you all had a good time giving it to Mary Frances that night at the Mine. Better you than me. Who'd want to get in there right after Mickey Dolan?"

"Dolan went last," Ned reminded Tim. "I made sure of that. Yeah, Tim, you missed out."

"Big deal," Tim said.

Shitfoot patted Tim's shoulder. "Don't feel bad, Timmy. The one lousy Wednesday I don't feel like going upda Mine, and doesn't Mary Frances decide to have a free-for-all. All along, she acts like the Virgin of Mount of Olives. Suddenly, she— I could kick myself! That was our only chance. She never looked at any of us again."

Bruce swiveled his bar stool around. "Wasn't that strange? Now that we're talking about it, that was really strange."

"What was strange?" asked Ray.

"Mary Frances, that night at the Mine. You know, Mary Frances was like, well, I know you're all gonna laugh when I say this. It's almost poetic, and I'm this big clunker talkin'."

"Like what? Mary Frances was like what?" Tim snapped, sorry immediately that he showed interest.

"Like this exotic flower I saw on a National Geographic special. Down South America or Cambodia, some exotic place. It blooms only once in a lifetime. And even then, this big, wonderful, beautiful blossom comes out in the middle of the night. By morning, poof! It's gone. The local people look for the signs it's about to bloom and they camp out, waiting for that chance of a lifetime to behold that one bloom. They don't go grabbing it and yanking it off the plant or anything like that. They just look at it."

Shitfoot smiled at Bruce like a proud brother. "And just think, Bruce, you were there for Mary Frances's one big bloom night. I hear you went first, Bruce."

"First, last, middle," Bruce said angrily. He gnawed on his lip. "Now, I wish I didn't do it to Mary Frances. You know, I thought of her the night I saw that show. Dammit, why do they have to put TV shows on like that flower thing anyway? Makes me feel like shit now." Bruce pushed his wineglass away and drummed his thick fingers on his forehead.

"Well, boo, hoo, hoo," Tim sang out. "Poor Mary Frances McDonald. She was lucky we even looked at her. She was going nowhere. A lowlife. Her mom worked in the cigar factory. Her dad dug coal, they said. That's if she even had a dad. They say he died when she was little. Sure. For all we know, she was a bastard kid herself. And like I told you, she was far from a virgin by the time you guys got at her. She got it from me first, remember."

"I don't believe you," Bruce said, staring into his wineglass at the bar. "I mean, yeah, word was all around town about you and her. I had my doubts, but what the hell. It was easier to be in on the gang bang if I could think of her as some low-life whore."

"Oh, you think I'm a liar. So now you're blubbering in your booze like some remorseful monster because you think I made up that good time with her in the Thunderbird and you gang-banged a virgin. Well, you can hereby give your conscience a rest. That boyfriend of hers, Catman Berkoski, he made sure he got his from her after I told him what a time she had with me. So see? She got it from two boys before you got in there, Bruce. Me, then Catman. So don't go sobbing over this poor, rare, virgin flower. Catman told me all he ever got from Mary Frances was holding hands and a kiss good-night at her doorstep. She always sent him home with lover's cramps. After she did it with me, he wasn't about to put up with her phony shit, 'No, honey. Please, honey. Not till we're married, honey.' Catman took what was coming to him. She must've liked it. Couldn't get enough then. So she had Mickey Dolan arrange that gang bang up the Mine. Rare flower, my ass, Bruce."

Bruce put his head down. "It haunts me. No matter what you say, it haunts me. Makes me sorry I ever came back to Mount of Olives after I quit the pros. Back in the old home town, scene of the crime, workin' in my dad's old box factory. I guess that's what you'd call going somewhere, Timmy."

"You're not working on the line, are you? You're not folding boxes, are you? You get to walk around and give the orders—turn up the line, slow down the line. You own the damned place, Bruce. What more do you want?"

"Nothin', nothin', forget it."

"Same thing I want, probably," Ray said. "Some connection with my neighbors. I took over my dad's business, too. But I live in a fucking limbo. I thought I could have this chummy little hometown store like my dad had. He loved that store! He loved the people. And they loved him. Why? Because he grew up with them. I mean *with* them. All of them. Sledding with them, playing ball, going to the movies. Their fathers worked in the mines together, their moms in factories. Their grandparents were all different nationalities—Polish, Irish, Tyrolean, German, Lithuanian. Couldn't even speak the same language, but they were friends. That's how the town was at one time. When some guy got killed on the job, other families helped the ones left behind no matter who they were, where they came from. Then a few people get a little better off, and the next generation a little better off. Like our families. Our parents tell us not to play with those grubby ones. My mother did, at least."

"Both my parents did," Bruce said. "My mom caught me playing kick-the-can on the schoolie with those kids from the coal patches and she dragged me away. I got a good talkin' to. 'Stick with your own kind,' she told me. Christ, is there anybody in this room whose grandfathers didn't dig coal? My parents decided I was going to marry a doctor's daughter some day. Or a lawyer's. I better put that in my pipe and smoke it." Bruce threw the last ounce of his wine down his throat. "Funny, I couldn't play kick-the-can with the patch kids when I was six, but Mom and Dad looked the other way when I practiced giving it to patch girls in high school. That's what I called it, practicing, when Dad caught me in the garage with Ginny from Wrenville. You know, that wreck of a coal patch in Coal Township. 'Just don't get her in trouble,' Dad warned me. He winked and patted me on the back. The next day he hands me a pack of rubbers. I shoulda never laid hands on that girl. I'm sorry I did."

Tim groaned. "What is this? Confession night? Bless me, Father, for I have sinned?"

"Why not confess, after all these years," Ray said. "Isn't that what we were all doing with the Mary Frances McDonalds in town? Practicing for the ones we would someday take seriously? Why not come clean? Speaking of television, I saw a show on Confucius a few months ago. Honesty was a big thing with him. He said that—"

Ned waddled to the middle of the room and stretched his eyes to slits. "Confucius say, 'Man who fart in church sit in pew.'"

Shitfoot, bowing, said in choppy English, "Confucius say, 'Woman who fly upside-down have crack up.'" Shitfoot and Ned grabbed each other's shoulders and skipped up and down the room, making mock Chinese sounds. Ned said, "Confucius say, 'Mys-ter-ree solved. Mary Frances daughter live in Maine. Big, big, big fat redhead. Father be Bruce Moose on Loose from bing-bang night.'"

"Shut up!" Bruce yelled, rattling glasses as his fist came down on the bar.

Ned and Shitfoot crept backwards into chairs.

"Forget it," Ray said. "Let's call it a night."

"Look, Ray," said Tim, "if you and Bruce invited us here just to get us to feel like shit for taking advantage of a bunch of going-nowhere, coal-town cunts—"

"No," Ray said, "that's not why. I wanted to be with old friends. I'm lost in that town now. I meet people every day, sure, but I might as well be from Mars. They're polite to me, but I just can't get a handle on them. With the exception of Mickey Dolan, who saved my ass a hundred times in chemistry lab, they're the kind of people I didn't want to know when I was younger. Now it's too late. I just can't fit in now. Frankly, I can't think of anywhere on Earth I'd fit in. I thought it would be good to see you guys, old friends. Be like old times. But the old times are gone. Who the hell'd want them back now anyway?"

10

Chaff Is Chaff

On Sunday morning, as Tim, Ray, Bruce, Ned, and Shitfoot finished up a sunrise breakfast before heading to the airport, Tim announced that he was extending his stay in Maine for a few days. "I found an antique car dealer here. I'm gonna propose a swap. Wouldn't mind adding a little more variety to my lot in Illinois. Good to see you guys. Thanks, Ray, for the invitation."

Tim showed up at the Vine Street Friends Meeting, an old clapboard building with a U-shaped driveway. A rugged teenage boy and a stooped woman with hair like a cloud were posted at the door, greeting people as they came in. The boy, offering Tim a yellow card, said, "First time here?"

Tim noted the heading on the card: *If This Is Your First Time at a Quaker Meeting for Worship.* "Oh, I've been to plenty of Quaker meetings elsewhere, but may I have one of these cards anyway?"

"Sure. Welcome." The boy twisted around and pointed to an open door near a corner of the foyer. "See that door? Go through there for Meeting for Worship."

"Thanks!" Tim crept toward the door and looked in. Several adults and school-age children were seated among concentric rows of wooden fold-up chairs. In one of the few double-seaters sat a man and woman around eighty, holding hands. Tim took note of a nice piece in the center row, a woman with straight brown hair hanging down to her lap. Next to her, two toddlers on their parents' laps played silently with tiny human figures made of cloth. Everyone was silent. Tim, noting that everyone else was in ordinary street clothes, felt conspicuous in his suit, tie, and topcoat. Even the room was plain, nothing but brown wainscoting, cream-colored walls, and a bare floor of wide, wooden planks. No statues, no altar, no pulpit, no pictures or candles. No furniture, apart from the chairs. So far, Tim noted with irritation, no Sharon, at least not for as far as he could see without rubbernecking.

On the door jamb, he saw a little plaque that would give him an opportunity to roam about the building to see if Sharon had squirreled herself away in some corner: *Please enter Meeting for Worship through the parlor to your left if you arrive after 10:00.* It was 9:54. He would have to find some excuse to go back outside and come in late. Standing with his back to the greeters, he sneaked glances at everyone who entered as he made a show of reading a quotation on a wall hanging, a large swatch of burlap with words stitched onto it:

> *Be patterns, be examples in all countries, places, islands, nations, wherever you come; that your carriage and life may preach among all sorts of people, and to them. Then you will come to walk cheerfully over the world, answering that of God in every one.*
> *— George Fox, 1656*

Tim scratched his head at the notion of a bunch of people with no better taste than burlap setting themselves up as examples. Standing on public streets and staring at the ground, doing nothing, while nut cases like Saddam Hussein ravaged little countries like Kuwait, jeopardizing our access to some of the world's best oil supply.

A pear-shaped shadow appeared on the wall as a woman with a hooded black cape came and stood beside Tim and whispered, "Good morning." Her lips moved as her eyes followed the words on the burlap. A look of astonishment crossed her lightly wrinkled face. "Thank you for drawing my attention to this. I've seen these words of Fox a million times, but today they're speaking to me in a new way. Thank you so much!"

Tim, leery of being drawn into a conversation, simply smiled.

"Hi, Marie," a man whispered to the woman in the cape.

"Good morning, Joe," she answered.

"Morning," the man said to Tim, who nodded in response. Marie and Joe walked into the meeting room.

Tim hung around, scouting furtively for Sharon while re-reading Fox's words till he knew them by heart. Except for Tim and the greeters, the foyer was empty. The greeters hung their coats on wall pegs. The old woman looked at Tim in a way that made him squirm. The boy, pulling the door to the worship room half closed, also eyed Tim.

"Oh, sorry," Tim whispered, taking a step toward the boy. "Ouch. I must've gotten a little stone in my shoe. I'll be right back." He tapped on the wall plaque. "Don't worry, I'll come in through the parlor." Putting on a hint of a limp, he went out and looked over the lawn and parking lot, hoping to see Sharon lumbering along. A city bus stopped, letting off a man with a seeing-eye dog, no one else. Glancing back at the tall windows, he removed his shoe, banged it on the stone step, and poked his finger inside the shoe before putting it back on. Thinking someone could be watching from the window, he traipsed a few yards along the driveway and back, looking satisfied at the improved feel of his footwear.

He went back inside, turned left, and walked past a staircase leading to the basement and to a floor upstairs. In the parlor, juice pitchers and baked goods were set out on a long table. The door to the meeting room was standing open and Tim checked out people's sizes and the backs of their heads. No sign of Sharon. Maybe she was going to take him up on his suggestion of waiting for him on the porch after the service if she didn't want to go to it. Taking a seat at the end of a row close to the center of the room, he was thankful for the good view of the woman with the long hair, but annoyed to find himself right in the line of sight of the two greeters. He copied the stillness and the downward gaze of the other worshippers and waited for something to start. Through a cast iron grate in the floor, he could hear toddlers playing in the basement. He heard an occasional cough or squeak of a chair from different parts of the room. More latecomers came in through the parlor behind him. Though itching to know if one of them was Sharon, he did not twist around for fear of appearing impious.

In the ongoing silence, Tim read the yellow card he was given by the boy in the foyer. According to the card, something was happening. People had set their own willing and daily clutter aside to discern God's will for their lives, to hear the "still small voice" that would lead the way. The card said that someone might stand and give a message, but Friends were asked to discern carefully if the insight they were given was meant for themselves or meant to be shared.

Tim wished someone would stand up and say something. It was maddening, sitting like stone for twenty minutes with nothing to do but wonder if Sharon had come in through the parlor. Was she sitting in a chair somewhere behind him? Would she show up later on the porch? His thoughts wandered to Ray Moleski and his confession party. To hell with Ray. To hell with Bruce. Ned and Shitfoot were still all right. Tim calmed himself by saying a little prayer for Ned and Shitfoot to have a safe flight home.

He noticed that the old couple holding hands had fallen asleep. Their heads were leaning against each other's. The man's lips quivered as he inhaled, and his free hand twitched. The pair shuddered when a man with a deep voice began to speak, but then they slumped and resumed dozing. The speaker, standing somewhere behind Tim, said, "While I was driving here today, the drawbridge over the harbor went up to let a big ship go by. I was stuck behind a red pickup truck with a bumper sticker that said, 'On the Day of the Rapture, this vehicle will be empty.' I picture this guy turning transparent and being drawn through the roof of his truck. Suddenly he's up there with God, congratulating himself as he looks down. His bumper sticker scoffs at all the flawed human beings left behind to read it while they wait to be tossed into the fire with the rest of the chaff.

"I— I have a lot of trouble abiding people advertising how saved they are. I arrived here at worship, crushed by the weight of my own hostility towards the man with the bumper sticker. Then, in the long silence of this morning, I was reminded of what Jesus said.

'The Kingdom of God is within you.' And I was brought to a place of peace." The man sat down.

What does this guy mean, Tim thought, reinterpreting the Bible to his own liking! Does he think he can gab his way out of Hell on Judgment Day?

A few minutes later, the woman with the long hair stood up. Tim expected to hear her take on the bumper sticker. He wondered if her voice was as beautiful as her face. But she glanced around in silence till all the children stood up in various parts of the room and followed her out to the foyer. Tim could hear them going down to the basement. So much for her, he thought. She's probably no fun anyway.

After another period of silence, a chair near a window creaked as someone stood up. Tim recognized the speaker as the woman who had thanked him in the foyer. Seeing that no one else was staring at her, he turned his eyes to the floor. She spoke with groping pauses. "Until this morning, I've been troubled by George Fox asking us to be patterns and examples in all places, assuring us we'll walk cheerfully over the world if we do. Because I travel so much for my job, I go to many places. I've tried to live up to Fox's standards, but I get worn out. At night in my hotel room, I confront myself. I demand an accounting of what kind of example I set that day. I fess up to my shortcomings and brood over my failures.

"This morning I re-read Fox's words. Suddenly, I saw a way out of this terrible cycle of striving and failing to demonstrate to people everywhere I go how to live right, how to do something I can't even manage myself. Today I see it's not a question of demonstrating how good I am. All I have to do is consent to being led inwardly by the Light of God. I don't have to ransack my own soul for every little flaw to make myself presentable and admirable in all places. The Light of God will search out my failings for me. Only minutes ago, I was brought to realize how rudely I had spoken to a co-worker. The insight just came over me in this worshipful silence. Sure, I felt ashamed of myself, but I'm not left writhing in relentless shame the way I am after scrutinizing myself. I feel a promise of help and hope. More insight to come and the grace to help me do better, if I simply wait calmly for it and consent to receive it. What a gift! So now I see. I don't have to be an example of someone who always gets things right. I can be an example of someone willing to be changed, of someone willing to be led day by day to a better path." The woman sat down and a long time of silence resumed.

Three cheers for you, Tim thought. Jesus! How did I ever manage to grow up in the so-called Quaker State without ever noticing this do-it-yourself religion? They just make it up as they go along! A bunch of scofflaws who question the call to war, even question their Christian duty to examine their own conscience. And that whacko on the bridge behind the red pickup truck. Chaff is chaff. What the hell!

From behind him, a young female voice, quivering, said, "I'm not sure if it's okay for me to talk. This is my first time here. I don't know if you people say prayers. If you do, please pray for me and for my mother. My birth mother. I'm gonna meet her for the first time. A nice man here said he'll introduce us. Please pray that she's not disappointed."

Tim almost laughed out loud. Disappointed? Horrified! That's the whole point, you dummy! Mary Frances McDonald searching for her little darling and finding the likes of you. Chaff.

The people sat in silence till the meeting ended with handshakes. The clerk introduced herself and asked if visitors would like to stand and introduce themselves. Two brothers brought greetings from a Friends Meeting in Ohio, and a woman brought greetings from one in Kansas. A college student from Harbor City stood up and said his visit was an assignment for a history class. He was supposed to check out a religion that came to flourish during the time of the Restoration.

Sharon popped up, blurted, "I'm Sharon from Harbor City," and sat down.

"I'm Howard Parker," Tim Giovannini said. "I grew up in Pennsylvania, and I attend different Quaker meetings in my constant travels. I can really relate to the woman who said how worn out all that traveling makes her." He stood there smiling confidently. From among the smiles of welcome came a dubious stare from the cloud-haired woman who had greeted everyone on the way into the building.

"Welcome, everyone," the clerk said. "That door over there to the right leads to our library. A member of Ministry and Counsel will be in there to answer any questions anyone may have about Quakers or our Friends Meeting. The other door leads to the parlor, where we have refreshments. Everyone is welcome."

After the clerk made a few announcements, people exchanged greetings on their way to the parlor or library. A woman around forty-five, her arms outstretched, hurried over to Sharon. Slim and as tall as Sharon, she wore sharply creased slacks and a crisp, green blouse. Her dark hair, freshly trimmed in neat, straight bangs, was tied back with a crisp, green ribbon. Sharon's clothes, pulled from her suitcase that morning, were crumpled. A jagged line of white residue from the salted streets stained her brown boots, which had a series of scuffed bulges over her toes. Sharon looked herself over and recoiled as the woman got closer.

"Good morning, Sharon! I'm Michele. What a wonderful story! How exciting! Meeting your birth mother after all these years! I'm on Ministry and Counsel here at the Friends Meeting. Maybe you'd like to talk some more."

A pleading look swept across Sharon's face as she met eyes with Tim, who was shaking hands with the old couple who had dozed through the whole meeting. "I'm— I really don't know any more. I need to talk to Mr. Parker. Sorry, I—" Sharon was near tears. Michele gathered Sharon against herself and said, "It's all right, Sweetie, you've had a rough time, I can tell."

Sharon pulled back and stood stiffly like a frightened soldier trying to look brave. Michele kept hold of Sharon's hands. A man passing by greeted Sharon and told her he'd hold her in the Light.

Tim came and stood next to Sharon and called out, "I hope you'll hold both of us in the Light."

"I sure will."

Sharon said to Michele, "This is the man who knows my birth mother."

Michele shook Tim's hand. "Hi, there! I'm Michele. Uniting Sharon with her birth mother. How exciting! Since you're not from this area, perhaps we can help, help with travel arrangements or something."

The cloud-haired greeter looked up from her bent walk to the parlor. She eyed Tim and raised a palm to Michele as if stopping traffic. Michele moved closer to Tim, and the two stood looking at Sharon like a pair of investigators deciding together how to proceed. Sharon's fingers crawled across her shoulder till they found the frayed right tip of her blouse collar and covered it.

Michele asked Tim, "Is her mother coming here? Perhaps I could suggest some places her mother could stay, even make a few calls for you."

"No," Tim said. "I don't think her mother'll be coming here. She'll want to show Sharon lots of places connected with her roots. It's a little coal mining town. A place with a proud heritage. For starters, Sharon will get to see where she came from." Tim, caught up in his own scheme, was momentarily convinced that Sharon really was Mary Frances's daughter. He held back a big guffaw as he imagined Sharon standing before the old United Mine Workers Building, now a hardware store, listening to the tale of the top floor and the four boys giving it to her mother among the Olympic hopeful's barbells. "So Sharon will probably have to travel to Pennsylvania."

"Oh. Then maybe I could suggest—"

The cloud-haired woman, laying a hand on Michele's arm in a gesture of restraint, said to Sharon, "I hope you'll think about this carefully, dear. Sometimes these sorts of reunions don't turn out as you'd hoped."

Michele puffed her cheeks out, as though her mouth were filling up with words she'd rather not say just then. "Claire, can I talk to you a minute? Out in the foyer. I'm sorry, Sharon, Howard. I have to catch up with Claire on something this morning. This will just take a minute. Have some refreshments in the parlor."

Michele and Claire went out to the foyer and stood by the burlap wall hanging below the upper staircase. Michele shut the door to the worship room. Tim told Sharon he had to get something from his car. "Wait for me in the parlor." Instead of going outside, he went through the parlor and dashed up the stairs in the foyer, listening.

"Claire, what are you doing?" Michele demanded in a sharp whisper.

"Wondering what *you're* doing, encouraging this. You don't know anything about those people."

"You heard Sharon speak. She's dying to meet her birth mother."

"All the more reason to make sure she isn't being taken advantage of before you jump in to try to help. I watched that man lurking out here in the foyer before Meeting."

Michele cast a skeptical glance at Claire. "Lurking?"

"Lurking, yes."

"He was waiting for Sharon. She said herself he'd invited her."

"True, but after Sharon spoke in Meeting, he had a smirk on his face. And there was something about his speech right now that— I saw that smirk again."

"A smirk. Ohhhhhhh, Claire. Even you said your eyes aren't what they used to be. He's respectable-looking. And he's a Quaker."

"So was Richard Nixon. Even Nixon probably had some idea what went on in a Quaker meeting. This Howard Parker had no idea. He copied any hints he could pick up. But he claims he attends Quaker meetings all over the place. I think he's up to no good. Maybe I'm wrong. I could be wrong. All I'm asking you to do is to step back. Make sure before we encourage Sharon."

"What possible motive could he have for tricking Sharon? One look at her will tell you, well, he couldn't be trying to con money out of her."

"Maybe this long-lost mother is loaded with money or something, something this Howard Parker thinks he can get his hands on through Sharon. Or maybe— Could be anything. Look at Sharon? Take a closer look at *him,* Michele."

"All right, I will. But you look, too. To be honest, Claire, I think you have some personal, unfinished emotional business that's coloring your perspective on this. Not only this situation. Other things, too. That's what I meant just now when I told Mr. Parker and Sharon I had to catch up with you on something this morning. This conversation is long overdue."

"What?"

"You have issues, Claire, unresolved issues in your own life. This isn't the time or place to go into that. I'd be happy to discuss it another time."

"I'd like to hear what you mean. I'll call you."

Michele patted Claire's arm. "Good. I'm glad to hear you're open to examining those things. Yes, let's get together and talk about them. As I said, I've been meaning to catch up with you on this. But, as you can imagine, it's an awkward thing to bring up. As for Sharon, it's obvious that she has issues. Possibly grief issues she never reached closure on. Certainly abandonment issues. Dreads being rejected by her birth mother."

"Dreads being— Who wouldn't in a situation like that?"

Michele appeared not to have heard the question. Her left hand was cupping her chin and her eyes were alive with ideas. "If Sharon's going to stand a chance at being accepted, she'll need some decent clothes. And did you notice her boots? She'll probably need help with bus fare, too. Let's talk more later. I need to get back in there."

"Me, too."

"Don't help if you're afraid, Claire, but please don't interfere."

Tim followed the two women into the parlor, where his efforts to get to Sharon were impeded by greetings. Sharon, pinching her frayed collar, was stammering at everyone who tried to be friendly. Tim listened from across the table as Michele sidled up to her. "Took longer than a minute, Sharon. Sorry about that." She placed a hand on Sharon's shoulder. "So where do you live?"

"At the M-WIT. Well, right now I'm on a six weeks time-out. You can't stay there more than two years at a time."

"Yes, I know. I'm a volunteer with New Steps for Women while working on my degree in social work. Actually, I'm done with my classes, just writing my thesis now. Anyway, some women in the support group I lead have stayed at the M-WIT. So I'm familiar with the policy. So where are you staying in the meantime?"

"Oh, I have lots of friends around town."

"And do you work here in town?"

"I sort donations at the Salvation Army Store."

"Full time?"

"Weekday mornings." Sharon backed up. "Um, I need to talk to Mr. Parker."

"Sure," Michelle said. She turned away and approached the man who had spoken about the bumper sticker on the red pickup truck.

Sharon took three cookies from a plate, and waved to Tim. Tim worked his way around to Sharon. Gesturing with his elbow toward Claire, who was at the other end of the table pouring herself a glass of orange juice, he whispered, "Watch out for that white-haired lady in the blue dress. Two women out in the foyer just warned me about her. They say she's a little—" He tapped his index finger on his temple. "A little—you know. Let's just say she's got issues." Tim stretched his neck and looked around the room till he spotted Michele in a cluster of other people. He made an exaggerated gesture of yanking his overcoat closed and buttoning it.

Michele hurried over. "Leaving?"

"Yes. It was nice to be here. This is a lovely meeting. Say, I wonder if you could do me and Sharon a favor. If you wouldn't mind giving me your mailing address," Tim said, backing toward the door and lowering his voice, "Sharon mentioned she's staying with different friends at the moment. I have some things to mail to her, a picture of her mother, and we'll need to correspond about arrangements. If I had an address I could write to—" He opened his briefcase and took a leather-bound notebook out, setting it on the table while pretending to root for a pen, which meant pulling out the case with the opera glasses. With a practiced hand he snapped open the little case, letting the opera glasses slip out and making a quick grab for them before they could hit the floor. Michele and Sharon dived for the glasses too, but it was Tim who caught them.

"Lovely opera glasses," Michele said. "And a lucky catch. What a shame it would be if these got broken."

Tim watched Sharon behold the opera glasses with the same sort of delight and fascination she had for the sunlight shining through the rotting leaf and making patterns on the back of her hand. Satisfied with Michele's reaction, he said to her, "About that address."

"Sure!"

Sharon pressed her hands against her cheeks. "Um, um, what about, I mean, what if I had a post office box? I've been thinking of getting one anyway. I can rent one tomorrow, right after I get off work at noon."

Tim and Michele exchanged a look. Tim shrugged. "Why not? But it would also help to have a phone number I could call on short notice." He handed the notebook to Michele.

Michele wrote down her name, address and phone number.

"Thanks. I'll be in town till around five tomorrow." Tim turned to Sharon. "How about if we meet at the post office around three? You can give me your new box number. I'll be on the road a lot for the next two months, so there's no use trying to write to me. It's better if *I* get in touch."

"Okay," Sharon said.

Tim gave Michele a nod and ushered Sharon out the door.

Sharon's arm flew around Cindy, whose feet slipped when the canvas cart they were pushing to the Salvation Army donation bins skidded in the icy parking lot. "Thanks, Big Sharon! Next time, I'll catch you."

Sharon shook her co-worker's hand. "It's a deal, Little Cindy."

The latches on the bins were eye-level to Cindy. When she popped them open and swung the first metal panel out, she was nearly bowled backwards by a big stuffed bulldog. She shoved the dog's mouth onto Sharon's wrist and growled. Sharon treated the dog to a bite of Cindy's neck. A brown monkey twisted the dog's tail, and soon a stuffed bear held by Sharon broke up the fray and ordered the women inside and back to work. They wheeled the new donations through the employees-only door and parked the cart alongside a long table, where they disentangled shirt sleeves from toys and pot handles. Sharon heaved a plastic bag onto the table and the contents belched out. As she sorted clothing, Cindy, her short, blond hair tied into a tail that stuck straight out like a basting brush, slipped her tiny hands into shoes and boots, exhuming one Barbie doll and one G.I. Joe.

Soon Sharon was pushing a cart of sorted merchandise through the green double doors to the sales room, one arm steadying books perched on a pile of toys. In the back corner, she took one book at a time from the cart and flitted about, looking for just the right spot for it among the shelves. So graceful and lithe were her movements, she could have been a ballerina in a stage play, putting ornaments on a Christmas tree. Her next cartload was more books atop sheets and blankets. The aisles had become crowded. Sharon, keeping her gaze low, looked at customers only long enough to avoid bumping them with the cart. Surprised by the new-looking black wool coat on one woman she dodged, she wondered why someone with a coat like that would be rummaging through a rack of used jackets. "Hi, there, Sharon," the woman said. Sharon found herself eye to eye with Michele, who asked cheerfully, "How you doing today?"

"Pretty good." Sharon retreated to the corner where the bookcases were. She began taking the books from the cart and sorting them into neat stacks on a wooden bench.

"So you're doing okay?" Michele asked as she approached. Sharon uttered a few sounds. Michele broke in with a cheerful voice. "I'm on my way to New Steps for Women right now. I think I mentioned yesterday, I volunteer there as a support group leader. I had some free time, so I stopped in. I was hoping to catch you here."

"Me?"

"Yes. I wanted to say hello. And I was wondering, do you type?"

"Well, yeah. I took— I took typing in high school."

"Do you keep up with it?"

“I type up papers for women at the M-WIT. Some of them take classes.”

“Do you have your own typewriter or computer?”

“The library has computers. I use those.”

“Good. Good for you!” Michele popped the clasp on her briefcase and took out a red plastic folder. She showed Sharon a few sheets of paper with handwriting. There was a floppy disk in a clear pocket. “I have a report here. It should come to about four pages typed up. Something for the Friends Meeting. I was wondering if you’d type it. It sure would save me a lot of time. I’ll pay you, of course. Twenty-five dollars. In fact, the money’s already in an envelope in the folder.”

Cindy, who was passing by, whistled in astonishment. She flashed Sharon a thumbs-up with both hands.

“Oh, no,” Sharon said. “I only get a buck a page at the M-WIT. Or I swap for a few cans of soup. I don’t think—”

“It’s worth it to me, believe me. I’m so goshdarn busy. I hope my handwriting’s clear enough.”

Sharon looked at the first page and read aloud, “‘Recorded Quaker Ministers in New England: a report compiled by Michele Arbalester.’”

Michele chuckled. “After attending our Meeting yesterday, you’re probably wondering what this is about.”

“Uh, ummm, no, I didn’t mean to— I just wanted to see if I could read your handwriting. And, and make sure it wasn’t columns of figures. I’m not great at typing numbers.”

“It’s just words,” Michele said. “As for the content, you didn’t see any minister leading our Quaker worship yesterday.” She jostled Sharon’s shoulder in a reassuring way and continued, undaunted, when Sharon took a step back. “Don’t worry. Recorded ministers are just ordinary Quakers. They’re not ordained authorities. It’s just that their vocal ministry—that’s when someone stands up and speaks in Meeting—has stood the test of time. It’s inspired. Helpful. They get recorded as having special gifts in ministry. Their gifts often carry over as a ministry in everyday life among other people.”

"Oh. How soon do you need it typed? I could finish it in an hour."

"No hurry. A week or so would be fine. The report isn't due for a while. If you type this up and bring it on Sunday, we can talk more."

"Uh, uh, I don't know. Could you pick it up here on Monday?"

"Monday I can't. How about Tuesday?"

Sharon shrugged. "Okay. Remember, I get off work at noon."

Michele rubbed Sharon's shoulder again. "Thank you so much for typing this! You'll save me so much time. Hey, what about lunch? There's a Chinese buffet up the street. I'm free till two, and I remember Mr. Parker said three o'clock for you at the post office. That gives us plenty of time for lunch."

"I can't. Sorry."

"Maybe next Tuesday. See you then." Michele waved and went out.

Sharon put the report in her backpack and pulled out a pack of peanut butter crackers, which she ate on her walk to the library. At first, she was glad to be doing the report, glad to have something purposeful to do while she filled in the hours till she met Mr. Parker. But by the time she finished the report, she felt uneasy. She went down to the waterfront to find Tina, who was lifting the lids of trash cans along the curb. Tina's black plastic bag of deposit cans had only a small bulge in the bottom. Probably not enough for a meal, Sharon thought. She took some bills from her wallet and held them up like a fan. "Bonanza!" she shouted. "I earned these typing up a report. Let's go to Muffler's Chowder House."

At the restaurant, Sharon explained how she happened to get the job. "I'm glad for the spare cash," she said, "but something about the job smells fishier than this chowder. Don't ask me why, but I get the feeling this Michele Arbalester really didn't need my help to get that thing typed."

"Why'd she ask you then?"

"I think so I'd read what it says."

"What's it say?"

"It's pretty confusing. It's about Quakers. It starts out saying God can inspire anybody—even a first-timer—to speak in a Quaker meeting. Like everybody's equal. And we all should be open to receive God's inspiration through anybody. Yesterday in that meeting—hold on, have you ever been to a Quaker meeting?"

"Nope."

"Well, everybody sits there totally silent for a while. Then somebody—could be anybody anywhere in the room—gets up and speaks about, oh, I don't know. It's hard to describe it. Something they discovered about God or life or, I don't know. Yesterday two people spoke about personal events where they ended up more at peace somehow because of some new understanding. And then—you're not gonna believe this, Tina. I don't know what the hell possessed me—I stood up. Me. Me!"

"You?"

"Yeah, and I blurted out that I came there to meet up with a Quaker who was going to introduce me to my birth mother. And oh, God! Ohhhh, God! And I asked the people there to pray that she wouldn't be disappointed in me."

"You did?"

"Yeah. And then I felt like such an asshole. God! I mean it. I don't know what the hell possessed me. I'm amazed they didn't laugh out loud. There I was, standing up in front of the world in my rumpled clothes and my big fat ass. I didn't know a soul there, and I go and spill my guts. I couldn't wait to get the hell outa there. Anyway, as I'm typing this thing today, I'm thinking this Michele saw how embarrassed I was and must've felt bad for me. So she shows up at the Sallies and asks me to type this thing so I'd know it really was okay to stand up and speak like anybody else. We're all equal."

"Doesn't sound like you feel a whole lot better about it," Tina said.

"I did at first. A little, anyway. But then the report goes on. It makes it sound like some Quakers are more equal than others. It goes on about Weighty Friends. And a few are so notable that their names go down as Recorded Ministers. The list at the end is pretty small. Only a handful in all of New England."

"Oh, and—let me guess—she's on the list?"

"Yeah."

"Aha!"

"What?"

"That's why she wanted you to type this report."

"So I'd see her name on the list?"

"Sure. *Now* you know she's the big cheese. If she was a cop, she'da flashed her badge."

"Aw, I don't know. I think she just wants to help me. Yesterday she offered to help me get connected with my birth mother. She gave Mr. Parker her address and phone number as a way of getting in touch with me while I'm on a time-out from the M-WIT."

"She thinks that Pennsylvania guy's on the level?"

"I guess so. I was a little put off by the way she launched right in on Sunday, so I told her I was going to get my own P.O. box. And I am. Today. At three o'clock Mr. Parker is going to meet me at the post office. I'll give him the box number before he flies back home. He's gonna send me a picture of my birth mother, he said. I'm glad because, honestly, Tina, I don't know what the hell to think. He also wants to send the woman in Pennsylvania a picture of me as a child. I remembered a nice color picture of me in the newspaper when I was nine. I had a big bright smile. I was throwing bread to seagulls on the East End Beach. I'm down on one knee on the dock, reaching up to the sky. A gull's beak is right at my fingertips. I was a slim little kid. That bird could have carried me off with the bread. Yesterday afternoon we found that picture in the library collection. We couldn't print out a color picture there to show how red my hair was, so Mr. Parker said he would go to the newspaper office this morning and ask for color copies of the original. It's an old picture, I know, but it should be enough for her to get an idea if I really could be her kid. Only trouble is, now I'm big as a house. She'll pass out when she sees me. That's if I go."

"Why exchange pictures? Why not just look up the records?"

"That's what I wondered. Mr. Parker said this woman couldn't find any records, that there was something funny about the whole adoption setup. I guess that's why it takes a lawyer to do some digging. Jesus, Tina, I don't know why I'm even looking into this. My mom must have bitched ten million times about how she was on her way to stardom in that New York chorus line. They began to give her the lead. Then *I* came along. Why would she adopt a baby just when her dancing career's taking off? It doesn't make sense. She must've meant she was pregnant with me. Still, I wouldn't mind having some nice mother somewhere out there. Why not?"

"Why not, that's for sure. Wouldn't mind having one myself."

"A nice father, too. One that wouldn't fly the coop. Haven't heard about any dear old dad in Pennsylvania dying to meet me, though."

"Maybe that comes next."

"Could be he didn't even know that woman in Pennsylvania was pregnant. So what do you think, Tina? Do you still think I should meet this woman?"

"Why not? What the hell. Like I said the other day, could be like winning the lottery."

Sharon looked up at the wall clock, a round face embedded in a ceramic seashell. "Guess I better get up to the post office. Why don't you order a coffee? Kill another cold hour till the shelter opens."

"Think I will. What about you? Where you going after meeting this Parker guy?"

"The laundrymat, then the library. Close my eyes, run my finger along that big set of encyclopedias, pick a book, pick a page, see where my finger lands. Yesterday I read all about the history of teabags."

"I bet that put you to sleep."

"Actually, it kept me from my usual nap in the library. I went from reading about shapes of teabags to tea ceremonies around the world. The trail was so fascinating I kept at it till supper at the Sallies."

“Maybe I oughta try that. Well, see you later. Good luck with that lawyer.”

Sharon pulled her suitcase to the post office and had six months’ rent paid on a box by 2:55. Her mailbox was just inside a recessed area. She tried the key, unlocking and relocking the little door with delight. Tipping sideways to look in the main area, she spotted the man she was waiting for and beckoned him to the alcove. “Hi. This is my place,” she said, opening the door of the box.

Tim was surprised to find himself charmed by the proud grin on Sharon’s face. Her open palm swept toward her “place” as if she expected him to step inside, hang his hat and coat on a peg, and make himself at home. He had an impulse to back out of this scheme while he still could, to say, “Sorry, but there’s been a mistake, a terrible mistake. I got new information that— Sorry, but I’m afraid that Ms. McDonald is not your mother after all.”

Memories of Ray’s big confession party at the Harborview Inn barged into his mind. And Bruce with his rare-flower speech. This nonsense about practicing on the local nobody girls. All this guilt over privileges families like his spent decades building to provide for the coming generations. Tim welled with resentment for Ray’s dirty trick of inviting him all the way to Maine for that. Looking at the scuffed bulges on Sharon’s boots, he reclaimed his status like a king returning to his rightful place on a throne. “Great! So you’re all set up here. I’ll write down the number and be on my way. Oh, and here’s your copy of that newspaper photo I ordered. I’ll be in touch. Bye now.”

11

Lurking

"Oh, hi, Claire. . . . Yes, I am coming to the vigil this Saturday. . . .Talk at your place first? You mean— Are you referring to what I said after Meeting last Sunday? . . . Good. I'm glad. We can have a talk and walk to the vigil from there. And Claire, thanks for your willingness to work through your issues. . . . Hello? Are you still there? . . . I thought we had gotten cut off. Let's see, the vigil starts at 9:30. How 'bout I come by at 8:30? . . . See you Saturday, then. Dress warm! Bye."

On Saturday Michele, holding a houseplant and a cardboard tray with coffee and muffins from the Victory Deli below Claire's apartment, knocked on her door. Claire greeted her with a bittersweet smile. "Hello. Come in."

"Good morning! These are for you," Michele said, directing the goods toward Claire's hands.

Claire, indicating the coffee table, said, "You can set your things down there. Have a seat." Michele sat on the sofa and unpacked the coffee and muffins, setting them on napkins. "Look—creamers, sugar packets, stirrers—they remembered everything!"

Claire sat on the opposite side of the coffee table. She shook her head when Michele slid a muffin and cup of coffee toward her. When Michele went to remove the cellophane from the houseplant she'd brought, Claire said, "Please don't. Leave it wrapped."

After a few sips of coffee, Michele sat with her mouth pressed against her clasped hands. Finally, she said, "As you can imagine, this isn't an easy thing to bring up. I hardly know where to start."

Claire waited in silence for Michele to say more.

"I suppose I should start where we left off our talk at the meetinghouse. Mr. Parker. You were suspicious of him."

"Yes."

"And, frankly, I felt that your suspicions— Well, to be honest, I felt that they said more about you than him. You immediately pegged the man as a deceiver."

"Not immediately. It dawned on me little by little as I observed him."

"You didn't even give the man credit for being a Quaker."

"I really don't think he's ever set foot in a Quaker meeting before. For heaven's sake, even if he is a Quaker, so what? Are we a race apart? Can't possibly be up to no good like the rest of the human race? Is that the credit you mean? Sorry, but I really do sense that he's up to some devious scheme."

"Another deceiver, Claire. Like your father? Like your husband, Henry?"

The hunched woman's eyes widened, but she said nothing.

Michele smiled, conceding, "It's somewhat understandable, given your history. Your father ran off with a younger woman, abandoned you as well as your mother. At nineteen, you marry Henry, a man twenty years older. You turn thirty, and that's too old for him. You find out he's been running around with a girl just out of high school. Protest, and he knocks your head against the wall. Henry's been gone for forty-some years. But his deceitfulness is as fresh in your mind as if it all happened yesterday. Your next husband puts you in the hospital with a broken arm. It's no surprise you'd be slow to become attached to a man again, but what I see in front of me now is extreme. I see a woman who is just plain afraid of men."

Claire choked back a sound from her throat. "Are you— Is this what's become of the things I revealed about myself at that weekend retreat? On that night, you were all sympathy and understanding, gathering me in your arms when those bottled-up tears burst out. Today? Today those same revelations are damning evidence of my distorted judgment."

"It's not as if I'm twisting your words."

"No, you got the story right. Those things happened to me. It's how you're using that history. That's what I'm protesting."

Michele folded her arms. "How can I not notice what's behind your suspicions? I'm a trained social worker."

"So am I. With forty-three years of work in the field."

"True, but you've been retired for how many years now? And how many years ago did you get your training?"

"Interesting how my history with men has everything to do with my assessment of this Mr. Parker today, but my professional training and decades of social work have no useful—"

"A lot has been researched and written about since your day in the field, Claire. Co-dependency, the influence of unfinished business on people's perspectives, dysfunctional families, being in denial about one's own problems and dysfunction. You said yourself the bond between you and your mother snapped after your father left."

"No, those were your words."

"But you agreed. That bond was broken. What was that, if not dysfunction?"

Claire looked squarely into Michele's eyes. "All right, what was that? What was that experience, that life we lived? Answering that question takes thought. It takes time and care and deep insight. Compassion. Noticing what was unique about someone, what made another person special, what wounded them so deeply that it's amazing they even want to stay alive. Understanding their experience takes humility, realizing one cannot fully grasp what's going on within another human being. A handy, instant buzzword for any family with problems doesn't get at the heart of it. It says nothing. Nothing at all."

Michele pressed her hand against her forehead. "I see you're into denial. Claire, you come from a dysfunctional family. That's clear, but you're just not willing to admit it, much less explore its effects—how it skews your perceptions, the problems it causes for other people. At Meeting, in particular."

"Tell me about these problems."

"I should have said all this months ago. I should never have put it off. It's only causing more problems."

"More problems! What were the first ones?"

"I'll get to those. You have issues with men, Claire. Until you admit that, the old lens you view everything through will distort your here-and-now. Like your suspicions of Mr. Parker."

"I am suspicious. Sharon needs to watch out."

"Like you? You've become so hypervigilant you're spoiling our Meeting for Worship."

"What?"

"It's about time someone took responsibility to elder you about that."

"Spoiling our— What have I said during worship that makes people think I'm ruining it?"

"It isn't what you say. It's that hypervigilant state you sit in. Like you expect some evil, deceitful man to walk in any minute. It spoils the gathered meeting, the sense of being together in a loving presence of the Divine."

"Spoils the gathered— Is that what Friends are saying?"

"No, but it's true. I'm just the first to say it out loud. Take last Sunday. You talk about a smirk on Mr. Parker's face. And how he didn't seem to know what was going on. How did you even happen to notice these things? You were watching him. That's how."

"After the way he acted in the foyer, yes, I watched him. I don't think I made a show of it."

"No, but the very spirit of your extreme watchfulness has a damaging effect. As the worship evolves into a gathered sense of God's light and love, it's—it's like a hole in a net, a rip, a— It got really out of hand when David started coming to Meeting. If he wasn't already seated when you walked in, your eyes turned to the door the second anybody stepped through. If he *was* already seated, your whole demeanor was like a guard's at the snap of a twig in the dark. That was one of the problems I was referring to."

"Oh, yes, David. David with the loose interpretation of what a greeter does. Especially if she has a pretty face, like Laura. No more of this simple handshake nonsense. On the morning he kissed her on the mouth, he should have been sent out. No, it was Laura who ended up leaving. After that, he made a point of lurking in the foyer till Laura came in."

"Lurking," Michele said. "That word seems to come up a lot with you."

Claire continued. "He'd pick a seat right next to her, press up against her. He'd cling to her hand when the worship ended with handshakes. She took me and you aside one day to express how uncomfortable he made her, and what happened?"

"You brought it up to Ministry and Counsel."

"And then?"

"We tried to see how we could help them."

Claire chuckled bitterly. "Some help. The Meeting coddled David. Gave him an ongoing support group, for heaven's sake, to help him deal with Laura's leeriness of him. That was your idea, Michele."

"I suggested it, yes. We have to look for the Light of God in every person, not just people we feel comfortable with. And the support group wasn't formed only because of Laura's leeriness. The man had psychological issues, too. I wasn't blind to those, but we have to be patient with troubled people."

"We? We have to be patient? We weren't the ones he pressed up against during worship. Shame on Laura for not being as patient and Quakerly as his support group."

"We, yes we, the community, all had to be patient. Laura was part of the same community as the rest of us. And so we handled it as a community. Once Laura was afraid of him, *we* made sure one of us sat on each side of her during Meeting."

"You've still got it backwards. Yes, we posted a safe person on each side of Laura, but it wasn't because she was afraid. It was because David was a threat to her."

"Laura *was* afraid. I can't go into details without breaking confidence about some of the things Laura's shared with me. Let's just say you could see for yourself how attractive she was. Some of the men she attracted over the years didn't make for a pretty history.

Laura had some serious issues with men. She was afraid of men. How about Arnie? She was afraid of Arnie when he started coming to Meeting."

"For heaven's sake, Michele! She'd be working in the meetinghouse garden alone in the evenings. How about the time Arnie showed up with a shovel and started digging a hole in the middle of the flowerbed? When Laura protested, he rose up and screamed at her in a rage, grabbed her and started kissing her all over the face and neck. Somehow she got away and ran to the nearest restaurant."

"Oh, stop it, Claire. I already know about that night in the garden. I'm the one she telephoned. You bring up graphic details for the drama. That's typical of someone with unfinished business. Rehearsing the same details over and over."

"And you portray Laura as a woman who's just afraid of men? Arnie gave her cause to be afraid. So did David. After David asked her out and she turned him down, he started stalking her, even at work."

"Laura worked in a campus library, a place open to the public. David was part of the public. He had a right to go there."

"Yeah, and follow her in the stacks during her shift. And just happen to be on the elevator during her break times as she headed for the staff room at night. When she started using the stairwell, so did he. She told both of us that herself. And who was lurking by her car after she left work at eleven?"

"There's that word again. Lurking."

"Lurking, yes. That's exactly what he was doing. And when Laura gave up her apartment and moved into the Y to save money, who started going there to swim every single night? David."

"The pool at the YWCA was open to the public, not just the residents."

"Why suddenly switch from the pool where he'd been swimming for years? He'd show up in the lobby well before the public swim and take his time leaving. Laura couldn't walk in or out of her own home without passing him at that time."

"You talk as if David were an out-and-out predator. David was a troubled human being with low self-esteem due to a troubled past. He was impulsive. Grabbing for anything that would bring him solace."

"Like Laura, you mean?"

"We must honor that of God in him. Same as in anyone else."

"Since when does that mean sniffing out the personal histories of the Lauras among us and probing their mental state? As if their suffering is caused by some flawed inner state, not by what someone like David is actually doing to them. Since when does it mean requiring women to tolerate the revenge of men who won't take no for an answer? Have you ever thought how unnerving it must be to have a guy like that show up at every turn? Laura was so relieved when he quit coming to worship on Sundays. And who walks up to him in a restaurant and says, 'I think I know why you don't come to Meeting anymore. Because of Laura's accusations'? You, Michele."

"Indeed, I did. And, indeed, that *was* why he quit coming. He said Laura must have complained about him to her employer. Another worker started jumping in to answer any questions David asked Laura for help with. That must have been the guy who went to testify when she went for that restraining order. She didn't need to take David to court."

"She did," Claire insisted. "Most of the time she worked alone at night."

"And David told me he thought Laura was speaking ill of him at our Meeting, and that made him feel too embarrassed and uncomfortable to keep coming. Friends were probably thinking he was out to hurt her somehow."

"He was. He was stalking her, just like she told us. I went to the library and watched him do it."

"Did he see you?"

"Yes."

"Ah, see? No wonder he thought Laura was speaking ill of him to Friends. What did you say to him?"

"Nothing. Not a word. He left when he realized I could see for myself he was up to no good. He was right on Laura's tail when she was reshelving books. He hung his jacket in the first study carrel near the Reference Desk to claim that spot during her shift. From there he could stare relentlessly when she helped patrons standing at the computer station, and he could stare at her from that carrel whenever she sat at the desk. And you know those big red binders they have with the list of serials the library has on hand?"

"I've used them."

"There are copies of those binders all through the library. I counted ten placed around the Reference area alone. All identical. All available to everyone. I watched David return to the Reference Desk again and again, bending over the counter and leaning into Laura's face to check the list in the Reference Desk copy. When he caught sight of me watching him torment Laura, he left. Same as when other Friends came to see. Marie, Joe, Dennis. Only with them—and with me too after my first time of watching him stalk her—he'd get off the elevator, see one of us sitting there, and get right back on the elevator and leave the building."

"That's why he was embarrassed to come back to Meeting. He probably felt ganged up on."

"What we did was answer that of God in David. That was our ministry. Simply showing up in the same spirit of seeking the truth as we show up for worship at the meetinghouse every week. We trusted the Light to shine on the truth, the good and the evil, and let him respond to it. And he did, if only for the times one of us was present. A little respite for Laura. All four of us told you what we witnessed. This shouldn't be news to you today. We told you, yet you encouraged David to come back to Meeting, which would have been fine if—"

"I told David our sign on the lawn means what it says, *All Welcome.*"

"Which would have been fine if he came in the spirit of truth, but his intention was only to gain another venue to torment Laura. And an opportunity to put a different spin on what he was really only doing at Laura's workplace and the place she lived. He must have been thrilled with such a weighty Friend supporting his right to show up at any public place as often as he wants, as if that were really all there was to what he was up to."

"All welcome, Claire. When there's a conflict between two people in Meeting, we can't just welcome one and not the other."

"That was the trouble, the heart of the trouble, right there—considering what David was doing a conflict between two people. Stalking is a crime. Not on a par with two honest, well-meaning people who can't agree on something."

"Oh, Claire, that's all water under the bridge. David is gone now."

"Sure, he's gone. His uncle died and left him a house in Utah. Lucky us. We were rid of him. Not so lucky for Laura, though. She had to leave months before that because she couldn't get a restraining order. Left Maine, her friends, her family, her job. Had to change her name so he could never look her up. That means people like me, who really love her, can't find her either. She told me she'd never burden me with that secret."

Michele sat back in her chair and looked at Claire with utter exasperation. "It's better that Laura left. It got so that she'd sit in worship in such a hypervigilant state. I can't see what good that did her, and it was spoiling the worship, our gathered worship."

"Oh, no! You didn't say that to her, did you?"

"I did. I did because she was indeed. And it was time she took a good long look at her fear of men."

Claire got to her feet and went to the window, pushed the curtain aside and looked out, her fingers clutching the window sash as if she were hopelessly trapped inside. "Ohhhhhh, of all the— Oh, I wish I knew how to find her."

"Let it go, Claire. Laura is gone. David is gone. He's not lurking, as you like to put it, around the meetinghouse anymore. Okay, maybe we didn't handle it so great. We've been mulling it over in Ministry and Counsel, hoping to come up with a strategy in case another troubled person like David shows up. Yes, I know, preparing for another possible David was *your* idea, Claire."

"Mine and quite a few other Friends from this Meeting. This didn't sit right with quite a few Friends. Most didn't even know about David stalking Laura until she failed to get that restraining order and had to leave town. She tried keeping it quiet so she wouldn't make the whole Meeting uncomfortable. In the end, her concern for everyone else's comfort backfired. She left our Quaker community tarred and feathered in your psychobabble."

Indignation flashed in Michele's eyes. "Call it what you will, but what matters now is that David is gone. Done. Finished. None of that has anything to do with whether this poor Sharon gets connected with her birth mother." Michele took a priority mailer from her canvas tote bag. "If it will put you at ease, Claire, I have a picture of her birth mother. You can see the resemblance yourself."

"You do?"

"Mr. Parker mailed it to me."

"You gave him your address?"

"I did, last Sunday." She laid the newspaper photograph of nine-year-old Sharon next to a photocopy of a page from a high school yearbook. Under Mary Frances McDonald's name Tim had written in green ink, "She has auburn hair and catnip-colored eyes, like this ink."

"Amazing," Claire said. "The resemblance really is amazing."

"Satisfied?"

"No. No, I'm not. I'm not convinced."

"I plan to stay in touch with Mr. Parker. We'll be talking on the phone. Sharon's on a time-out from the M-WIT, so he won't be able to call her. If it makes you feel any better, if I detect anything underhanded when he calls, I'll take note of it. But really, Claire, I don't expect to."

Claire stood up. "Of course not. The man says he's a Quaker. I'd like to go for a little walk before the vigil. If you'd like to sit awhile, you can let yourself out when you're ready to leave. Please take the plant with you."

Claire walked out the door with one arm through the sleeve of her coat. She walked along the cobblestone streets, feeling bruised and worried, wishing she could phone Laura and assure her that her presence in Meeting was always treasured, that this talk of her ruining the worship experience for everyone else was just that, talk. Less than talk. The inane, rote babble of one person. Honor the Light of God in people like David! Yes, we must. And that means encouraging them to submit to that Light, to let it shine on the truth in their hearts, as we all need to do, the good and the evil. And when evil is plain, to consent to receiving the Grace that will help them change their ways.

Claire arrived at the statue of the lobsterman close to the end of the vigil. The weather was mild. Melting snow from a shrub bed glistened as it trickled across the sidewalk.

Sharon, who had slept in the shelter, was making her way toward the sunny benches near the lobsterman statue, pulling her suitcase. Her plaid backpack bulged behind her shoulders. She had forgotten the clerk's announcement that the vigil would continue at the same place as long as the war continued. She wasn't about to put herself on display with all her belongings on a bench now that she'd be recognized by the group. She strode directly inside the Green Mountain Coffee Roasters. She was standing by the counter, scouting about for a place to sit when some of the people from the vigil came in. Sharon panicked, at first, but then she saw an advantage. She could give the report she had typed to Michele and be done with it.

Claire, the first to step inside, asked Sharon if they might share a table. Sharon recalled Mr. Parker's warning about the white-haired woman all the Quakers thought was wacky. Yet, Sharon could not refuse. She imagined that no one would want to sit with an old woman everybody thought was nuts, so that was all the more reason to say yes. The woman was probably lonely like herself. What could it hurt? They chose a tiny table and hung their coats on the backs of the two chairs. They were seated only a moment when Michele borrowed a chair from a table for four and dragged it over. She set the wrapped plant down on the table and said, "Mind if I join you two?"

Sharon, digging in her backpack, stammered, "No, it's fine. I mean, I'm glad. I finished typing that report for you. It's here. I can give it to you now."

Michele opened the folder and looked over the report. "Beautiful! This looks beautiful!"

Sharon shrugged. Michele slid the report over to Claire. "Look. Sharon typed this for me. Didn't she do a nice job?"

Claire glanced at the paper and looked at Michele with a puzzled expression.

Michele slipped the folder into her bag and pulled out the priority mailer. Her smile had a touch of mystery. "Now, Sharon, I have something I want to show you."

Sharon pulled her shoulders back. Michele patted her hand. "It's only a picture. I want to show you a picture of your mother. That is, unless you've already gotten your copy from Mr. Parker."

"It could be in my post office box."

"Oh! Well!" Michele said, sliding the photocopy of Mary Frances's yearbook photo from the envelope. "No need to rush up there. You can have a look at my copy. Wait till you see. I think you'll be amazed."

Sharon backed her chair away from the table, placed the picture on her lap, and studied the pretty teen with hair teased into a beehive. Michele leaned sideways. Her eyes darted from Sharon's face to the photograph. Sharon, hunching her shoulders, endured the scrutiny with the same dismal resignation as when she sat at the M-WIT supper table in front of windows with only broken, vertical slats to shield her from the eyes of the men at the Harborview Inn.

"That green ink," Michele said, "It's the same color as your eyes. Amazing!" Michele took a small mirror from her purse and offered it to Sharon. "Have a look."

Sharon slapped the picture onto the table and jumped to her feet. "I gotta go!" She worked her way through aisles narrowed by winter coats bulging over the backs of chairs. She ran through downtown Harbor City. At the post office she found curled up in her mailbox a priority mailer with a return post office box in Illinois. She hurried down to the waterfront, her pull-along suitcase flying up and flipping as the wheels hit the cobblestones. She darted into the maze of lobster traps stacked high on Widener's Wharf. Falling to her knees, she pulled out the picture and exclaimed, "What a kind face! And you do look like me. At least the tiny me I used to be." She studied the face some more, detecting a terrible sadness despite the lovely smile. “This was taken after you had your baby, wasn’t it? After you had to give it away.”

Pressing the image against her chest, she cried out, “Are you my mother? Are you really my mother?” She dropped back against the traps. The edges of the paper shuddered in the salty breeze that blew through the wooden slats. “Even if you are, what would you want with a big, fat piss ass of a daughter?”

Sharon took a pack of cigarettes from her backpack and smoked into the evening, not bothering with supper at the Sallies. She smoked till the last cigarette was gone.

That night, when she arrived at the shelter, she was stiff with cold. She washed quickly and shoved some vinyl triangles between double pads and her underpants. She fell asleep quickly. Deep in a dream, she sloshed through tide pools in her black flip-flops. Soupy sand oozed between her toes. Smiling away at barnacles that opened like eyes as seawater lapped the boulders they were stuck to, she waved her fingers at the squiggly black things poking out to suck in a meal. She walked along a vast stretch of plain gray beach until she came to a salt marsh. Patches of cattails lined the paths. Clumps of iridescent sea pickles with pink, star-shaped flowers grew among rocks. She bit into a sea pickle, scrunching up her mouth at the sour salt flavor. The misty salt air caressed her with such a carefree kindness that she rose to her toes and twirled happily, arms over her head, till she spun herself giddy, shrinking as she spun to the size of a child of nine. Suddenly, her feet were in frilly white anklet socks and black tap-dancing shoes with curlicued patterns of rhinestones across the straps. Puffy yellow sleeves capped her shoulders. She swayed with her arms out and tap-danced her way down a flagstone path, zig-zagging to a stairway of rocks, where she tapped toward the top until she tripped. Her chin skidded across the rough stone platform. Pushing herself up on scraped elbows, she looked about. Every lovely thing of Nature was gone. She was now indoors, sprawled on a short wooden structure with a few steps leading up to a platform and a few leading down the other side. Her fingers clung to the lip of the other edge of the platform. Hot theatre lights, burning down between rows of short black drapes, lit the rhinestones on the strap of her splayed left foot like a constellation. The footlights shining up on her cast a dim light over the first few rows of an audience. People, some with smirks, some with frowns of pity, stared. Some, pop-eyed, sat with mouths frozen in a gasp. Two seats in the middle of Row 3, where Sharon's parents always sat, were empty. When the door below a red exit light opened, she saw the two of them scurrying out. She let go of the platform. Hot pee trickled down her thighs.

12

Rebekah

NOW, MARY FRANCES MCDONALD WAS BORN near the Ebony Gem Colliery in a coal patch called Black Hollow. That's where her grandfather, Joe McDonald, mined down on Level 4, Breast Number 6, with some mad Pollack named Casimir until the breast was all mined out by 1917. When she was in fifth grade, she moved to Otterdale, the coal patch with the sweet-smelling crick along the slagpiles. Anyway, the house Mary Frances rents in Black Hollow after she retires from the Navy is the very same house that that Casimir lived in back in the early 1900s. The very same, 255 W. Saylor Street.

There's a legend connected with that house. Among the mules at the Ebony Gem was one named Rebekah. Casimir was the only one she'd behave for in the mine yard. Oh, she was okay with the regular mule drivers, hauling coal cars and all that. But the daily walk for fresh air in the mine yard, a treat for all the mules, well, Rebekah would go only with that Casimir fella. They say she was as crazy as he was, sitting her stubborn rump half in the cage, half in the mine yard if anybody else tried to walk her.

Casimir was found one day, down on Level 4, alone, all snuggled up dead behind the boarded-up opening to Breast Number 6. Since all the breasts along that gangway had been cleared of minable coal, there was no reason for Casimir or any other miner to go down that gangway anymore. So the circumstances of Casimir's death were fishy, to say the least. But that's another story. What's important to know about now is this legend about Rebekah. She was missing from the underground stable, and when they found her, they found Casimir's body. They found her leaping back and forth in the gangway like a giant rocking horse, braying and gnashing her teeth.

To get her back to the cage—that's what the mine elevator was called—and up to the level where the stable was, they had to tether her to the back of an empty coal car and have it pulled by another mule, Isaac. Rebekah busted out of her stall again and again and stood by the cage, waiting for somebody to lead her down to her beloved Casimir. One day they took her back down to Level 4 to see what she'd do, and blind though she was, like most of the mules who lived for years in the dark, she went right for Breast Number 6, Casimir's old workplace. She went wild! They couldn't get her to work again no how.

After a week of her madness, the mine owners were getting impatient. What good was a mule that wouldn't work? It's not that they were quick to part with a mule. No! Whenever there was an accident at the Ebony Gem, the first question the owners asked was, "Were any mules killed?"

They decided to give Rebekah one more chance. If that didn't work out, she was due for a bullet between the eyes. They decided to try putting her in the mine yard for a day or so. She busted outa there, too. She ran wild for blocks. Two Philadelphia & Reading Coal & Iron policemen—Coalies, the people called them—followed with whistles, nightsticks, and rifles. Women with children in tow, pushing wheelbarrows of coal they had gleaned from the slagpiles, scooped up their little ones and scrammed out of the blind mule's way. Suddenly, Rebekah stopped and let her head droop. Slowly, she bumbled, blind, through the streets of Black Hollow, bumping into carts and lampposts. The Coalies kept back a ways.

By and by the mule chanced upon 255 W. Saylor Street, which was on a corner across the street from the school field. Casimir's boots stood on the porch next to the railing. Beside them was the brush he used to clean them with every night before taking them down the stone steps that led to the cellar from the back yard.

Rebekah sniffed those boots like a bloodhound. Casimir's children, three sooty little girls with a skinny brother who was two, were in the yard sizing bootlegged coal through a makeshift breaker, a series of screens with different size holes. The sound of someone cracking coal with a sledge hammer came from the shanty at the end of the yard. It was Victoria, their mother.

"Look!" Felicia said, "There's a mule! I think he wants to come in!"

"That must be Rebekah," Anna Chrissy said, "the one Daddy told all those stories about. See? She's sniffing his boots. She remembers!" Anna Chrissy, a seven-year-old blondie, was the oldest.

"Let's open the gate," Felicia said. The gate was on the side fence, close to the porch. The children made a run for it.

Rebekah tried to squeeze her face through the porch banister and get at the boots. But she couldn't. She began to kick and bray.

Victoria came out of the shanty, blackened from her work of cracking coal. As she was running to grab the children, the two Coalies turned the corner and took aim, but the children stood between the men and the mule and begged them not to shoot.

"Out of the way!" the Coalies kept shouting.

Victoria joined hands with her children. She'd seen her husband soothe that mule in the mine yard. Huddling the younger children against her, she sent Anna Chrissy for the boots. "Stay on the porch," the mother said. "Just set the boots on top of the banister."

The child did as she was told. Rebekah, her sightless eyes like stones, knocked one boot to the ground. She jerked her head in spasms. Victoria took the other boot from the banister and brushed it along the side of Rebekah's face. "There, there," she said.

"Out of the way," one of the Coalies said. "It's plain that mule's no good to us anymore. She'll cost us, that's all. Move!"

A crowd of women and small children began to gather.

"I'll take her off your hands," Victoria said. "Leave her here. Don't shoot."

"We have our orders," the same Coalie said. The other one whispered something to him, but the first one only repeated, "We have our orders."

"Fifty dollars," the other one said.

"We were told to shoot, Michael, not sell the damned thing if she won't straighten up. Out of the way, everybody."

"I'll take responsibility for this, Floyd." Michael said. "Let the woman have the good-for-nothing mule."

"Long as you're the one catches hell for it."

Victoria, her fingers tucked in Rebekah's halter, said, "Fifty d— I don't have fifty dollars."

"You can pay so much a month."

"It would take me years!"

A woman standing on the sidelines took a change purse from her pocket and gave Victoria a nickel. Others did the same. Victoria handed the nickels to Michael.

"Forty-five cents," he said. "That's a start." He circled the mule in final appraisal and gave her a pat on the hind end. "I'll come back with an agreement you can sign."

So Rebekah came to live in the back yard of 255 W. Saylor Street. Neighbors helped to build a stable there and donated straw. Casimir's boots were kept in the stall. Rebekah joined the family's bootleg coal operation, pulling chunks of coal from abandoned bootleg mines in the mountainsides.

The only time they had trouble with her was when there was an accident at the Ebony Gem. When miners died, their bodies were heaped on buckboards, driven to their homes, and dumped on their front porches.

Rebekah went mad the first time a buckboard with three dead miners rolled past her yard. Even when a buckboard went down some other street, Rebekah knew. They say she knew which whistle pattern was which at the colliery—the start-and-quit blasts, the blasts that predicted rain or snow. She kicked and brayed the minute the whistle began to blow that series of long, long blasts that gave notice of disaster underway.

And here's where the legend comes in. They say that, whenever a coal miner died, even if he died at home in his own bed, Rebekah knew. She knew, and she went mad all through the night for nights on end. Scraps of kicked-up straw flew through the streets of Black Hollow. The braying didn't stop till after the wake and the last flower was laid on the newly filled grave. If you think that was the end of it, you're wrong. Long after Rebekah was dead and

Casimir's family had scattered, they say that any children living at 255 W. Saylor Street could hear Rebekah going mad in the back yard whenever a coal miner died, even decades later.

In the fall of 1990, old Jimmy Gallagher, who worked at the Ebony Gem till it closed in 1952, dies. He dies in bed of the black lung. The big lugs kicking soccer balls around the patch have told the children of the Davis family living in Casimir's old house the legend of Rebekah. And, whenever some old miner dies, wunna them lugs climbs up to the high porch off the kids' bedroom and makes mad mule noises by their window. Then the lugs go stick a piece of straw in a splintering banister post on the back porch below. There's no consoling them two little kids when they find it. They hop into their parents' bed night after night, insisting they could hear that mule. Now, Jimmy Gallagher, you see, is only one of many old miners dying off in the 80s and 90s, but his death is the last straw for the Davis family. They put the house up for rent. And who rents it? Our Mary Frances!

She's not in her new home a month when she wakes up to straw strewn over the snow drifted up onto her back porch. There's straw in the yard, straw all along the fence and up the three wooden steps leading into that raggedy tan tarpapered shanty at the end of her yard. Mary Frances's neighbors, Chet and Barbara Whalen, a couple in their seventies, are standing on their side of the porch banister. They got jackets on over their pajamas.

"That prankster again," says Barbara. "Only we never saw it this bad. Used to be some brat just wedged one straw under a splinter in the porch banister. One. That was enough to scare the kids who lived here before you. The father had a mind to redo that whole porch come spring if they'da stuck around. Now. Now looka this. Get the newspaper, Chet. Let's look at the obituaries. There must've been a whole slew of old miners died at once."

"I already know," Chet says. He pulls the rolled-up paper from inside his jacket and spreads it on the banister. "That's why I drug you out here so early. Four of them this time. Ollie Welsh, Jackie O'Connor, Tom Deutsch, and Rockface Zamboni. All dead of the black lung."

Barbara looks at her husband funny. "Rockface? Is that what the obituary says? Rockface?"

"No, it says Guido. But who the hell ever called him Guido? And I bet he's the one's responsible for that straw along the fence and up into the shanty."

"Get out. How could he be responsible? He's been bedridden for months. And now he's dead."

Rockface Zamboni, by the way, was called Rockface because of the broken cheekbone he got when a Coalie caught him haulin' off a lump of coal from the Ebony Gem and let him have it with a rock when he was a kid.

Mary Frances, who's been standing with her arms folded across the top of a snow shovel, says, "Tell me what you mean, Chet, about Mr. Zamboni being responsible."

"Well, I'll tell you. But come out of the cold. Come in for a coffee."

Mary Frances hops over the banister and sits at her neighbors' kitchen table.

Chet begins his tale. "Rockface, you see, was a little touched in the head by the time he was in his seventies. He'd wander about the patch, arguing with himself. And he had more than a touch of the black lung. Fact, he had it so bad, he'd walk hand over hand along picket fences or poke his fingers through wire ones, grabbing for dear life, struggling for his breath. It was awful to watch him. He'd come up to your yard near every day, Mary Frances. He'd make his way along the cinder sidewalk. His fingers was all gnarled. Sometimes he'd get them caught in the wire fence and I'd have to come around and help him out. Between the grunting and gasping and babbling, he'd scare the children in the yard. The family that lived in that house before you, why, their kids was just little."

"Yes, and poor Rockface," Barbara adds. "He was clear into his second childhood by then. He wanted to come into the yard and swing on the swings with the kids. Naturally, the parents didn't let him in. He'd make his way around the back of the alley and sit on the stoop at the back door of the shanty. He'd mope there for hours."

"That's right," Chet says. "And one day in the summer, he came in through the door at the back of the shanty. He appeared in the doorway to the yard like the Ghost of Christmas Past himself. Startled the hell out of the children. I was pulling weeds outa the irises over here. I called to him, but he paid me no mind. He hung onto the railing and eased himself down to the grass on his rear end, one step at a time. The children ran into the house screaming. After that the father replaced the back door of the shanty with drywall, painted the whole insides over, and made the place a playhouse for the kids. I don't know if you've had much chance to look over that shanty yet, Mary Frances, but you can see where the back wall dips in where the door to the alley used to be."

"I haven't, really. I just poked my head in when I first looked at the property."

"But tell her, Chet, it wasn't just because of Rockface. Some brat—and I'd like to get my hands on whoever it was—told those kids that Rockface was that crazy Casimir come back to life. Really that Casimir coming to get them and haul them off to the Land of the Dead. And that rotten little brat filled their heads with all kinds of scary tales about Casimir coming after children through the shanty from the alley. They say he used to come after his own children that way. Walling up that door now would do no good. Casimir's spirit would be able to walk right through it."

Chet said, "But, you know, that brat had the story all wrong. Mrs. Stutzman, who lived on this side—she died years ago and my mother knew her—said Casimir never came after anybody through that shanty door. That was the door Casimir's wife and children used to escape through. They'd wait till Casimir dozed off in the kitchen after one of his mad rampages, and the mother'd sneak the children through the yard, through the shanty, and out the back door to the alley. That's the way it really was."

Mary Frances sighs and says, "And now that prankster is trying to scare me with the straws. Kids. Well, they'll get bored with that after a while. Meanwhile, look at all that snow. I think I'll shovel my way to the gate."

There's more straws appears, one at a time, as old miners die off. Mary Frances is not alarmed by them. She just says a little prayer for the miner and sweeps the straws off onto the red cinder sidewalk. It amuses her to wonder how long it will take the prankster to give up the straw game. But she's not amused—in fact, she's downright pissed, if you'll excuse the language—when she finds an unsigned note clipped to her clothesline near the end of March:

> Say, Miss Mary Frances McDonald, you ought to be ashamed of yourself, looking for your kid, dredging up dirty tales your poor mother spent years living down. Asking around for who might know anything at all about your baby. Let's say you track down your kid. Then what? Ever think about how the kid will feel to learn what the rest of us know? The father could be any one of a dozen or two from a gang bang up the Mine. Think about that before you go digging any deeper.

Every word is a cut-out from a newspaper or magazine, except for "Frances" and "McDonald," words her mother probably couldn't find and had to handwrite in. Yes, Mary Frances recognizes the handwriting despite the forced, uncharacteristic slanting of the letters to the left. She doesn't let on to her mother that she's received this note. In fact, she steps up her efforts to spread the word that she's looking for her baby, asking in bars, at the supermarket, in the waiting room of the doctor's office. Please, anybody who knows anything, please speak up. Write me a note, anything. You don't even have to put your name to it.

Soon a certified letter comes in the mail from Illinois:

> April 1, 1991
> Dear Ms. McDonald:
> I am an attorney who has been contacted by a party in Mount of Olives, Pennsylvania, to arrange a meeting between you and your daughter. She has been hoping to locate her birth mother as well. The arranging

party's name is to remain anonymous for now. If you are interested, I can set up a meeting with the proviso that the details leading up to it remain private and confidential.

Within a week, a package will be waiting for you at the Mount of Olives Post Office, General Delivery. For the sake of your privacy, the package will arrive in a plain brown wrapper. It will contain items related to this matter. After reviewing them, please let me know whether you wish to pursue the matter further.

Sincerely,

Howard Parker, Attorney-at-Law

A plain brown wrapper, Mary Frances thinks. Letter dated April 1, April Fool's Day. Is this a prank? Why bother with privacy? The whole town's heard the story of how she got pregnant. Prank or not, it's the first lead she's got. A few days later, she picks up the package at General Delivery and opens it in her car. She finds a shiny gray box that once held 80 sheets of 25% cotton fiber antique laid paper. Through a triangular hole, which was part of the box's design, a coarse black cloth is visible. Black fringes dangle through the hole. The box opens like a book.

Mary Frances lifts the cloth out of the box. It's a beautiful black shawl with flowers, pink ones, yellow ones, along the edges. It reminds her of the shawls tied over the heads of the old Slavic ladies hunched and hissing over their rosaries at Mass on Sundays when she was a kid. Pinned to the shawl are a note and a photo of a little girl feeding seagulls. Mary Frances, removing the safety pin, goes right for the photo, awed by the resemblance to herself as a child. She unfolds the paper that was pinned to the shawl:

Dear Ms. McDonald:

Two reservations have been booked for you and your daughter Sharon at the Everheart Hotel in Harrisburg, Pennsylvania, a block from the Amtrak Train Station. This is an extended-stay hotel, so both units, 818 and 820, have a bedroom, a sitting room, and a small kitchen furnished with dishes, and so on. Sharon has already agreed to this arrangement. If you agree to meet her, she will arrive by train in Harrisburg at 3:17 pm on May 11. Her return ticket is for May 18. If you decide to meet Sharon, wear the enclosed shawl over your shoulders. Sharon will be wearing an identical one. That's how you'll recognize each other. Please fax your response to the number below by April 15. I will be in court most days between now and then; however, if you would like to speak with me, please fax a number where I can reach you in the evening.

Sincerely,

Howard Parker, Attorney-at-Law

"Sharon! A girl! A girl with a name!" Questions whirl through Mary Frances's mind. Did they count her fingers and toes when she was born? Did she have hair, or was she bald as a cue ball like herself? That round, white head. What happened to that picture of herself at six months old, dozing on Daddy's lap? That picture, all the pictures? Sharon would want to see family pictures. The whole family. What would she think when she walked into her new-found grandmother's parlor and saw four walls of photos of her dead Uncle Jack? Jack on a tricycle, Jack hosing down the car, Jack busy on every wall but one, where his eight-by-ten school portraits, all twelve, were arrayed in rows. Sharon would look about for pictures of her mother. Ah, there! On the coffee table, her school portraits crammed helter skelter in brassy frames, first-grade braids bumped up against twelfth-grade beehive. Would Sharon count them? Two, four, six, eight, ten, eleven. The missing child noting the missing portrait that stands for her entry into this world. How long would that moment drag on? If only there were more pictures. What did happen to that cue-ball picture, to all the other photographs that used to get passed around at gatherings of cousins and uncles and aunts? The albums. They must be around somewhere. Probably the attic.

Mary Frances decides to call her mother and ask if she could go up the attic and look for some old pictures, but she sits quietly on the couch for a few moments to banish all excitement before she picks up the phone. After four rings the voice of that Rick Trounov comes on, "Hello! You've reached the home of Joyce McDonald. Please leave a message after the beep."

"Mom? Mom, please pick up the phone. I just want to know if you'll be home this afternoon so I can stop by. Pick up the phone!"

Mary Frances pictures her mother in the brown recliner, listening to her plea. The tape on the answering machine rolls on. There's another beep, and then a dial tone. Mary Frances decides not to call again. She won't call to beg about more pictures. She won't call to announce her good news, news that her mother will only shrink from. No, the thing to do is keep it all to herself and just bring Sharon to the house in the flesh.

A giddy feeling rises up in Mary Frances, the kind of giddiness that kept her wide awake on Christmas Eve. When she got old enough for Midnight Mass, it was the Christmas story, as much as the presents that thrilled her. Now, keeping her own secret, she remembers how intrigued she was by Mary's response when shepherds came to see her newborn child: "And all that heard, wondered; and at those things that were told them by the shepherds. But Mary kept all these words, pondering them in her heart."

Mary Frances composes a note with her phone number and runs uptown to fax Mr. Parker. That night, Mr. Howard Parker, Attorney-at-Law, rings the phone of Mary Frances McDonald. She immediately detects a Coal Region accent.

"Oh, yes," Tim says, "still got that accent. Isn't that something? My folks are from the area, but a bit farther north of you. Fact, I was born there. We moved to the Midwest when I was eight, but I still spent summers there with my grandparents. I was just back that way recently. That's when someone approached me to make this contact with you."

"Someone? What someone? Not a soul in this town will talk to me about my baby. Not even my own mother."

"I'm not at liberty to divulge my source. Let's just say it's someone who's willing to come forward as a matter of conscience."

"Conscience."

"Yes."

It occurs to Mary Frances that it could be one of the boys from that night at the Mine, someone with a conscience after all, but someone with a wife and kids, a guy who just wants to make good without stirring up trouble. Just be glad you found your baby, she scolds herself. Don't press to know who took pity on you now. "Can you at least tell me where my baby was born? Not Vermont. I know now it wasn't Vermont."

"No, it wasn't Vermont. I've been given to understand that your mother's been telling people you broke your leg at a relative's in Vermont that summer. I didn't realize she's been telling you that's where you gave birth."

"Where was it, then?"

"Sorry, but I'm not at liberty to—"

Mary Frances, encouraged by the fact that this attorney admits the truth about Vermont, says, "Okay, never mind about that. That can come later. Is there any chance your source is willing to talk to me if we can be really discreet? I mean, meet me somewhere where neither of us will be recognized."

"I can ask. I'll get back to you on that."

The next day, Tim calls back with the disappointing reply. "Sorry, they said they can't."

13

Godzalez

I GOT A KUZZINT IN HARBOR CITY, MAINE, a mighty wharf rat. It really pisses off tour boat owners when the tourists see him leap up to dodge a looped rope a deckhand is trying to fling over a piling as the boat sidles up to the dock. The owners look on from the little ticket booths, seething. The captain looks out from the wheelhouse, beholding the backup at the top of the gangway that bridges the deck and the wharf. No tourist in their right mind wants to be the first to go down.

Now, people don't go giving rats names like they do for dogs and cats and pet birds. However—my kuzzint is known throughout New England as Godzalez, a cross between datdare giant Japanese monster, Godzilla, and Speedy Gonzalez, a cartoon character renowned as the fastest mouse in Mexico. Feral cats, who run in packs along the wharves, feasting on scraps from fishing boats and dumpsters, would love to feast on Godzalez. No chance they'll ever catch him.

He tells me he first saw Sharon when she was nine. He was enjoying an apple cob in a dumpster behind the Maine Center for the Arts, when this tall couple came busting out to the parking lot, jabbing accusing fingers at one another. Their faces blazed and their mouths opened like shouts heard 'round the world, but only cat-like hisses came out. Godzalez says he couldn't make out a word.

The man got into a beat-up old car, drove to the mouth of the lot, backed up into another parking spot, got out, and slapped the car keys into the woman's hand as she caught up with him, her arms held out in supplication like a panhandler's. "Here," he shouted, "you can keep this rusty old tub. It matches the kid's hair. Have a nice drive back to Lewiston-Auburn, you and that loser of a kid of ours. Bet you can't wait to see her flopping on her face on the evening news." And he sauntered out to the sidewalk.

"Wait!"

But the man didn't wait. He disappeared around the closest corner.

"Damn her!" the woman screeched. Her beautiful long legs, a dancer's legs, moved like wooden stilts as she thudded back toward the building, her hands balled into fists.

Sharon, escorted out to the parking lot by a woman petting her head, made big bug eyes at the sight of her mother. Godzalez followed the child, who ran off, ducking into a doorway till the women pursuing her passed by. She made it to the waterfront, where she tucked herself in among the stacks of lobster traps on Widener's Wharf. Godzalez says she bawled her eyes out in her yellow dress with the big, puffy sleeves. Sunlight beaming through the slats on the traps made the rhinestones on her tap-dancing shoes gleam like stars.

Not to scare her or anything, but Godzalez, who loves children, figured she needed somebody to talk to, so he made an appearance. He kept his distance at first, sniffing this and that as he shuffled around. Once he had her attention, he decided to act cute. He got on his back and kicked his legs. Then he stood up like a squirrel begging for a treat. He twitched his nose, working his whiskers into a charming rhythm.

"Sorry," Sharon said. "I don't have anything to give you. Plus, I have no money to buy you anything. Plus, I couldn't go to the store now anyway."

Godzalez, being a rat, couldn't ask why or anything like that, since rats can't talk, of course, not people talk, at least. He got down from his begging posture, slouched forward, and tucked his front paws under his chin, as if to say, "I'm all ears if you wanna talk."

"I know you won't tell anybody, so I guess I can tell you why I have to stay here. I gotta hide till my clothes dry. Look." Sharon fanned out the front of her dress, displaying a big wet stain. "It's pee. I peed myself on the stage. Now I'm eliminated. I was supposed to be the winner and go to New York. Now I'm— And I don't know where my dad went."

That was all she had to say. She sat against the traps, occasionally flapping her wet dress and blowing on it. Soon dozens of people were swarming the waterfront, calling, "Sharon, Shaaaaaaron." That's how Godzalez learnt her name.

"I can't let them see me," she told him. "My dress is still wet."

Taking the hint, Godzalez made a verminesque appearance on the open area of the dock, going right up to people's toes and sniffing them, drawing soft giggles from Sharon as searchers screeched and ran off. A lobsterman came by and tipped his hat, saying, "Afternoon, Godzalez," and walked right on, hopping onto his little boat, whistling as he tinkered with this and that. Godzalez, knowing the child could not hide there forever, was hoping she'd notice that Doug, the lobsterman, would be an okay guy to ask for help. See? He didn't shoo the cute little animal. There! Even tossed him a corner of his sandwich.

Now, it wasn't long before Godzalez saw that Doug had not only spotted the little girl, he was giving her a chance to come out on her own.

When Sharon's dress was dry, she crawled among the traps, standing up, but not quite coming out in the open when she got near the boat. She waved at Doug, as if he'd just sailed up to her front door. He waved back.

"I gotta get home," Sharon said. "Lewiston-Auburn. And I'm hungry."

Doug tossed her a pack of peanut butter crackers. Soon he persuaded her to let him walk her to the police station.

Godzalez, satisfied that she was in good hands, twitched a good-bye with his nose.

Sharon was about twenty the next time Godzalez saw her. She was on her first time-out from the M-WIT, traipsing through the snow on the docks, mapping out the sunny spots where one could kill an afternoon, becoming a sort of wharf rat herself, befriending the homeless, picking up bits of their survival wisdom. She was huge, he said, huge. He wasn't even sure, at first, it was her.

"You're Godzalez!" she said, when she woke from a quick shut-eye against a ticket booth. "Godzalez that helped me hide with my wet dress."

He got all toasty, blushing bashfully under all that ratty-looking fur. So it *was* Sharon. To show that he was indeed Godzalez, he did the same tricks as the first time he saw her.

"I never said thank you," she said. "When that nice man got me to the police station, all safe, I told them how you showed me who it was safe to go with. I wanted to run back and tell you thanks, but the cops wouldn't let me. They knew which rat I meant, though. Godzalez, they said. And they promised they'd tell you themselves. Oh, I hope they did! Even if they did, I want to say it myself. Thanks!"

Sharon fiddled with a loose button on her coat. "And thanks for scaring everybody else away when my dress was still wet. Tell you a secret. I've been pissing myself ever since. At night, I mean. That made things even worse at home. You know, the pissy sheets and all. The pissy, smelly pajamas. Anyway, I got a job flipping burgers after graduation, saved a few bucks to get to Harbor City. I'm on a time-out from the M-WIT now."

Godzalez still keeps an eye out for Sharon. He got hold of me after he saw some guy follow Sharon last January and learnt he was from Pennsylvania. He said the guy was dressed in a fancy topcoat at first, keeping to the other side of the street. And when Sharon mixed herself in with these people having a vigil at the lobsterman's statue, that man did, too. Godzalez was too far away to hear what the guy said to her, and to tell the truth, he didn't catch on that something was up until the guy went into the Army Surplus Store and came out with a plaid jacket and wool hat and followed Sharon about all day, checking her out with some goofy-looking, tiny binoculars.

Godzalez knew for sure something was up when Sharon came down to Long Wharf and told Tina about this Mr. Parker who wanted to introduce her to some beautiful, kind birth mother in some Pennsylvania coal town. And there he was, this Mr. Parker, right behind the shack they were leaning against, eavesdropping and jotting down notes.

"I smell a rat," Godzalez tells me. Sure enough, it turns out to be Tim Giovannini. If that isn't bad enough, he tells me some woman from that vigil group, Michele, keeps showing up at her workplace, the Salvation Army Store, somebody who thinks Mr. Parker is the cat's pajamas. Naturally, Godzalez is not fond of cats in pajamas or any other garb, and he's worried that Sharon's gotten all starry-eyed over the true friend she thinks she's found in Michele, who has started telling Sharon a few things about herself—the basic getting-to-know-each-other stuff people say at the start of a new friendship. Michele has three daughters a year apart—all in college now. Back when the youngest started kindergarten, Michele started on her masters program, taking a course here and there, no need to rush. Always enjoyed dabbling in psychology. Husband's a banker, so she's been fortunate to have that sort of luxury and plenty of time on her hands with her girls all in school all day. Volunteered a lot at a place that helped single mothers get on their feet.

Sharon, who's always been a wallflower, always private about her own story, begins to open up to Michele, one petal at a time.

Godzalez only ever sees Sharon downtown or around the waterfront, so he picks up these tidbits from when she wanders down there and talks to him or Tina. Soon Sharon is talking Michele this, and Michele that. Tina thinks it's a bit screwy the way Sharon laps up this woman's attention and kind ways. "Slow down," she warns Sharon.

But Sharon, a bit flattered to think a banker's wife would see anything at all in a creature like herself, starts going to datdare Quaker meeting. She blurts out a thing or two during worship, no details, just says she has hard things she hopes God will help her get over some day. Tries not to cry, but chokes up anyhow. The minute announcements are over Michele zooms over to console her. At first, Sharon hangs back, but the first time she breaks down and lets herself get folded into those motherly arms and soothed by the petting, motherly voice every child craves, that's it. She's hooked.

Sharon tells Tina about the Sunday she hung around the meetinghouse, feeling like she could finally tell another human being about a hurt she's kept buried inside for years. "It had to do with a dance recital. I knew it was bad, but when I told Michele what happened on that stage, she helped me see just how deep that wound really was. She helped me see how the effects of that day were still dragging me down, influencing my here and now. She called it the day the bond snapped between me and my mother."

"The day the bond snapped between you and your mother?"

"Yeah, the woman who claimed to be my mother, at least, the one who raised me. Seeing that day for what it was—the day that bond— Man! I must have bawled in Michele's arms for an hour!"

Sharon gets drunk on this weekly dose of motherly indulgence. By April, the mommymoon's over, or should be, considering. Somebody with a sadder story has started showing up at the Quaker meetings on Sundays. It's a single mom who grew up in a miserable family. Never any peace in that home. Now her own thirteen-year-old daughter has started going wild. Drinking, staying out all night. This single mom is never able to finish what she starts to say. She breaks down in tears. Michele goes zooming up to her right after the announcements, arms open and ready to console. Soon Sharon finds herself waiting in line for those motherly hugs. One Sunday she has to wait out in the parking lot till lunchtime. She struggles to wrestle down the green monster rising up in her heart, a heart she's ashamed of.

When she tells Tina this, Tina's all sloshy drunk, slurring out her two cents. "If you ask me, Sharon, that Michele is bad news for lonely people."

Sharon takes a long, thoughtful look at the flask of booze in Tina's hand. "Oh? How's that?" Sharon asks, but she asks it in a tone that hints she's already decided to chuck whatever Tina's explanation is.

"You think you've been ousted. But you've never been in her circle in the first place."

"I don't know what you mean."

"What about all those times you said you ran into her in the supermarket? Tells you she's picking up this or that for her dinner party. Does she ever invite you?"

Sharon shrugs. "Why should she?"

"You say she's your friend. That's what a true friend would do. Include you in her everyday life. Does she ever come to the M-WIT?"

"Lots of times."

"I don't mean to analyze your wretched childhood. I mean just to hang out with you like I do. Play cards. Sit in the lounge and watch *Jeopardy* on TV with you."

"Well, no, but— But I've called her lots of times. Bent her ear a long time on the phone. I'm embarrassed, to tell you the truth. Took up lots and lots of her time. But she's always listened to my problems. Always. Never turned me away."

"And what about her problems, her troubled childhood?"

"What do you mean?"

"Every family has its problems. Does she confide in you about hers?"

"Just a remark once about her mother always so busy volunteering for church events and her father always off on business trips."

"Didn't go sobbing on your shoulder, though, I'll bet."

"I told you, it was just something she mentioned once. So what."

"Your friend is your equal. Friendship isn't where one person thinks the other is so much more screwed up than herself. Some damaged thing she thinks she knows just how to fix, or even has a right to fix. Not a hobby she dabbles in, something to fill her days when her kids go off to school and her husband leaves for the office. Not some good deed to assure herself she's being a good citizen or whatever that minister thing was you typed up for her."

"Oh, so maybe *you* can do better by me."

"Forget it. Do what you want."

14

At the Amtrak Station

THE BIG DAY IN PENNSYLVANIA ARRIVES. By then, Tim's shoe-brush hair has grown into a pile of fluffy locks, which he has had tinted brown. He has a mustache to match. He's got himself a pair of glasses like Buddy Holly's, big frames, black as the ace of spades. He sits on a bench beneath the beautiful vaulted ceiling of the Amtrak Station in Harrisburg, Pennsylvania. Taps of high heels echo as women cross the marble floor. Tim pulls the cheesy spying bit he's seen in a million movies. He holds up a newspaper and peeks over the top and out the sides.

Finally, there she is, Mary Frances McDonald, Russian shawl and all. A black skirt hugs her petite hips. The squash heels of her black shoes pad along as she makes her way to the schedule board and looks up. The face of an angel, Tim thinks. As if she's looking up at God himself, listening to instructions on where she's to fly next and do good in this world. Then he pictures her with legs spread, getting it from boy after boy on the hard wooden floor of the Mine. Mickey Dolan, too. Whore. Uppity little bitch. A miner's kid turning her nose up at a chance with a Giovannini in the plush back seat of a Thunderbird. Now she'll see.

Tim follows Mary Frances across the room and up the short, broad staircase leading to a long, narrow room. Windows on each side look down onto a series of tracks separated by brick platforms with droopy-head lamps on iron posts holding up pointy red roofs. Between the windows are doors marked with track numbers. Mary Frances looks down at Track Number Three. A silver train approaches, nosing up slowly between the platforms. Mary Frances flings open the door and flies down the stairs as a loudspeaker announces the train.

Tim, standing at a window, takes out his opera glasses and watches Mary Frances descend to the platform. She paces a few steps in one direction and then the other. She stops abruptly, does an about-face toward the tracks, and takes a step forward, sliding her feet together and standing with shoulders back. Tim grins. What, is she going to salute? The black fringes on her shawl lift in the breeze. The train stops. Doors open. Mary Frances's head swivels. Above the two steps one car down, a Russian shawl puffs up like a parasol snapping open. To Tim's delight, Sharon is even bigger than she was in January. He's dismayed, though, at the sight of her black slacks and pale green blouse that look like they came from a store far above her means. Her hair has been neatly trimmed to a straight, blunt cut much like Mary Frances's. Tim's spirits soar when the puzzling grace of her movements deserts her, and she stumbles on the steps, jerking sideways like a fridge strapped to a hand truck. Our Mary Frances dashes over and grabs Sharon's upper arms to steady her. Mary Frances is all smiles and tears. All smiles and tears. She steps back and beholds Sharon, letting her make her own way onto the platform. Mary Frances's head comes up to Sharon's neck. Sharon, blushing like mad, is slow to slip her big hands around the little woman who's smiling and reaching up to her, whose shoulders are shaking with joyful sobs. Sharon's face is frozen in a look of utter disbelief. Then she smiles and lets her cheek come to rest against Mary Frances's head. The wind picks up with a passion and stirs up their auburn hair.

"All right," Tim says through clenched teeth. "Be a martyr. Be the good, kind mother after all, no matter what. No matter how big this tub of lard is. But there's a father, too, remember. And she'll want to know about him. If Plan A hasn't sunk your heart, it's on to Plan B then." He leaves the women to make their way to the hotel, which Mary Frances has already checked into. Through the peephole in his own door across the hall, he's already had a good view of her coming and going. He takes a long-distance phone card from his wallet, goes over to a pay phone and gets Bruce the Moose on the Loose on the line. "Hey! Bruce! Tim Giovannini here! . . .

You don't sound too happy to hear from me, and I don't blame you. In fact, that's why I called. I owe you an apology. Those things you said in Maine. You were right. . . . Well, I'm in Harrisburg at the moment, and I just saw Mary Frances. That's what brought this on. I mean, it's not like I haven't been mulling it over, but seeing her face to face. . . That's right. I got a guilty conscience. She's here with her daughter. I'm not sure, but I think it's that girl we saw in Maine. . . . That's what brought on this overdue apology. I'm sorry, Bruce, for making a jerk out of you, for taunting you that she must be your kid. . . . What? . . . I really couldn't say. It's not like I can go staring at her to get a better look. But I'll tell you, Bruce, it's easy to see she's a picture of Mary Frances when you've got them side by side, only two heads taller. So I wouldn't be surprised if this girl did turn out to be your daughter. You can come and see for yourself if you want. They were just checking into the Everheart Hotel just as I was checking out. . . . No, sorry, I can't wait. I'm just on my way out of town. Anyway, the hotel has a restaurant downstairs. You might catch them at breakfast." Tim lets out a fretful sigh. "You know, you're not the only one I owe an apology to. There's Ray. I wasn't too nice to him either up there in Maine. And most of all, there's Mary Frances, me bragging about the great time I had with her in the back seat of that Thunderbird. Man! If only teenage boys could understand how much harm they do when they don't keep it to themselves! Especially in a small town. . . . No, not today I won't. She's got her daughter with her and all. . . . So how are you doing? . . . That's good, that's good. Glad to hear it. And how about Ray? . . . Good, good. Tell him I said hello."

At eight the next morning, Tim strolls into the Everheart Restaurant with his fluffy brown hair, mustache, and black-framed glasses. Lo and behold, who's sitting at a table in the center of the room? Bruce the Moose on the Loose. No Sharon or Mary Frances yet. Tim takes a table in the same row as Bruce, but picks a chair against the wall. Not too sure Bruce will be fooled by his new look, he pulls the old hide-behind-a-newspaper trick. He catches a look on Bruce's face when the waitress sets a plate of bacon and eggs before him. Bruce nods and grins a thanks like a shy little kid. Oh, God, Tim thinks, that trusting smile. Hoss on that old TV western, *Bonanza!* Big, clunky Hoss. That's who he looks like. Just as gullible, too.

Soon Mary Frances comes in. She pauses to check her watch, looks around, and takes a table near the window, not too far from Bruce. Sharon steps into the restaurant a few minutes later. She doesn't seem to see Mary Frances at first. Her head darts left and right and her eyes are wide with panic. But, ah, there. There at that table by the window, she sees Mom, relaxed and looking at the menu. Sharon hunches up as she approaches, walking almost on tiptoe, yet smiling a shy, hopeful smile.

I'll be damned, Tim thinks. Same smile. Hoss, Jr. Except Junior is a girl. Tim remembers following Sharon around the streets of Harbor City, her smiling like that at every living thing. Even non-living things, like the shadow of a half-rotted leaf. Holy shit, he exclaims to himself. What if she really is Bruce's kid? Tim pictures Bruce blushing his way off the football field, shying away from any credit, even when he clearly saved the frigging game.

Sharon reaches the table by the window and stands there with her hands clasped in front of her. She's wearing nice clothes and a brand new backpack, a black one.

"Good morning," Mary Frances says, squeezing Sharon's hand with her fingertips. She gestures for Sharon to sit down. Sharon, shimmying out of her backpack, sits down, smiling her sheepish smile. She reaches into her backpack and pulls out a square, white envelope. "Happy— Happy Mother's Day!"

Bruce looks up. He stops his coffee mug just as it reaches his lower lip. The cup rests there and he stares over it, his face pure astonishment. He sets the cup down, blushing and clamping his hand over his mouth. Then he throws two bucks on the table, hurries to the cashier to pay for his breakfast, and exits through the archway to the hotel check-in desk. Tim has an urge to tackle him. He rubbernecks and sees Bruce writing a note on a sheet of paper. Bruce folds the note, writes something else on it, and hands it to the desk clerk, who slips it into a key cubby on the wall behind him. Then Bruce goes out the front door of the lobby. He crosses the street, glances through the window at Mary Frances and Sharon, and then walks on.

Tim's in agony, what with Bruce gone and Sharon and her phony mother fawning over one another, probably for the next hour. He's kicking himself for picking a table too far away to listen in. Then there's that note Bruce left. What does it say? He shoos away the waitress when she offers a coffee top-off, pays for his meal, and saunters over to the hotel desk.

"Good morning, sir," the desk clerk says.

Tim, seeing his boyish, conscientious face, immediately pegs him as a hard sell. "Good morning. I'm a guest here at the hotel, and I wonder if I can ask you for a favor."

"Yes, you're in Room 819. Certainly. What can I do for you?"

Tim's struck dumb by the clerk's instant matching of guest and room. With a memory like that, well. . . But Tim's boulder-sized wants cast a big shadow over his pebble-sized wisdom and he proceeds. "That man who just left. The big guy who handed you a note?"

"Yes?" The clerk looks cautious. He stands like a loyal soldier, hands at his sides.

Tim takes a twenty-dollar bill from his wallet, slides it across the counter, and bumps it up against the clerk's stomach. "May I see it?"

Now it's the clerk that's struck dumb. He looks about, as though ready to summon the rest of the army. Looking highly offended, he slides the bill back to Tim. "No, it's not addressed to you. I can't do that."

"But he's an old friend of mine. At least I think he is. An old friend from college I haven't seen in years. By the time I realized it was him, he was out the door. I'm hoping the note will say how to get in touch with him."

"Sorry, but I can't give it to you. I suggest you speak with the party he addressed it to. Maybe they can help you."

"And who might that be?"

"Actually, I can't tell you that, either. I thought you might've noticed which box I put the note in."

Tim scoops up the money. Now he's really kicking himself. He's drawn attention to himself and pissed off a hotel clerk who never forgets a face. "Never mind," Tim says. "I have an appointment right now. In fact, I have to check out early. Let me settle my bill." Tim signs the papers. He takes the elevator upstairs and packs his things. He's out the door before the two women are out of the restaurant. He drives his rented car north, toward Mount of Olives, not sure if he's going there or not. But he does go. Sixty miles later, he pulls off I-81 and heads over a high mountain, passing abandoned coal breakers and black slagpiles with the rounded ridges of the beautiful Appalachians rising behind them.

He swears he won't drive to the last block on Bloke Street, where the old Mine is. He can't pass that yellow brick building without seething over Mary Frances doing it with all those other boys up there on the top floor. Nonetheless, where's the first place he goes? Right up to Bloke Street, to Tom Collar's old gas station on the corner of Bloke and the Avenue. Across the street stands the Mine. As the station attendant pumps the gas, Tim stares and stares at the Mine, thinking, why? Why did she do that? Why those boys and not him? If only he had an answer to that question, he thinks, maybe, for once in his life, he could let it rest. The attendant approaches, announcing the price of the gas. Tim pays and gives the dashboard a mighty punch as he pulls out to the street.

He drives on, wondering if he'll see Bruce. He pulls the car into a nose-in spot in front of the library across the street from Worker's Paradise, Ray's store. Next to the library is a small deli with fresh farm goods, cheeses, homemade jellies and hot food you can get on a plate. There are three booths in the front window. Tim goes inside and buys deviled crabs, pickled eggs, and German potato salad. He takes a seat in a booth. Across the street, he sees Ray at his register, taking cash for a pair of muck boots. Tim doesn't know it yet, but at a restaurant two doors down sits Bruce, brooding over a mug of coffee. Soon Bruce steps outside and heads toward Ray's store. He waits on the sidewalk till the customer with the new boots comes out. Then Bruce looks through the display windows, as if to make sure the place is all clear. It's plain to Tim from Bruce's face that the man's all in a dither and is going to pour his big, hefty heart out to Ray. Tim's kicking himself for his stupid disguise. Between Bruce and Ray, they'd see through it if they stood close enough to him, and they'd want to know what for. No way can Tim stroll over there and pretend to be a browsing customer. A great conversation is about to happen before Tim's eyes, and he won't be able to hear a thing.

Bruce steps inside the store, closes the glass door, and leans back against it. Ray looks up. Tim reaches for his opera glasses, but puts them right back in his pocket. Stupid. Who else but him would be observing people through those things in Mount of Olives, Pennsylvania? Ray crosses the room, puts his hand on Bruce's arm and leads him over to the bench where customers always sit to try on boots. The talk begins. Ray leans forward in earnest attention. Bruce shrugs and shakes his head from time to time. From the looks of things, Tim would have to say Bruce has taken the bait and is up to his gills in guilt. If Bruce doesn't find some way to ease his troubled conscience, he'll go belly up. It's just a matter of time before he shuffles up to Mary Frances, and maybe even to Sharon, with that sheepish Hoss face of his and fesses up. Bruce the Moose on the Loose who started high school a year before Mary Frances and finally graduated a couple of years behind her. Big, dumb clunky Bruce producing a big, dumb clunky daughter. Somehow, pondering all these distasteful revelations about to hit Mary Frances does not give Tim the thrill of victory he expected. Watching the two buddies across the street, he feels jealous, though he'd never admit it, even a little absurd, like a character from a play whose part has been cut from the script, yet who's still backstage, rehearsing. Suddenly, he feels a surge of fresh spite. He has a mind to go get his hair buzzed back into a flattop and lightened to its normal blond shade. If somehow the whole gang gets together and figures out he's behind the whole thing, let them. Let them.

Besides, he'd like to stop at the dealership and see his mom and dad. In their seventies and still not retired. Always a pleasure to see them making such a go of things. And Betsy, his sister. He'd like to see her, too. He can hardly show up at anybody's door, though, with fluffy brown hair and Buddy Holly glasses. He leaves Bruce and Ray to their chummy tête-à-tête and gets his shoe-brush hair restored at a beauty shop three towns away. The bleached shade is not quite his usual. It's as light and bright as it was when he was five. He'll think of some excuse.

Soon he's sauntering into the dealership, pondering the old high school days with Sylvia in her V-neck sweater behind the reception desk, twirling her long brown hair around one finger and placing it on her breast, trying to get him to look. She must be a fat old hen with five kids by now, Tim thinks. He heads right for the tall counter to see whatever young babe is sitting at the desk behind it these days.

He's not two feet into the door when Bum-Knee, a lot more bent and hobbly, wheeling a gray trash can and nodding to Tim, crosses his path like a black cat bringing him bad luck. And bad luck it is from Tim's point of view. The woman behind the desk is the very same who worked the desk at the dentist's office when he was a kid. "Aw, quit yer blubberin'," she'd say. Between her and Bum-Knee as employees, Tim asks himself if his parents are running a charity ward for people who ought to retire, but who just don't want to face the music.

"Aw, quit yer blubberin'," the woman says when Tim catches her eye. Instead of the familiar glare, she offers a grin with better teeth than Tim has seen among people he graduated with. "Your mom's not here. Your dad's in the back office."

"Thanks."

Ricardo Giovannini stands up when Tim enters. "This is a surprise. Hello! What brings you to Pennsylvania unannounced?"

"Cars, classic cars. And a chance to swing by here on the same trip."

Ricardo stares at his son. He twists his mouth to one side and bites on his lower lip. "Why don't I believe you?" he says.

"You don't believe me?"

"No."

"How should I know why?"

Ricardo shrugs. "Anyway, you're here. How about supper at Mattucci's?"

"What about Mom, and Betsy and Bob, and that lazy, good-for-nothing kid of theirs? What's his name? Rick? Maybe they can join us."

"Yes, Rick. You know that's his name. Your sister and Bob are down the shore. Rick's probably home. I'll call him."

"No, don't. I really wanted to see Betsy. If Rick tagged along, fine, I could hardly say no. But since she's not around, forget it."

"You know, son, it wouldn't have killed you to show that boy a little more attention over the years. After all, you're the only uncle he's got. You have no children of your own."

"True, I don't. Not that I know of anyway. And that means no child support to pay month after month for kids I'd hardly get to see. Half the guys from my class got married and ended up on that carpet. The rest are being taken for every penny they got. Poor Hal Jones, he's been in court so many times he could be a judge. Me, I had enough smarts not to tie myself up in a marriage in the first place."

"Let me call Rick," Ricardo Giovannini says, reaching for the phone. "He likes Mattucci's."

Tim's got a note of irritation in his voice when he says, "How do you know what he likes? He spent more time at the babysitter's than at his own house. Betsy let him get so attached to her, you'd think he was *her* kid. Bob shoulda never let Betsy work in that chiropractor's office. Maybe if she'da stayed home and paid more attention to her own kid—speaking of giving him attention—he might seem more like one of us. He's not like us. Not at all. No ambition. He oughta be in here learning the car business. No, he's probably still playing with the chemistry set he had that time I came home and tried to take him to a football game. I couldn't coax him away from the damned thing no how. Sorry, Dad, but the kid's a weirdo. I don't want to have supper with him. For all that chemistry stuff, you'd think he'd at least want to go to college. No, he scrapes by on some low-budget carpentry business, doing odd jobs. Going nowhere."

Ricardo Giovannini has slumped under Tim's rant. His face sags with disappointment in Tim's attitude, though he can't say he's surprised. "All right, Tim, I'll call your mother. It'll be just the three of us." He dials the phone. "Hi, Sophia. Tim's in town. . . . Right here in my office. Blond as the day he was born, only brighter. . . . I don't know. Dyed it, I guess. Musta found a gray hair since his last visit."

15

Plan B

THE NEXT MORNING, TIM TAKES A RIDE to Bruce's box factory. He goes right to the office entrance and finds Bruce behind a desk, looking over some papers. "Hey, Bruce!" he says, all cheery. "I wrapped things up early and stopped in town to see my folks. Had a nice dinner last night at Mattucci's. How 'bout lunch?"

Tim notes that Bruce's Hoss smile is a bit dragged down. Ah, a man with something on his mind. Bruce stands up and taps Tim on the arm with a friendly fist. "Sure. If you've got the time, there's a little hot dog stand on the way to Catawissa. I'd like to talk about, you know, about yesterday. And I'd rather not sit in a booth in town."

"No problem."

"Give me ten minutes?"

"Great! I'll be outside in my car. It's a red convertible. I'll put the top down. Yeah, I know. It's only May. There's still frost in the morning. But when I saw this little red baby in the rental lot, I couldn't resist."

Bruce's worried mind puts a bounce in Tim's step, but only a slight one. In fact, he's more irritated than glad. This has all become a lot of work, this Plan B. There shouldn'ta had to be any Plan B. Mary Frances shoulda let out a shriek on that Amtrak platform like a village peasant seeing Godzilla rear its massive, scaly head over a mountaintop. Then this would all be done. No Plan B required. They'd be even. He could hop a plane back to Illinois and forget he ever set eyes on Mary Frances McDonald, ungrateful little bitch. Forget he ever grew up in this godforsaken, grimy, going-nowhere, ungrateful place. Then to hell with her, to hell with Bruce, Sharon, everybody.

The top on the red convertible is down and Tim waits for Bruce behind the wheel. He doesn't notice Bruce approaching. He just hears, "Okay, here I am."

They hit the road, the cold mountain air walloping their faces. "This is refreshing," Bruce says.

Refreshing, Tim thinks. Refreshing? Can't he think of anything better than some old-lady word for a treat like this? "Cooooooooool!" Tim hollers with a menacing, adolescent grin as he hits the accelerator. "Cooooooooool!" They zoom down one mountain and over another as Bruce shouts directions to the roadside stand. It's an old green wooden place with the windows for outside service still boarded over with winterizing plywood. There's a lunch counter inside and two rows of Formica-topped tables. Bruce and Tim, the only customers, stand at the register and put in their order.

"I'll bring your food over to you," the man says. "Have a seat anywhere."

Bruce leads the way to a table in the far corner.

"You said you'd like to talk," Tim coaches.

Bruce sighs and shakes his head. "Boy, oh boy. I think you were right, Tim. I think that young lady is my daughter."

"Oh, so you went to Harrisburg and saw her?"

"Yep, in the hotel restaurant. They came in for breakfast, just like you thought they would."

"Is that right?"

"Yeah. And, I'll tell you, Tim. My heart sank when I saw her."

"I guess so. She's huge!"

"That's not why," Bruce says. "Yeah, so she's huge. She's also twenty-five or so. In those twenty-five years, I never even met her. Never saw her grow up. Never provided her with anything she needed. I always had plenty. I could have seen to it that she—"

"Jesus, Bruce! Don't you already have a pile of kids to provide for?"

"Yeah, but we could've made room for one more. I love kids. Sandy does too. She woulda welcomed that girl, no question. I almost went over to their table yesterday, but I lost my nerve. What could I say? 'Hello there, I think I'm your dad?' I just paid my bill and left. Actually, I dropped off a note for Mary Frances at the hotel desk first."

"You did?"

"Yeah."

"What did it say?"

"It just said something like, 'Hi, Mary Frances, I saw you in the restaurant. I've owed you an apology for years, but this wasn't the time or place. Please give me a call in the next day or so.' I signed it and wrote down my phone number and my pager number."

"Has she called?"

"Not yet. This whole thing's eating at me, Tim. I gotta think of something to make things right."

"Well, I'm sure you'll think of something." If Tim could think of a way to scram outa there without stranding Bruce, he'd go. He's groaning inside at the prospect of listening to Bruce's tedious, guilt-ridden deliberations, but Bruce comes to a snap decision. "Mind if we get that food for a take-out?" he asks, getting up from his chair.

"No, I don't mind."

Bruce goes over and speaks to the man behind the counter. Then he comes back and says, "Thanks, Tim. I've made up my mind. I'm heading right back to Harrisburg to see if I can catch them before my daughter goes back to Maine."

"Sounds like a plan," Tim says. "But how do you know she's really your daughter?"

"She's got Mary Frances's face and my build. She's gotta be! Even if she isn't, I still feel obliged somehow. I at least have to look into things more. What about you? Will you be staying with your folks for a few days?"

"Till the weekend. Then I'm heading back."

After supper that night, the phone rings at the Giovannini house. It's Bruce, calling for Tim. Tim's parents, hearing small exclamations of astonishment, look at him questioningly when he comes back to the table to finish his wine. "That was Bruce the

Moose on the Loose. Seems he's located a long-lost daughter of his."

"Oh?" Tim's parents say together.

"Yeah, a girl from Maine. Bruce is with her in Harrisburg at the moment. Her and her mother. They're bringing the girl here to meet her long-lost grandmother."

"But Bruce's mother died last year," Sophia Giovannini says.

"Not Bruce's mother. The other one. The unwed mother's mother." Tim chuckles. Plan C has manifested all on its own. Maybe Sharon didn't draw shrieks of horror from Mary Frances McDonald or Bruce the Moose on the Loose, but she sure as hell will from Joyce McDonald. This time she won't be able to fix it by shuffling those eleven portraits around her coffee table. What Tim wouldn't give to be a fly on the wall during that reunion!

"You look mighty amused," his dad says.

"I am."

"So who's this grandmother here in town?"

"Joyce McDonald. You gotta admit, Dad, Joyce McDonald's been the town joke with her broken-leg-in-Vermont cover-up for Mary Frances going on thirty years now. She's still at it! The more she tries to hide the story of her bastard grandchild, the more attention she brings to it. Everybody knows she's got all of her daughter's school portraits crowded on a coffee table in any old order, hoping nobody'll notice there's only eleven. Remember Ned? Only last January he was telling me what his mother said. She said the Avon lady wanders into Joyce's parlor and acts surprised to see there's only eleven."

"Oh, and why does she do that?" Ricardo asks.

"To get a rise out of Joyce McDonald. Why else?"

Sophia chimes in. "No, Tim, your father can figure that much out. I think he means, why does she do a mean thing like that?"

"Oh, forget it." Tim pouts and his parents exchange a look of concern. They all sip their wine in silence. Finally, his mother says, “So when are they bringing the young woman to meet her grandmother?”

“Some time tonight. Why?”

“Tonight?” Sophia gets up from her chair. “They’re coming from Harrisburg tonight?”

“That’s what Bruce said. He said they were just leaving the hotel.”

Sophia stands with her hands resting on the back of her chair, giving her husband a look which he responds to by getting up from the table too. They take their coats from the closet under the staircase in the front hall.

“What’s going on?” Tim says. “What, are you going to warn Joyce McDonald? What’s it to you guys anyhow?”

The parents don’t answer. They go out the door. When Tim hears their car drive away, he hops into his rented convertible. It’s a five-minute drive to the edge of town. He parks the car among the many at the Acme Supermarket across the two-lane from the stadium, and he walks the quarter mile to the coal patch of Otterdale, where Joyce McDonald lives. He cuts through the abandoned colliery and walks along a narrow path, where the thorns of wild blackberry bushes catch on his pants and sleeves. Finally out the other end of the path, he stands at the bottom of the road and sees his parents’ car up ahead. “What the hell!” he utters. It’s killing him, wondering what the hell they could possibly be doing in Joyce McDonald’s house. He wants to go in there too, but his last shred of sobriety prompts him to turn back onto the path.

Tim gets home, changes out of his prickled clothes, takes the same seat at the table, gulps down a full glass of wine, and pours himself another. He notices for the first time the scratches on his hands from the blackberry bushes. He counts them. Four. No, five! “Goddamn them! If everyone would just mind their own business. Hear that, Mom? Hear that, Dad?”

They’re not back so, of course, they don’t hear. It’s at least a half hour till they walk in the door, hang up their coats and come and stand near the kitchen table. Tim cannot read their faces. He puts his hands on his lap so they don't see the scratches. Finally, he asks, "Well?"

"Well?" his father responds.

"Well, did you warn her that her long-lost grandchild was about to show her face, even though Grandma's had a helluva time showing her own face in this town? I mean, after what her wild little Mary Frances did upstairs in the Mine."

"Shut up, Tim," the father says. "Just shut up." He leaves the kitchen, and so does Sophia. Never in his whole life has Ricardo Giovannini spoken those words to his son. Never. A fist in the chops couldn't have been more stunning. Tim rubs his fingers over his mouth. Then he pours himself more wine.

Meanwhile, back in the coal patch of Otterdale, a light blue car pulls in from the two-lane, followed by a black one. They come half the loop around the green and park on a spot where the grass is worn bald. Sharon and Mary Frances get out of the blue car, Bruce out of the black one. Bruce says, "Just give me a wave from the window if you want me to come in."

"Okay," Mary Frances says. "See you in a bit. Ready, Sharon?"

Sharon hangs back and Mary Frances says, "She won't bite. Like I told you, she'll be stunned at first, but we'll be fine."

Mary Frances presses down the latch on the white picket gate. "Oh, I forgot to tell you. We're not allowed to use the front door. We have to go through the side yard to the kitchen door."

Sharon shrugs and follows Mary Frances. The streetlamp shines on the daffodils and tulips along the walkway leading to the porch farther down the side of the house. Through the sheer curtains on the windows of the parlor, dining room and kitchen, Joyce can be seen pacing in a fret.

"You didn't tell her we were coming, right?" Sharon asks.

"Right. I didn't want her to get all worked up before we even walked in the door."

"She looks pretty worked up to me. Now I'm not so sure I want to go in there."

"Okay, we don't have to go in tonight. Me, I can't imagine a time she won't be upset. She just wants to forget her daughter was an unwed mother. I'm tempted just to get the first meeting over with, but if you'd—"

"Yes, let's get it over with."

Mary Frances knocks on the kitchen door. Joyce, visible through the glass pane, covers her ears, then her mouth, then her ears again. Mary Frances stops knocking. She's about to knock again when the door flies open. Joyce whirls her arm for the women to hurry in off the porch. She pokes her head out to the porch and looks in both directions. Then she shuts the door and pulls the shades down over the glass panel and the window overlooking the porch.

"Mom, what's wrong? I—"

Sharon has taken a step slightly behind Mary Frances. Joyce, advancing, pushes Mary Frances to the side. Her eyes burn into Sharon's. "I was warned you were coming. You conniver! You lousy, stinking conniver!"

Sharon, lifting her left arm to shield herself, catches a glimpse of the strawberry mark on her hand and whisks it out of sight.

"You know damned well you're not her daughter! Came here to con us. What! Is it money you want? Is that why you're doing this? Look around. Go ahead. Take a good look. Do we look like a family with money? Same kitchen table near fifty years! Same throw rugs on the kitchen floor near twenty. I made them myself. Made them from old neckties and strips of cloth from dresses and shirts worn to rags. That's the sort of thing you'll find in this house!"

"Mom!"

"Don't mom me! She cannot be your child!" Joyce declares with a firm thump on the stove. "You had a baby boy, Mary Frances. I know. I was there."

"You were there?"

"Yes, they handed me the boy and I handed him over to his new family myself. So don't go letting this gold-digger imposter take you for every dime she can get."

Sharon turns her head every which way, looking to escape. Joyce is standing in front of the kitchen door. Sharon spies the archway leading to the next room. She sprints through the dining room, through the parlor and out the front door, leaving it open. Mary Frances runs after her. From the porch she sees Sharon running across the green, across the two-lane, and into the cemetery. Bruce gets out of his car and follows her. Mary Frances, torn between a wish to help Sharon and a craving for the truth finally spilling out in that house, grips the porch banister. She trusts Sharon to Bruce and goes back inside. She glares, speechless, at her mother.

"Don't look at me like that, Mary Fran. The girl's a fake! You should thank me for sending her packing. Your baby was a boy. I was there, I tell you. And, yes, you were right. The child was not born in Vermont. That's why you couldn't find any birth records in that state. He was born here in Pennsylvania, up past Scranton. I drove you halfway to Pittsburgh and then back east again, and then up north beyond the coal towns, letting you think you were driven all the way to Vermont. You agreed to be blindfolded and travel lying down on the back seat, remember, so you wouldn't be reminded of the child you gave up every time you traveled those highways. Nobody forced you. You agreed to it."

"And who did you hand my child over to?"

"I promised I'd never tell. We all agreed it was the best thing."

"I didn't agree."

"You were sixteen."

"I want to know. Where is my son?"

"I can't tell you. I struck a bargain. I gave my word." Joyce sits down onto the plastic-covered sofa behind the coffee table with the eleven school portraits of Mary Frances. She slouches down, barricading herself behind the cheap, glitzy frames. She folds her arms, and stares at her feet.

"What kind of bargain? What kind, Mom? Tell me."

"Never mind what kind of bargain."

"For Christ's sake, Mom! What kind of bargain!"

"I promised I'd never tell."

"Where's my son? You know, don't you? Or was it a girl? How do I know if you're telling the truth about anything? Maybe Sharon is your granddaughter, but you don't want anybody seeing her around, asking embarrassing questions. She looks just like me. All those tongues wagging once again about your wild daughter's gang bang up the Mine."

"You weren't wild! Mickey Dolan forced you up those stairs." Joyce slouches lower on the couch, her legs sliding out under the other side of the coffee table.

"Let's not start that again. We were getting to the truth. Let's stick with it. Stop trying to lose your pregnant child among those mixed-up pictures. Stop trying to hide your face behind them." Mary Frances shoves the portraits off the coffee table with one sweep of her arm. "There! There, now they're gone. Now let's talk."

Joyce looks up. "Mary Fran, now, don't be mad now. Yes, it was a boy, and, yes, I know where he is, but I promised I'd never tell you. Even tonight, I promised I wouldn't even tell you it was a boy. Let you think this girl from Maine was really your daughter. But when I saw her conniving, gold-digging face, it made me so mad, I— Oh, I'm kicking myself!"

There's a light thump against the front door. The knob turns. Joyce topples the coffee table in an effort to get her legs out from under it and get to the door before it opens. "I'm not letting her back in here!" Joyce manages to fling her body against the door before it opens more than half a foot. It slams shut.

Mary Frances reaches for the knob, fighting her mother for it. She manages to pull the door open, sending Joyce stumbling back to the couch, where she lands on her side. Joyce looks up and says with a huge smile, "Why it's Rick Trounov! Betsy Giovannini's kid!" She sits up and tugs her skirt smooth and pats her hair. "Oh, you rascal! What are you doing here?"

"It's Wednesday night. I brought the pizza. It was my turn to pick the movie, remember?" Rick steps in, holding a pizza box with a VHS of *Amadeus* on top. His alarmed eyes take in the table toppled on its side and the framed portraits strewn on the floor.

"But, Rick, I left a message for you on your answering machine not to come tonight."

"When?"

"Half hour ago. I said I didn't feel like a movie tonight. Or a pizza. I don't feel so good."

"I was already out the door by the time you left that message. What happened here? Are you hurt?" He glowers at Mary Frances. "What did you do?"

Joyce wags her finger at Rick. "Now, don't look at her like that. This is Mary Frances, my daughter. You've seen her popping in and out on leave from the Navy over the years. She'd never lay a hand on me. I swooned. If she hadn'ta been here to break my fall, well, what's a few pictures on the floor?" Joyce sets the coffee table upright and starts filling it up with her daughter's photographs, grunting each time she bends down. Rick stoops down to help.

"Sorry," Rick says, looking up at Mary Frances. "There I was accusing you when you were helping out."

"It's okay." Mary Frances can't stop staring at Rick. Something familiar about his green eyes. She watches the care he takes when he picks up her tenth-grade school photo. A crack in the heavy glass goes from the shoulder and down across the plaid vest. Rick shakes his head as he runs his finger over the crack.

Joyce waves the back of her hand at the damaged object. "Oh, that's nothing. We can buy another frame. You'll pick one up for Joyce tomorrow, won't you, Rick?"

Rick ponders the damage a moment longer.

Joyce winks at Mary Frances. "Cat must have his tongue. Why, I've never seen him so mum. He's always such a talker. And lively too! Puts me in mind of our Jack, he does."

Mary Frances stoops down by the coffee table, almost knee-to-knee with Rick. He says, "Don't worry. I'll get a new frame tomorrow and have this fixed up for you in two shakes of a lamb's tail." She sees a look of impish merriment in his eyes and an earnest wish to patch everything up, make her feel better.

She, too, sees Jack in Rick. She remembers Jack putting a Band-Aid over the smarting welt on her finger after their mother dug out a splinter with a needle she'd charred and sterilized in a match flame before poking it under the sliver of wood. Jack put the Band-Aid on, crossed his eyes and stretched his mouth, making her laugh as he flitted around the room like a drunken dancer. Mary Frances twists her head around and looks at the pictures of her brother on the walls. Her eyes fix on the one of Jack offering her the kewpie doll he won at the Bloomsburg Fair. She glances back and forth from the many faces of Jack to Rick's face. Jack as an infant raising himself up on his forearms. Jack getting bigger and bigger and bigger. Betsy Giovannini's kid? Mary Frances remembers that it was Tim Giovannini Bruce had called when they were leaving Harrisburg tonight with Sharon, called to thank Tim for mentioning he'd seen me and a girl that must be my daughter. A big girl that just might be his daughter, too. Bruce told Tim we were on our way to Otterdale. Ah, so Tim must have told his sister Betsy, and then they—Betsy and her husband—they came to Otterdale and warned Joyce she'd better keep the bargain. And Mom, she—how could she look me straight in the eye and say this is Betsy Giovannini's son? No, Mom, it's my son!

Mary Frances shoots a hard look at her mother. "Scoundrel!" she wants to scream. "Liar! Conveniently getting tendinitis from the repetitive motion at the cigar factory so you could quit and take up babysitting. Betsy gets a baby and you get to replace Jack. Replace him with your daughter's bastard child and call the birth a broken leg. You've had all the joy and none of the shame!" But Mary Frances says none of these things. Her rage is softened by the tender perplexity in Rick's eyes. She sees a little disappointment even. He was trying to help by offering to replace that glass, but it didn't do any good. Tears fill her eyes as it dawns on her that he must have heard the ugly tales about how her baby was conceived. As much as she wants to hold him, she cannot make him walk the streets of this town knowing he was that baby.

Joyce, seeing Rick and Mary Frances gaze so thoughtfully at one another, starts chattering and rearranging the school portraits, quickly swapping a second-grade one for a sixth-grade one, the senior portrait for the photo taken in first grade. She talks fast. Her voice is shrill and panicky, like she's running alongside a train that has begun to pull out without her. "Of course, he's not *that* much like our Jack. A little around the eyes, maybe, but— Mary Fran, quit staring at the poor boy. Don't take it so, so— I don't know. I don't know what I mean." Joyce leans over the table and thrusts another photograph between Rick and Mary Frances. "This is my favorite picture of you, Mary Fran, your fourth-grade one. The happiest picture of all!" To Rick, she says, "Her father was still with us then, you know. Lucky for us all he was. He was near sent to Pearl Harbor on datdare ship that took the worst pounding on December 7, 1941. Let me see now, what was the name of that ship?"

"The *Arizona,*" Rick says in a rote tone, as if reciting the same catechism question for the millionth time.

"Our Mary Frances would never've been born if he hadda been on that ship. I was pregnant with our Jackie then, my first one. Our Jack was such a good boy. Only twenty-one years old when that Dolan's boy took him drag racing down that Centralia highway. Twenty-one and dead already." The wistful tone in Joyce's voice is swept aside by bitterness and spite. "Dolan's boy, that conniver! They say his brains were spread all over the road like cottage cheese. Served him right."

Throughout this barrage of history, gossip, and outrage, Rick does not wince. The expression on his face is almost blank, but somehow expectant, like the disciplined look of a military recruit prepared to carry out the next order the moment the tirade ends. The picture with the cracked glass is resting on his knees. Mary Frances reaches for it, and Rick places it in her hands. The tears that had begun to fill up her eyes pour out.

Joyce shakes her daughter's shoulder. "Why, Mary Fran, what's wrong? The boy *told* you he'd get you a new frame."

Mary Frances squeezes Rick's hand. "Thanks," she says, standing up. "Mom's back to her old self now. I think I'll go."

"How 'bout some pizza?" Rick says.

Joyce wags her finger at him. "Now, our Mary Frances has had a long day. She needs to be getting home." Placing her hand on her daughter's shoulder, Joyce prods her out to the porch. "That's a good girl. Go home and get some sleep now." She beelines it back inside and shuts the door.

Mary Frances sees that Bruce's car is gone. A piece of paper flaps under her windshield wiper. She goes over and reads the note: "Sharon is with me. Don't worry. I'll see to it she has a place to stay tonight. Please give me a call tonight or tomorrow morning."

Mary Frances pockets the note. She puts her hand on the door handle of her car, but she doesn't want to drive. She wants to walk and walk and walk. She walks across the green, crosses the two-lane, and goes into the cemetery. The tombstones are all in rows with the edges facing her. She begins a climb up the hill, where life-sized statues glisten in the moonlight like ice sculptures.

At the foot of an empty cross a mother holds her murdered son, her head bent in inconsolable sorrow as two robed figures look on. Sinking down onto the grass, Mary Frances squeezes the lifeless hand dangling from the mother's lap.

16

Home to Roost

"WHAT'S THE MATTER with *her?*" Tim Giovannini says, standing in the front hall of his parents' stately Victorian home and jerking his thumb in the direction his mother is heading—up the staircase and out of range of his big, drunken mouth, which has been treating the old homestead to calls for a festive night.

Neither mother nor father has answered anything Tim's said in the last seventeen minutes. Continuing in this newfound family tradition, Ricardo Giovannini sits on the parlor sofa that faces a coffee table and a pair of wingback chairs on a Persian rug in the center of the hardwood floor. His hands are clasped and his elbows are resting on his knees. His face is a picture of defeat. "So the chickens have come home to roost," he blurts out to the walls in a massive sigh.

Tim's face lights up. He thinks he's got a response. "And the peeps too, don't forget. The peep, I should say. Mary Frances McDonald's little peep must be with her in Otterdale right now, snuggling under her wing." Tim stares at his stone-faced father for several minutes. Then he shrugs, flicks off the hall light at the foot of the stairs, and goes back down the darkened hall to the kitchen. When he gets there, he gives the heavy swinging door a shove. It jerks back and forth past the door jamb with a spiteful th-wwwoosh, th-wwwoosh, th-wwwoosh before it settles into place.

Now and then, Ricardo looks up from the couch at one of the empty chairs, as if somebody sitting there has just put a question to him. Then he goes back to pondering. An occasional creak on the staircase in the huge old house bids for his attention. He turns and looks past the hall, hoping to see the slippered feet of Sophia coming back down the staircase. But he knows she hasn't changed into nightclothes. She didn't go up there to sleep. Like him, she's up there waiting, waiting for the knock on the door. Both of them knew this night would come. Someday the mother of that child would find her way to their door. Finally, the bell rings. Ricardo turns the porch light on and looks Mary Frances over. Her cheeks are wet with tears. He knows damned well it's her, but he opens the door slightly and says in a casual, innocent voice, "Yes?"

Mary Frances is not fooled. In fact, she surmises that her mother has already called to warn these fine, upstanding pillars of Mount of Olives, Pennsylvania, that the jig is up. She strains to be polite, at least till she gets her foot in the door.

"Mr. Giovannini?"

"Yes?"

"I'm Mary Frances McDonald." As if you don't know, she thinks to herself. "Could you please tell me how to get in touch with your daughter Betsy?"

"Tonight?"

"It's very important."

"I—" Ricardo flinches when she flicks away a tear. He turns slightly away, like he's been slapped. "I'm sorry, but Betsy's down at the shore with her husband." Once he gets that much out, he looks directly at Mary Frances and takes up the polite tone of a butler. "If you'd like to leave your phone number, I can pass it on to her."

Sophia Giovannini walks down the stairs. She turns on the light in the lower hall. Her husband's eyes beg for mercy, but Sophia opens the door wider. "Please come in. We can talk in here." Sophia leads the way to the parlor and extends her hand toward one of the wingback chairs. Mary Frances sits down. Sophia sits on the couch, but leaves a gap between herself and her husband.

Tim pokes his drunken head out from the kitchen. "Who's zat at the door?" he hollers up the hall. "I heard the doorbell. Who is it?"

Ricardo hops to his feet, grabs onto the archway, and swings into the hall like a monkey. "Somebody looking for Betsy."

"Who?"

"Never mind who. Please! Just stay where you are." He goes back to the couch and sits right next to his wife.

Tim comes through the hall anyway. "Aaahhhh!" he croons, rubbing his hands. "And what have we done to merit a visit from a woman of such high honor?" He leans back against the archway, arms crossed, ankles crossed. He wears the proud smirk of a drunk who can barely stay upright, but who feels like he's just managed a full day of conquering the world.

Ricardo says, "Go upstairs and sleep it off, son. This doesn't concern you."

"Betsy! What does she want with our Betsy?"

Ricardo says, "Please, Tim. Stay out of this." And to Mary Frances he says, "He doesn't know. He honestly doesn't know. He was away at college back then. Really, he doesn't know."

"Know what?" Tim says. "Dad, clue me in already. What does she want with Betsy?"

Mary Frances says, "Don't bother pretending, any of you. I thought it was just my mother pulling the wool over my eyes, but you people are in on this too. All these years, every one of you knew exactly what became of him."

"Who?" Tim says.

"You know damned well who! You've all deceived me all this time. Please, don't talk to me now as if I haven't got a brain in my head when you can see I've figured out the truth."

Sophia shakes her head, "Honestly, Tim doesn't know about him. But now you do, so you're right. You're right. There's no use going on pretending."

Ricardo gives Mary Frances a look of resentment. "I just wish to God your mother had kept her word. When we learned you were about to go to her tonight with that girl from Maine, thinking she was your daughter, we begged her not to go upsetting everyone. We begged her to keep her word."

"Her end of the bargain, you mean. That's what she called it, a bargain. Don't worry, Mom didn't come right out and spill your precious beans. She just accused Sharon of being an imposter. Some gold digger trying to take me and my family for whatever she could squeeze out of us."

"She did?" Tim says with a big, fat, victorious smile.

"Oh dear. I'm so sorry," Sophia says.

"Sure."

"We're not heartless people," Sophia shoots back. Her husband pats her hand. They both fidget. Ricardo, half rising, balls up his fists and says, "Tim, wipe that grin off your face or I'll, I'll—" Now it's Sophia who does the hand-patting after grabbing Ricardo by the belt and easing his ass back down to the couch. Tim's mama and papa stare at their laps till a pounding on the door makes them swing their frightened faces toward one another.

"What, you expecting the Boogie Man?" Tim says. "Sheeze!" He shoves off from the archway and makes for the door, swinging it open with the flair of a carnival host letting the next brave soul into the Fun House. "Bruce the Moose on the Loose!" He gawks around Bruce, checking out the porch. "And where is the lovely young daughter you said you were bringing from Harrisburg?"

Bruce shoves Tim aside. Ricardo and Sophia jump up from the couch as Tim slides down the hallway wall into a squat. "Don't worry. He'll live," Bruce says. He puts a hand on Mary Frances's shoulder. "I saw your car outside. Good. We're both here." He turns to Sophia. "We need to talk to Tim. Is there some place in the house we can go and talk?"

"The kitchen," she offers in a shaky voice.

"I don't think so," Ricardo says. "Whatever you're so angry about, Tim's no match for you under any circumstances. Tonight, well, look, you can see he's had a bit to drink and, well, it's like knocking down a feather. No! Talk right here. Besides, what can there be to talk to Tim about? Mary Frances came here to speak with Betsy, not Tim. Betsy's down at the shore. We've tried to explain that Tim's had nothing to do with any of this, but Mary Frances seems to feel that he does."

"Oh, he certainly does," Bruce says. "He certainly does. Don't you, Mr. Parker? Mr. Howard Parker, Esquire."

Mary Frances gapes at Tim. "You're Howard Parker? You? You're the so-called attorney who wrote to me to arrange a meeting between me and my supposed daughter? The attorney I talked to on the phone?"

Tim, struggling back up onto his feet, looks at his accusers like they're nuts.

Ricardo pants before he can get a word out, "You really did that, Tim? You actually posed as a lawyer and got these people together to— Why? Why would you do such a thing?"

"Who says I did?"

"Sharon," Bruce says. "When she came running out of Joyce McDonald's place tonight, crying her heart out, I followed her. We had a long talk. Joyce accused her of being a con. Sharon told me how she got mixed up in this in the first place. Some lawyer named Howard Parker approached her in Harbor City, Maine. When? January, the weekend we were there. Me, you, Ray, Ned and Shitfoot. We were there that weekend."

"So were thousands of other people."

"Our hotel was directly across from the women's hotel where Sharon lives. We could see right into the lounge. We all gawked at her through those fancy little opera glasses of yours. We all agreed Sharon could pass for Mary Frances's daughter, if only she weren't so big. And of course, being so big myself, the joke was on me. I could be the girl's father. To everybody else, Sharon's resemblance to Mary Frances was just an amazing coincidence. Something fun for the old gang to shoot the shit about at a hotel party and shrug off on the way home. But you, Tim, you followed up. You went off by yourself all weekend. The rest of us wondered why you flew all the way from Illinois for a get-together with your old buddies, only to go off by yourself all day. Now I know why. To lasso Sharon into this scheme. At some point you showed Sharon those opera glasses. When Sharon mentioned them tonight, the light went on. I asked her to describe this Howard Parker. Sure enough, her description fit you. I stopped by my house and got the photographs I took in Maine. As soon as Sharon sees your face, she says, 'That's him! That's Mr. Parker!'"

Tim just shrugs.

"So you con Sharon into thinking her real mother is pining her heart out for her in Pennsylvania. Then you trick Mary Frances into thinking the child she's been asking around for has materialized. Oh, but that wasn't enough amusement for you. You had to rope me in too. You just happened to be at the Amtrak Station in Harrisburg just as Sharon's train pulled in. Called me up and urged me to take a closer look at that Mary Frances look-alike from Maine, see if she wasn't really my kid after all."

Tim chuckles. "Bruce the Moose on the Loose. Say, Mary Frances, you must have been so proud when the carnival wheel stopped spinning and the little leather flap wedged in on Bruce's number. Is that where you put your money? Or did you put it on Ray or Ned? Or on that low-life Mickey Dolan? Or on that boyfriend of yours, Catman Berkoski? Round and round and round she goes. Where she stops, nobody knows. The father could have been any guy in town."

Ricardo grabs Tim by the collar of his shirt. "Or you, Tim. Maybe that little leather flap points right to you!" When Tim tries to pull his father's hands off his collar, Ricardo sees the scratches on Tim's hands. "What happened to your hands? Those scratches weren't there when we went out to talk to Joyce."

"Blackberry bushes. I went for a wah—"

Mary Frances puts her hand on Ricardo's shoulder, turning him away from Tim. "Is that why your family took my son? Because you thought Tim was the father?"

"You took her son?" Tim says. Mary Frances, catching a look of surprise and innocence more genuine than even a longtime liar like Tim can pull off, says to Ricardo, "So Tim really didn't know. It was all worked out between my mother and the parents of the supposed father. I'd be tricked into thinking I gave birth in Vermont. I'd come away thinking I'd signed my baby over to a good home arranged by a real adoption service. But in reality, my child gets handed over to Betsy Giovannini."

"Yes," Sophia admits.

Tim confronts each of his parents with a stare. The father stares back. The mother looks down. "Rick? She means Rick?"

"Yes, Rick!" Ricardo says. "Somebody had to take responsibility. You can't just go bragging to your buddies about all the fun you had with a girl and just leave her to dig herself out of trouble."

"You really thought the kid was mine?"

"We heard you bragging," Sophia says.

"And so you thought *our* family should raise the kid?" Tim puffs up his chest with indignation. "I always knew something was wrong with that kid! He was *never* like us. This explains it. He's not a genuine Giovannini, that little going-nowhere—"

Tim's parents look at Mary Frances in helpless embarrassment. "That's enough, Tim." his mother says, "You've done enough damage."

Tim rattles on. "Okay, so kids brag. I was a cocky teenager, for Christ's sake. I bragged that I got some girl knocked up. And you believed it?" He gives his parents a taken-aback look like he's just stumbled upon the stupidest idiots on the planet. "You must've heard about Mary Frances's big night up the Mine. Everybody in town knew about that."

"The possibility that it could be our grandchild was enough for us," Ricardo says. "And Betsy was on that waiting list to adopt for so long. Poor Betsy, she wanted a baby so badly. Couldn't have one herself."

Tim scowls. "You never let on Rick was adopted."

"No," Sophia says. "It was all handled while Betsy was living up in Scranton. She and her husband moved back here with the baby and just went on like the child was born to them. Coming back to Mount of Olives was part of the agreement."

"And," Tim asks with of look of total incredulity, "Betsy was willing to adopt the famous Gang-Bang Baby just to get off that waiting list?"

"Watch your mouth!" Ricardo says, raising a fist. "Betsy was not to be told whose baby it was. She was told the child came from an adoption agency. That was also part of the agreement."

“The bargain,” Mary Frances says bitterly. “Something in it for everybody. Betsy gets off the long waiting list for a legal adoption. Ricardo and Sophia get to feel like they’ve done the responsible thing. And—and they get to enjoy their grandchild. My mother, well! She stakes her claim and gets to play babysitter. She gets to enjoy her little grandchild all she wants. No one need ever know the child is the very one conceived by her daughter in a dance-hall gang bang. Mam Mam Joyce gets to have it both ways. All the fun and none of the shame. And what does the baby’s teenage mother get? She gets the birth over with. She gets to pretend it never happened. After she graduates high school, she gets out of town so her mother can save face. This bargain, though, it had one major flaw. Tell them, Tim.”

“Tell them what?”

“There was never any possibility the baby was yours. No chance at all. None. I turned you down. That night my brother was supposed to pick me up on Third and Bloke Street, he forgot. Jack forgot. All my friends went home, but I stayed and waited for Jack. Who comes along and offers me a ride? God’s gift to girls, Tim Giovannini. That was the first time you ever spoke to me, Tim. It was late, so I got in. When we got to the edge of town, instead of driving on to Otterdale, you pulled in at the loading dock behind the Acme. I was supposed to feel honored that you’d want to make out with me. What a privilege!”

Tim looks at Mary Frances as if to say, “Of course, it was.”

“You were all over me. I asked you to stop, but you wouldn’t. You ripped my clothes. I punched and kicked. Thank God I managed to blow the horn. That’s when you shoved me out the door and drove off.”

Tim’s mother covers her mouth in horror. Mary Frances goes on. “Oh, but that wasn’t the end of the ugly story, was it, Tim? After that night, boys who never looked my way came flocking. Boys in your crowd. Boys who didn’t date girls in my crowd unless they already had a rep-u-ta-tion. Suddenly, I was the most popular girl in town.

“Then I saw it wasn’t popularity. I had a ‘reputation.’ I couldn’t walk up Bloke Street without some boy calling out to me with what he’d like done to his body, like he was ordering from a menu. ‘Hey! Mary Frances, I hear those pretty little hands give a handy, dandy handy.’ Some boys just grinned and made motions at their crotches. One night when I was coming out of the Mine Ned humped the back of my leg like a dog. A half dozen other boys followed me down the sidewalk in a pack, like I was a bitch in heat. Why? They felt perfectly entitled. In this town any girl who gave up her precious virginity had no right to turn down any boy.

“Only I never gave it up. Did I, Tim? You never got what you were after that night behind the Acme. So you were going to make me pay. You saw to it that I’d be tormented everywhere I went. Soon Catman, my longtime boyfriend, demands to know why I did it with Tim Giovannini and not him. He thought it was because you came from a big-shot family, while his people were just factory people.”

A smile of satisfaction oozes across Tim’s face. “Ah, yes. And so Catman took his turn. He told me he let you have it. None of this little-kiss-good-night-on-your-doorstep bullshit and leaving him with lover’s cramps.” Tim sighs through a smirk. “Yeah, Catman took what was coming to him. You must have liked it. Liked it so much you thought you’d try a gang bang up the Mine.”

“She was ruined,” Bruce says. “Finished in this town. Nothing left to lose. Done. But that wasn’t enough for you, Tim. After all these years, you hatch this scheme. Sharon, big fat Sharon, who could pass for Mary Frances as a young girl, if not for her size, was your idea of a joke. Daughter of a big, dumb jock.”

Mary Frances steps right up to Tim. “Was this the ultimate payback, Tim? Or is there more to come? Exactly how much is a going-nowhere girl supposed to suffer for turning down a roll with the high-class Tim Giovannini in the back of a car her family could never afford?”

Sophia reaches for the phone on the end table and dials. “Bob’s Taxi? Yes, I’d like you to send a cab to 319 S. 5th Street. . . . To the Pine Walls Motel. . . . Fifteen minutes? Great. Thank you.”

When she stands up, her husband grabs her hand. "What? Wait! Don't! Please! Sophia, don't go. We can—"

Sophia breaks free and goes to the closet under the stairs. She pulls out Tim's jacket and digs in the pockets, takes out the keys to his rented car, and clutches them in her fist. She throws the jacket to Tim. "Get going. I'll drop off your flashy red convertible in the morning. You're too drunk to drive."

Tim responds with a tough, adolescent sneer. "Throwing me out?" He raises his chin as though daring his mother to land a punch on it.

His father comes over and takes their hands. "Now there's no need for this. We can sit down like sensible people and—"

"Come on," Mary Frances says to Bruce. "Let's get out of here." Out on the porch, she says, "Where's Sharon? In your car?"

"No, she was gonna wait for me in the restaurant at the Pine Walls Motel. I got her a room there. She wouldn't come to my house, and she sure didn't want to come here. I better get over there before Tim shows up in that taxi."

"I'll come too. I'll take my own car."

"No, don't."

"Why not?"

"Sharon doesn't want to see you. She believes you think she was trying to con you."

"Why? Why would she think that?"

"Because you didn't run outside with her when your mother accused her of being a con artist. If you don't mind me asking, why didn't you follow Sharon out?"

"I saw you get out of your car and go after Sharon. I thought she'd be all right with you, and I could go to her later. For the first time in twenty-seven years, I was getting the truth out of Mom."

A taxi pulls up and sounds the horn. Ricardo Giovannini comes jogging out. He pulls his wallet out of his back pocket as he approaches the cab. Sophia is right on his tail. Ricardo, sticking his arm through the passenger-side window, says, "Here's for your trouble. We've changed our minds."

"Forty dollars!"

"No we haven't," Sophia says. She opens the back door of the cab and looks up at the porch. "Tim?"

"Sophia, you're making a scene," Ricardo says out the side of his mouth.

Mary Frances says to Bruce, "I'll drive over, but I'll wait in my car. Please ask Sharon to give me a chance to speak with her."

"Okay, let's go."

Bruce and Mary Frances get into their cars and drive across the viaduct leading to Black Hollow, where the motel stands facing the little coal patch across a two-lane. The one-story motel arcs around a combination bar and restaurant. Bruce sprints inside, past the register and glass display case with jewelry and figurines made of anthracite coal. Sharon is not in the booth where he left her. He walks past the booths to the dark bar with its dozen stools. Only two are occupied, both by men. He goes outside and crosses the parking lot to Room 6. The room is dark. Sharon doesn't answer his knock. He goes back to the register and notes that the number-six slot of the key rack is occupied with two keys. Bruce flags down the cashier, who's coming out of the kitchen. "Say, Jim!"

"Oh, Bruce, I have a message for you."

Jim, a lanky guy of fifty with a prominent Adam's apple, comes over and opens the register. He counts out some cash and hands it to Bruce. "Here. The room was never used. She left right after you. Just handed me the key and left this note for you." He hands Bruce a slip torn from a telephone message pad.

Bruce reads it. "Thanks for trying. Sorry. Sharon."

Jim says, "I noticed her walking back toward Mount of Olives with a backpack and suitcase."

"Thanks." When Bruce turns to leave, he finds himself facing Sophia Giovannini, who's standing between a pair of leather suitcases. Sophia, covering her mouth like she's gonna be sick, turns away and closes her eyes as Bruce goes out.

Jim, eyeing Sophia from behind the register, says, "Oh, Mrs. Giovannini, hello. May I help you?" She doesn't answer. "Mrs. Giovannini, are you all right?" Jim puts his hand on the telephone receiver. "Would you like me to call someone for you?"

Sophia looks out the window and watches Bruce drive away. "No. No, thank you," she says. She goes out and sits in her car. She pictures a young woman the size of Bruce with a face like Mary Frances McDonald's, walking and walking in a strange town. "This is all Tim's doing," she mutters. "All Tim's doing. I must help her." Sophia heads back toward Mount of Olives to search for Sharon, but when she reaches the viaduct, she decides not to cross it. She decides to search in Black Hollow instead. Black Hollow is only two streets wide and maybe a dozen blocks long, with big mining slagpiles behind the back street of houses. Sophia cruises along Front Street and then along Saylor Street. She cuts down to the alley between the mining slagpiles and the back yards of Saylor Street. Midway along the foot of the slagpiles is a playground with some monkey bars, a sliding board, a set of swings with wide board seats, and a hexagonal merry-go-round with wood planks around the rim.

Scrubbly bushes crowd the embankment in front of the playground. Baby pines and skinny white birches poke up here and there on the slagpiles. As Sophia cruises past a tangle of blackberry bushes, moonlight presents the silhouette of a large figure on a swing. The person's back bulges out with a backpack. The figure twists slowly on the swing, toes maneuvering on the ground, chains grinding as they tighten.

Sophia feels the turn of the screw with each twist, she's that ashamed. She drives farther down the alley, turns up a short side street, and parks. She waits, thinks. She's got no silly notions of being able to undo the damage her own son has done. She doesn't dare try to fathom how much damage that was. She fears she'll be too crippled by shame to help the poor girl out now. Already her legs feel like they're made of wood. She walks to the playground with no idea how she'll help, but knowing she must. Somehow, she must. She reminds herself not to call Sharon by name. She crosses a hump of grass in the middle of the dirt alley and sees the flame of a match as she starts the short climb up a path between two bushes. Blackberry thorns snag her skirt like whiny children demanding her attention.

“Spare a cigarette?” she calls out, though she hasn’t smoked since the day she found out she was pregnant with her first child.

“Shoo-uh,” Sharon answers in her Maine accent. She gets up from the swing, shrugs off her backpack, digs out her cigarettes, and whacks the top of the pack against the side of her hand, forcing a few cigarettes to stick out. Sophia takes a cigarette and puts it between her lips. When Sharon strikes a match, Sophia almost gasps. The young face in the flickering light bears the ravages she saw on a face like that nearly thirty years earlier, a face she turned away from at every encounter, telling herself she had done her duty, done right by the girl. Sophia takes a shallow drag and sits down on the neighboring swing. “Thanks.”

She keeps her mouth shut for fear she’ll send Sharon running. Sharon, toes straight down in a muddy puddle, rocks her swing in jerky starts and stops. Her voice is croaky. “I need to get to Harrisburg. Where’s the best place to stand to hitch a ride?”

Sophia’s so grateful for some idea how to help, she nearly pops up with an impulse to dangle her keys and say, “I’ll give you a ride!” But she stays put. “Harrisburg. Let’s see. Someplace on the edge of Mount of Olives. You’ll need to get to I-81 South. That’s about ten miles from here. Not many people heading that way at this hour, but there’s tons commute to Harrisburg in the morning. Around six-thirty.”

“I guess I’ll wait then. My train doesn’t leave till Sunday. I already have my ticket.”

Sophia feels giddy from the cigarette. Giddy and less jumpy, even a little envious of Sharon with her ticket. “A train,” she says. “I wouldn’t mind getting on a train myself.”

“Where to?”

“Anywhere. I just left my husband.” Sophia, hardly able to believe she blurted that out, clasps her hands and bites down on her thumbs.

Sharon, swinging a little, says, “Ever been to Maine?”

“Maine? No, never.” Sophia is surprised. This Sharon takes the news without the slightest start, as if she runs into women every day who announce they’ve just left their husbands.

"If you're interested—I mean, I'm not asking to know your business—there's a place in Maine where women can stay cheap. Two years while they're getting on their feet."

"Oh?"

"Yeah. The Maine Hotel for Women in Transition. The M-WIT, for short. Even after your two years, they don't exactly kick you out. You have to do a time-out for six weeks, but then you get to come back. I just finished up a time-out this winter. My third one. Now I'm good till 1993."

"Till 1993. If I could just get to the Fourth of July."

"You could stay just till the Fourth, then. You don't have to stay the whole two years, but you can if you want to. Or just stay a night or two."

Sophia waits for the big question, why the Fourth? She thinks back on her words to Ricardo: "Don't try to contact me before the Fourth. If you do, I'll *never* come back. I want that much time to think." She remembers the big pop eyes Ricardo made, the smirk on Tim's face tightening into a pout. Still braced for probing questions, Sophia gets none from Sharon, who's true to her word. Not asking to know somebody else's business, just passing along a helpful tip while facing her own disaster, though you'd never guess, Sophia notices, if you didn't happen to know from hearsay that this young woman must feel like she's just been flattened by a steamroller. How can she peel herself from the ground to even notice somebody else's troubles?

Sharon digs out a little travel clock from her backpack. The numbers light up green when she flips open the lid. "You said six-thirty. That's when the traffic starts heading to Harrisburg, right?"

"Yes, right around then."

"I'll set this for five. Give myself a chance to walk to a good hitchhiking spot. Where should I stand?"

Sophia suggests a place, and Sharon repeats the directions as she stands up and looks around. "I passed two old shanties tonight. Down that way, next to some taller building that looks like it has a roller coaster climbing up to one side of it. The place is all grown in with weeds. It doesn't look like anybody goes there anymore."

"Just kids. That's the Ebony Gem coal breaker. Sometimes kids go to abandoned collieries and play."

"Anyway, I guess I'll sleep in one of those shacks. What about you?"

Sophia imagines herself waking up in her fine skirt and jacket in a coal shanty. She near laughs out loud, picturing kids peeking in the window and running home with news about that fancy lady from the Ford dealers passed out drunk. Then she scolds herself, why waste time shocking the town? To Sharon, she says, "I just want to get out of town. Now. I mean tonight. Just hit the road. That's what I want to do, just hit the road." Now that Sophia's caught the skedaddle bug, she's not so prim about holding her tongue. "I have a car. Want a ride? I'll take you to Maine. You have a driver's license? We could take turns driving and dozing."

"Yeah, I do, but—" Sharon panics at the prospect of pissing herself in her sleep. Even all padded up and barricaded with plastic so she doesn't soak the car seat, there's the smell. The smell. Big fat piss ass.

"Wait!" Sophia says. "I know! We have a conversion van. I'll get that. We can pull in at rest stops. We can both sleep in that."

Sharon shakes her head. "I don't think— Maybe you can drop me off at I-81 so I can hitch it to Harrisburg tonight. There must be cars from other towns going that way all night. I'm good for a few more nights in a hotel there. And, like I said, I already have my train ticket."

"Let me take you to your hotel in Harrisburg, then."

"You sure?"

"Why not? It's a favor to me, too. It gets me out of town. That's what I want to do, get out of town. Tonight. I want to get out of here tonight."

"Me, too. I mean, if you really don't mind driving me that far."

"No, I'm glad to, and it's only an hour away. I do want to get that van first, though. I can sleep on the road and not leave a trail of credit card charges at motels. It might take me a half hour. I have to dig out some papers."

"Sure."

Sophia drives Sharon across the viaduct and into Mount of Olives, where she parks several blocks from the dealership in case Ricardo gets it into his head to look for her there. She asks Sharon to wait in the car and then walks to Giovannini Motors. Colorful strips of triangular plastic flags flap over the cars in the bright parking lot. The showroom is dimly lit.

Sophia pauses in the parking lot. The years of building up that business play in her mind like clips from an old film. She sees herself getting out of a car on a winter day, a diaper bag dangling from her shoulder. Baby Tim, a sweet little bundle in her arms, blinks when a big onion snowflake lands on his eyelash. People fuss over the baby in the showroom. Sophia sees herself walking down the hall to her office, sees herself tucking the baby into the white, straw bassinette next to her desk, hears the paper rolling on the adding machine. Now she stands stiffly before the building like a lifelong parishioner who's heard whispers about the goings-on in that place, who doesn't know if she can bring herself to ever go in there again. Yet, she knows it's not like she's had nothing to do with the goings-on. She's one of the culprits. In on the bargain, smiling like a proud grandmother when Betsy trots in with another sweet little bundle, little Rick, who sleeps placidly as Betsy parades him around the showroom.

Sophia goes around the back of the building and enters through the service garage door. First she feels her way through the dark hall to the office where all the vehicle keys hang on a rack. She flips on the light long enough to pick out the two sets of keys for the 1989 Chevy conversion van that was traded in. Then she goes to the office and gets the vehicle title, which has already been signed by the seller. Sophia fills in her own name as the buyer, embosses Ricardo's notary seal onto the title, and rubber-stamps his signature onto the witness line. She takes a temporary license plate from a cabinet, and without recording the number in the book, goes out and puts it on the van. Then she walks two blocks to an ATM machine on the side wall of her bank and withdraws the limit of $400 for one day.

17

The Latest Gossip

REMEMBER NED? He's the guy at Ray's party at the Harborview Inn in Maine, who loves getting the latest gossip from his mother, who gets a good bit of it from the Avon lady in Mount of Olives. Well, the day after Joyce McDonald screams in Sharon's face, the Avon lady tells Ned's mother that Joyce's next-door neighbor told her she saw Mary Frances pull into the patch with a big, big girl who looked just like her. Sure, it was starting to get dark, but the neighbor got a good look when the dome light lit up in Mary Frances's car. There was no doubt—*this* was the famous Gang-Bang Baby. Not only that, Bruce the Moose had pulled in too. So that accounts for the girl's size.

Ned's mother fills him in on the whole story over the phone. "That's right. Bruce showed up, too. But he waited in his car. Guess they figured one shock at a time was best for Joyce. Like I told you when Mary Frances first came back looking for her baby, Joyce could have died of shame. Why couldn't Mary Frances let sleeping dogs lie? Twenty-five years since she left town and by now people have forgotten. Nobody brings it up. . . . The Avon lady? Well, she doesn't come out and *say* anything to Joyce. She just wonders about that missing portrait. . . . Wonders out loud. Yes, out loud. Anyway, last night, when that missing baby shows up, they're not in the house two minutes when the neighbors hear all this screaming through the kitchen wall. Next thing you know this big girl comes flying out the front door, across the green, across the highway. I heard she was near hit by a Mack truck. . . . Well, Bruce went after her. Followed her up to the cemetery. Next thing you know the two of them are driving away. . . . Mary Frances? Still in the house, fighting with her poor mother. The only thing breaks it up is when Ricardo Giovannini's grandson shows up with his usual Wednesday night pizza like the loyal dog he's always been. Joyce oughta be ashamed of herself the way she latched onto that boy. She was supposed to be the babysitter, that's all. But they say Betsy Giovannini would have to go over there and beg her son back from her. Why she didn't fire Joyce only God knows." That's all the news Ned's mother has for him so far. She tells him to tune in later for an update.

Now, the Avon lady is itching to know what Joyce will do with those school portraits on the coffee table, now that the whole town is talking about the Gang-Bang Baby showing up in Otterdale last night. Joyce won't be able to keep up that that baloney about the broken leg in Vermont. The Avon lady would like to think up a reason to show up today, two weeks before her next visit is due. But surprise, surprise, she doesn't have to think up a reason. Joyce calls *her.* "I dropped my bubble bath," Joyce announces. "Spilled it all over the bathroom floor. . . .No, I don't want to order another one. It's time I tried a different one. I have the catalogue, but maybe you could bring some samples."

The Avon lady takes the bait. In 2.3 minutes she's in her car, heading over. Joyce, meanwhile, suddenly remembers the pizza. She wouldn't put it past that woman to find some excuse to open the fridge to see whether that Wednesday-night treat managed to get eaten after the big ruckus. She'd probably figure Rick, at least, would've eaten his half. After all, he showed up right after the big scene. Wouldn't even know about it. So why was the whole pizza still sitting in the fridge in the box? Hmmm.

Joyce gnaws on her fingertips, same way she did last night after Mary Frances left and Rick started shuffling along the walls, studying each picture of Jack like a visitor in a museum.

"Wwwwwwuh—what are you doing? Sit down, Rick. The pizza's getting cold."

Rick continued his rounds in silence. When he got to the big color photo of Jack flashing his driver's license from inside the white Studebaker, Rick spent a long time staring at the green eyes.

He took his own license from his wallet. He kept looking from his license picture to the many faces of Jack, much the same way Mary Frances had looked from his face to Jack's.

"Rick! What are you doing?"

"Cat must have my tongue," he said, and he walked out.

Now the Avon lady is knocking on Joyce's kitchen door. Joyce takes the pizza box from the fridge and shoves it into the stove drawer under the oven. She lets the Avon lady in. The woman damned near passes out when Joyce says, "Let's sit in the parlor."

The Avon lady has to steady herself against the archway. Not only have Mary Frances's school pictures been removed from the coffee table and replaced by the Avon catalogue, there's not one picture on the wall. Behind the couch, twelve evenly sized, evenly spaced, white rectangles stand out on the yellowing wall like tombstones. White squares and rectangles of various sizes mark the places where photographs of Jack have hung on the other walls for near three decades.

Joyce lets the Avon lady have a good gander at the stripped walls before she says, "I'm gonna ask that nice boy, Rick Trounov, to come by and put a fresh coat of paint on for me."

The Avon lady takes hold of the arm of the couch and eases her skinny rump onto a plastic-covered cushion. Her hands go for the catalogue on the coffee table, but her head still swivels and her eyes look upward.

Joyce says, "Guess you must be wondering what happened to all the pictures."

"No, I—"

"Well, I was sitting in the doctor's office, looking through magazines. Did you see that story in *Wise Women's Monthly* about that lady who came to see that she would never reach closure till she dismantled the shrine she'd made of her baby's bedroom?"

"I did see that. Her baby died of SIDS just before his first birthday. She left the crib in place, the mobile on the side rails, the wicker basket full of toys. She said it was as if the child might come back at any moment and play with them. Almost every inch of all four walls was covered with photos of her dead child."

“That’s right, that was the article. She cleared out the room. All the photos went into albums and up the attic.”

“Yes,” the Avon lady said, “and that’s when her grief began to lift. ‘Began to lift’ is the way she put it. I remember. After a few months, she selected one little photo to put on the bookcase downstairs in the sitting room. Just one. And it was okay. Ah, so that’s why Jack’s pictures are gone.”

“That’s right. I’ve been grieving long enough. Now, Mary Frances’s pictures, well— It didn’t seem fair to have pictures of her and none of Jack.”

“So you put hers away for a while, too.”

“I did.”

“Good for you!”

“Speaking of Mary Frances, you must have heard that she came back last December after she retired from the Navy.”

“I seen her in the supermarket plenty of times. I figured she must have moved back.”

“To look for her baby.”

The Avon lady’s jaw near drops to her ankles when she hears Joyce admit that Mary Frances did indeed give birth. After all these years of shuffling those portraits around the coffee table!

“Why she came back to embarrass me after all these years I’ll never know. Well, she found her baby. A girl from Maine.”

“Really!”

“Really. She brought her here to meet me last night. The spitting image of our Mary Frances, the spitting image!”

“And?”

“And I’m afraid I wasn’t very nice to her. My own granddaughter.”

“What happened?”

“It was Mary Frances’s fault, really. If she’da called ahead. No, she just springs her on me. All I could think of was the shame. My own daughter an unwed mother after all I did to bring her up right. The shame. I accused that poor girl from Maine of being a fraud, screamed in her face.”

“Oh, dear.”

"But I knew she was Mary Fran's girl. I knew from the birthmark on her left hand. A strawberry mark shaped like an hourglass. The same mark the infant had. The very same."

"So you were there when the baby was born?"

"I was. I was waiting in the next room in that Home in Vermont. I couldn't let this baby, my own grandchild, go without even a kiss good-bye. I saw that birthmark on her sweet, little hand."

"I can imagine that would be hard."

"So I kissed the little girl good-bye and handed her over to the social worker who was standing by to deliver her to the couple waiting to adopt her. I always denied to Mary Frances that I even knew whether the child was a girl or a boy. Figured the less she knew, the easier it would be for her to forget. Doesn't she come around after all these years asking questions!"

"You were saying you weren't very nice to your granddaughter when she showed up."

"No, I was so surprised by the visit, the disgrace suddenly back in my face, I took it out on the girl. She ran out the front door and that's the last I seen of her. Last I seen of Mary Frances, too. She didn't answer her phone this morning. I hope she doesn't plan on keeping my granddaughter from me now that she realizes I've known all along that the baby was a girl and I wouldn't tell. All I can say is I hope she'll find it in her heart to forgive me."

"I'm sure she will. By Thanksgiving, the three of you will be sitting around the table eating a nice turkey dinner."

"I hope you're right. Okay, now, let's have a look at those bubble bath samples."

While Joyce sits in her parlor sniffing bottles, that nice boy, Rick Trounov, who walked along the old dirt coal roads for hours after leaving Joyce's, is standing before the bathroom mirror, lathered in shaving cream. As each stroke of the razor reveals more of his boyish face, he sees more of Jack's face—the chin, the cheekbones—and the narrow, straight nose of Mary Frances. His face is all clear now. Staring into his green eyes, he recalls the pain in the green eyes of Mary Frances as she stooped knee-to-knee with him while he held the photo with the cracked glass. He remembers her studying his face for so long, remembers her tears. He wishes he had spoken up when Joyce chided her for bawling over some old picture frame that "the boy" had already told her he'd get fixed. Adding insult to injury, he thinks. And what a deep injury must have caused those tears! Even he could see that, and he hardly knew her, so Joyce had to know what brought them on. And now he knew, too.

Rick's phone rings. "Hi," Joyce says, "It's me. Did you buy that picture frame yet?"

"No, I—"

"Good, don't. I was hoping to catch you before you went to the store. I'll bet I near didn't. The Avon lady came by. She always picks the worst times to show up. I thought I'd never get rid of her. I don't need that frame. I'm putting all Mary Frances's pictures in albums. Jack's, too. Wanna know why? Because I finally realized—You know the other day when I went to the doctor? I read an article by another mother whose child died." Joyce gives Rick the same baloney she gave the Avon lady. "Maybe after a little healing, I can put one or two pictures of Jack in the parlor again. We'll see."

Rick recognizes the familiar tones and jabber Joyce uses when she's lying.

Joyce chuckles. "You know, I kept those pictures on the wall so long, near thirty years, that there's white spots everywhere. No kidding. White spots in the shape of all those frames, that's how long those pictures were on that wall. How 'bout you pick up two gallons of beige paint for Joyce?"

Now she wants me in on the lie, Rick thinks. Wants me to help paint over the truth. He puts the receiver down slowly. Before it reaches the cradle, he hears Joyce shouting, "Rick, are you there?"

Rick is standing before the mirror again. He envisions the white shapes on Joyce's parlor wall, can see every picture that created them. "Now I see why I've never looked much like Mom and Dad. Why there was such a tug of war for me between Joyce and Mom. Why Joyce shooed me out of sight whenever her daughter came home on leave. Made excuses for me not to come over."

Rick's phone rings again. He doesn't answer it. It rings twice more by the time he steps outside and heads for Black Hollow. As he walks across the viaduct, he wonders what he'll say.

He steps up onto Mary Frances's back porch. Through the window on the door, he can see her sitting at the table. She has a pen pressed against her lips, and there is a writing tablet on the table.

He knocks. When she turns to look, he sees a face swollen from crying. Her cheeks are dry when she opens the door. Rick bows his head for a moment. Then he says, "Can I come in?"

Mary Frances lifts hands aching to embrace her child for the first time, but she doesn't dare to touch him, doesn't dare to brand him as the one. She opens the door and gestures towards the table.

Rick takes a seat around the corner from where she has been sitting. He notices that the paper has no words on it. When Mary Frances sits down, he places his hands on hers. "I'm sorry," he says. "Last night. I could see you were hurting. I didn't understand why. Not right then anyway. I could just see that it was really bad. I thought for sure your mother would comfort you or— But it was right back to Pearl Harbor. I should have hugged you or—" Rick stands up and reaches for Mary Frances. She gets to her feet and takes one small, tentative step toward her son, who leans forward and gathers her against himself. "You're my mother, aren't you?"

"I wasn't going to say anything. Just go away for good this time and let you be."

"Because of the rumors of how I was conceived."

"They're not just rumors. They're true. All true. And I don't know who your father is."

"That doesn't matter. You're my mother." Rick steps back and runs his fingertips along his mother's cheek, grinning. "Let's tell everyone! Let's not be ashamed. You've suffered plenty already."

"What about Betsy? She doesn't know. It was all arranged between my mother and her parents."

"Betsy will always be my mother, too. I love her very much. She'll welcome the truth. Now she'll understand what she was up against. That she didn't just fail in a tug of war with some babysitter. She'll know it was all arranged before she ever took me in her arms."

18

Ricardo

Ricardo Giovannini has stayed home today. He keeps wandering out to the front porch, frowning at the empty parking spot, hoping Sophia will pull in any moment, hoping Tim, who has just driven away in his rented red convertible, will not. Ricardo goes back inside and checks for the blinking green light on the answering machine. Nothing. He's sure Sophia could not have really meant she'd stay away till the Fourth of July. Nearly six weeks! She'll call. When the phone does ring, it's Bum-Knee reporting the missing van.

"I think Sophia might have signed it out, so don't worry. I'll check later."

Ricardo imagines the van leaving the lot in the night. Why take a conversion van and not a car? His heart jumps when he pictures Sophia pulling into a truck stop, stretching out on the bed in the back, making a night of it. "Oh, call!" But the phone doesn't ring.

Ricardo thinks of calling Rick, Rick who couldn't possibly be his grandchild, he realizes now. He realizes this, but finds he feels the same love for Rick he felt in all the years before he knew. He frets, wondering what rumors will reach Rick's ears when he shows up for his afternoon job at the hardware store. And Betsy. She'll be back from the shore by then. How will she feel when she learns that Mary Frances has finally tracked down what the whole town calls "her gang-bang baby" and it's Rick?

Waiting for the phone to ring is driving Ricardo nuts. He takes a walk up to Bloke Street for a coffee. Gotta think things out. If only there were some way to keep this terrible news from Rick and Betsy, the two innocent ones in this whole mess. He prays as he walks. His prayers are answered when he takes a seat at a restaurant counter and hears lips abuzz with news that that girl from Otterdale has found her gang-bang baby. "Some girl from Maine," Fred Hawkins tells him. Fred winks. "Big as a fridge, I heard."

Ricardo double-steps it back to his house, hops into his car, and heads for Black Hollow. Mary Frances is licking an envelope when he knocks on her kitchen door. She looks at him with eyes full of disgust. Her cheeks are wet with tears.

"What do you want?" she asks, holding the door open just enough to speak.

"Please, may I come in?"

Mary Frances lets him in and watches coldly as he takes a seat at her table. "It's not too late," he says.

Mary Frances remains standing near the door. "For what?"

"To let things be as they were."

"What do you mean?"

"People think that girl from Maine is your child."

"Oh, they do, do they? And how did that bit of news happen to get about? Wait, I think I know. The Avon lady stopped by my mom's today and Mom—"

"Yes, Joyce confessed she's known all along that the baby was a girl. Even recognized a birthmark on her hand. She—"

"People confess a truth, not a lie."

"All right, all right, it's all a lie, I know. But Rick and our Betsy are completely innocent. Why expose them to— I'm sorry. I know now how you must have been wondering all these years about your child. You must have had pain that I can't even begin to grasp. But it's too late to raise Rick now. He doesn't even know you. What good can it do to tell him? What can it hurt if people think some girl five hundred miles away is the one?"

Mary Frances flips over the envelope. "This is addressed to her. She was already gone by the time I got around to seeing to her last night, after the way my mother attacked her. I'm hoping she'll forgive me. And now you expect me to ask this crushed young woman to play along?"

"No, no. She doesn't need to know. You can just— What would it take to convince you to—"

Mary Frances's eyes follow the movement of Ricardo's hand as it reaches around to his back pocket, but stops short of pulling his wallet out.

"To what? Pretend Rick is Betsy's child and leave town again for another twenty-some years? I rented this house in December. But it's a rental with the option to buy. I'm going to buy it. And no, there is no amount you can pay me to use Sharon the way Tim did."

Ricardo stands up. "Please, can you at least think it over before you go saying anything to Rick?"

"Rick knows."

"You told him already?"

"No. He came by here this morning and said, 'You're my mother, aren't you?' And we talked a long time."

"How in the name of God did he— Bruce? Was it Bruce who told him?"

"Rick put the pieces together himself. He plans to tell Betsy when she gets home from the shore. Don't worry. I'm not going to try to rip him away from her. My mother already tried that. But he's free now."

19

Back in Maine

It's just after dawn when Godzalez sees Sharon approaching Widener's Wharf from the bus station. She is wearing a shabby, blue windbreaker and threadbare jeans. She's got a red, canvas backpack whose smallest pocket, missing a zipper tab, hangs partly open like the mouth of a person in a stupor. Sharon stands on the sidewalk, watching the little lobster boats cut loose from the dock and sail on. When the last boat is gone, she shuffles along the wharf to the very end, where she sits with her back facing the city and lets her legs dangle from the dock. After a while, she twists her head around and says, "Godzalez, you here?"

And, lo, there he is, a few feet away.

"Been there all along, I see."

Godzalez comes closer and settles down by Sharon's knee. She takes a pack of cheese crackers from her windbreaker pocket and sets a cracker down for Godzalez.

"I'm trying to get up the nerve to go find Tina. Apologize. Haven't talked to her since the day she tried to tell me Michele was no friend."

Godzalez knows that Tina, on her way down the hill from the homeless shelter, has already spotted Sharon. He saw her sit down on a door stoop across the street. He can tell she senses that Sharon's been shattered by whatever happened in Pennsylvania. He'd love to nudge the two old friends back together, but he just waits, trusting they'll find their way.

Tina gets up, crosses the street, and calls to Sharon from halfway up the dock. "Hey, Sharon, it's me, Tina. If you wanna talk, I'll be down on Long Wharf."

Sharon twists around and sees Tina heading back to the street. She doesn't get up till she thinks Tina has staked out her spot. Tina is leaning against the same supply shack where Tim Giovannini first eavesdropped on her and Sharon.

Sharon heads over and settles down beside Tina, who offers her a cigarette. The women finish their smokes in silence.

"Thought you moved to Pennsylvania," Tina says. "It's nearly July."

"I was supposed to transfer to a bus in Boston on the way back. I got up to the door of the bus and pictured everybody at the M-WIT clamoring to know how my trip went, and decided no. I called the desk. My rent was paid for every week in May and one in June. I told them to let you have my room till then if you came by. Then just pitch my stuff and rent my room to whoever wanted it. Did you go there?"

"Did I go there looking for you?"

"Yes."

"No. I don't go forcing myself on somebody who doesn't want to talk to me. I only offered to talk today because I could see you were in deep shit. If you didn't come over to Long Wharf, well, going once, going twice."

"I'm sorry. I wouldn't blame you if you turned your back on me now."

"I'm not gonna. Let's just forget it."

"Thanks."

"So you stayed in Boston."

"On the streets. I had enough cash for a few weeks at the Y, but I just didn't want to be around anybody. That woman in Pennsylvania? She wasn't my mother. The whole thing was a setup. And Mr. Parker? He was no lawyer. Seems I was his idea of a joke, the last thing a woman looking for her child would want to find. And doesn't this sorry specimen of a human being, me, go like a fool and—"

"You're not a sorry specimen."

"Don't I go and get all dolled up—like it would really make a difference—new haircut, new clothes, new backpack, new suitcase, new shoes. Nearly four hundred dollars just for the suitcase and matching backpack. All on Michele's credit card. I dropped off every last thing at a thrift shop in Harrisburg and bought these clothes. You tried to tell me Michele was no friend. And, stupid me, I listened to her, instead of you.

"Actually, Tina, I almost didn't listen to her. On the day she showed up at the Sallies and offered to take me shopping, I nearly backed out of the whole trip. Something about it just didn't feel right to me."

"What was it?"

"I don't know. It was just a feeling I had. That's what I tried to tell Michele."

"What'd she say?"

"She got right in step with me when I was walking home, told me that what she saw before her was a sad, young woman who was afraid to connect with family. She reminded me of the day the bond snapped between me and my mother, meaning the woman here in Maine who claimed to be my mother. Said I was looking at family life today through an old lens. It was time I got up the courage to open new doors. Yeah. Some new door. I go with my newfound mother to the house she grew up in. My supposed grandmother opens the door and screams in my face that I'm not the one. The baby was a boy. I'm just some con artist, a gold digger trying to take the family for all it's worth."

"Holy shit!" Tina lit another cigarette. "If you had any notions like that, you can thank me for giving you the idea."

"What do you mean?"

"The day you told me this Mr. Parker said you were the missing daughter of some kind woman in Pennsylvania, I saw dollar signs. Remember? I said it could turn out to be like winning the lottery, and you'd be nuts not to check her out. Sorry for being such an asshole."

"Don't worry. That's not why I went. I wasn't thinking about money at all. I fell in love with the idea that my real mother was this kind, friendly— I had this longing. For years, this stupid longing. For years, nobody comes along to fill that longing, and then, suddenly, there's two great moms in my life: Mother Michele and Mother Mary Frances."

"If that's stupid, there's a lot of stupid people in this world. I'd be one of them. The only difference between me and you is that I quit looking." Tina takes a flat bottle from her pocket. "Here's my mother, right here. And my dad, too. Hi, Mom! Hi, Dad!" She takes a swig. "Hey, you want to hear something hilarious? She actually came down here last week."

"Your mom did?"

"Yep. I was dumpster diving when she showed up. As soon as I caught her eye, I gave her a good view of how I ended up, thanks to her. I flopped flat out in the trash and swallowed a big, loud gulp of booze."

"What did she do?"

"She—" Tina laughed long and hard. "She invited me to go bowling."

"Bowling!"

"Yeah, bowling. No shit. She had this guy with her, looked like a friggin' leprechaun. Bushy eyebrows, twinkle in the eye, pipe. All he needed was a green derby on his head. Looking at Mom like she's the treasure of his life. The Mona Lisa, Helen of Troy, Katherine Hepburn—all rolled into one."

"Her husband?"

Tina shrugs. "Maybe. And her sister, my Aunt Jackie, she was there, too. She had nothing to do with my mom for years and years. Now they're all chummy. The three of them, her and Mom and that guy, they're all smiling like they just swallowed a bottle of happy pills. It was kinda weird seeing somebody dote on Mom like that guy. She wasn't bad looking, but Dad always acted ashamed to be seen with her. Always comparing her to somebody prettier, classier. Somebody who walked nicer, had slimmer fingers, knew how to set a better table. You name it. One morning we got on a crowded bus and the bus driver's saying, 'Move to the back, move to the back.' Me and Mom squeezed past Dad a little and everybody new who got on the bus had to, too. He wouldn't budge from the front of the aisle. Then some pretty blonde gets on. Not just pretty, striking. People just about gasped at the sight of her as she walked way to the back. Dad nearly broke his neck climbing over feet and briefcases to get back where she was. Mom stuck her chin up, trying to look dignified, but she was crushed, embarrassed and crushed. She whisked me off the bus two stops early. When Dad caught up with us at the bank, the first thing he said was, 'Why can't *you* look like that?' He was always asking her that.

"Mom was a closet boozehound for years before I realized it. Lived in a slump. Could barely drag a word out of her at all, much less a kind word. A big crab when she did speak to me and my brothers. Hardly noticed we were even alive. Didn't even come to my high school graduation. She forgot, she says. Forgot. She was home nursing a hangover and setting up for the next one. Now, the bitch shows up and wants to take me bowling. Screw her."

Sharon picks up a seashell from the dock and starts scraping mud from the crevices with her fingernail. "Maybe that's as much as she really has to offer right now. Bowling. Some place to start again. Could be fun."

"What," Tina says, "you think I shoulda gone bowling with her?"

"I don't know. I was just imagining my mom coming down here and asking me to go bowling."

"You'd go?"

"I might. I don't know."

"It's not like ten frames of throwing a ball down a lane's gonna make up for twenty years of crabbing and neglect and beatings."

"No, that's for sure. Tell you the truth, Tina, I don't think there's any such thing as anybody making up to anybody for anything. I mean, I don't think that anymore. If I went bowling with Mom, it would have to be like me and you going bowling, two friends. Not me giving her a second chance to be a better mom, a pass/fail setup she's bound to fail. Bound to. And it wouldn't be me bullshitting myself, like the stuff she did to me didn't hurt. A dog that's lost its leg will always limp, but I think dogs have more brains than people.

They're glad for a chance to swim after a stick and enjoy the waves and the game if they can still manage it. Anyway, Tina, we had the parents we had. They had the parents they had. No gems either. Not all that lucky themselves. Parents, teachers, neighbors, friends, the grocer down the street. Nobody all good or all rotten. But some did things so rotten you didn't even want to wake up the next morning. Anyway, things were what they were. There's no going back. And there's no finding a better parent now. Too late to be a kid again."

"Maybe you should tell that to Mother Michele next time she comes down here."

"She came down here to the docks?"

"Yep. Somebody from the M-WIT described me to her, so she came and asked me if I knew what became of you. Guess that fake Mr. Parker wasn't returning her calls. I told her I had no clue where you were. All the while, she's looking me over, assessing the quality of my life, I can tell. Pitying me. Must've had a bad childhood. No shit, Sherlock. Fingering through her brain files for labels—dysfunctional family, need for closure—deciding what textbook fixes I must need. When she doesn't find you, she says to me, 'And how are *you* doing?' Like I'm gonna break down in tears she can soothe on the spot, blubbering about the day the bond snapped between me and my mother. Pissed me off. I told her to go dabble in somebody else's life if she needs a hobby."

"I'd tell her the same thing myself now, but I'm outa here. I came to close my savings account."

"Back to Boston?"

"For now. I got a full-time job sorting at the Sallies. I was able to get a good recommendation from the one up here. Hadn't missed a day in eight years. Think I'll try for a room at the Boston Y. Maybe even get a second job. I want to buy a car."

Tina shoves Sharon's knee. "Hit the road and see the world."

"Something like that. Chase a few sticks in Boston Harbor for starters. Oh, I got a new P.O. box in Boston. Let me know if you're coming down." Sharon writes the address on the back of an envelope and gives it to Tina.

"Don't worry, I'll be down."

"Speaking of P.O. boxes, time I get going to the post office, close the box up here. Guess I'll be seeing you, then."

"Yep." Tina takes a swig of Mom and Dad and waves.

Sharon finds three pieces of mail in the box, two from Michele, dated two weeks apart, and one from Mary Frances. The letter from Mary Frances goes into her backpack. She chucks the ones from Michele into the wastebasket on the way to the counter, where she turns in her key. "No thanks," she says when the woman asks if she'd like to fill out a card to forward any new mail.

The letter from Mary Frances stays put until she's in a park, sitting on the ground, leaning against the trunk of a tall willow, surrounded by its wispy branches. A large fountain that rains down into a pond drowns out the sounds of other people. I can curse here if I have to, she thinks. She opens the letter:

Dear Sharon,

I know it must have looked like I didn't care what became of you when my mother made it clear that you were not my child. I did not go out to you after she made those ugly, false accusations that had to hurt you deeply, so what else could you think?

Please know that I did run after you. I saw you running across the green, and when Bruce followed you, I trusted you to him. I stayed behind to confront my mother. It was the first crack in the wall of lies I'd been smashing into for nearly thirty years. I was afraid that if I didn't pry it open all the way right then, I'd never get another chance to learn the truth. I came by to be with you at the motel later, but you were gone.

I am sure you never meant to con me. We were both roped in by the same schemer, Tim Giovannini. Bruce told me you identified him in a photograph as the "Mr. Parker" who approached you in Maine. Had you turned out to really be my daughter, I would have been thrilled. We were just starting to get to know one another in Harrisburg. I'd be glad for a chance to pick up where we left off.

Since I don't know whether you even want to hear from me, I won't go into a long story about myself. I'll just say that I have met my son. Our paths crossed numerous times since he was born, but the secret was kept from both of us.

I will be at the address above until November. Then I am volunteering with *Médecins Sans Frontières* (Doctors without Borders) for nine months. I had some medical training during the Vietnam War, but I'll be able to help mostly as a translator. I picked up several languages in the service. After my time with MSF, I'll return here to Black Hollow. I'm buying this house, so it's more or less my home. A place to come back to. Then, who knows? Perhaps I'll volunteer with them again from time to time.

Sharon, you know how to reach me if you want to. You're always welcome here.

Take care,

Mary Frances

Sharon doesn't curse. She watches the fountain through the willow branches, surprised to find herself comforted by the letter instead of angered by some attempt to twist things or lie, something meant to make her think that night in Pennsylvania wasn't really so bad. "Both roped in by the same schemer," she reads again. She reads the letter a few more times and takes a tablet from her backpack:

Dear Mary Frances,

Thanks for writing to me. I'm glad it mattered to you what became of me. You were right. Bruce was somebody you could trust to treat me right. I don't know how to get in touch with him, but please tell him I'm sorry I ran off the way I did after the way he tried to help me. He was going to give me a ride back to

Harrisburg for my train, but I just left him hanging. I couldn't settle down. I had to go.

Some nice woman named Sophia saw me at the playground where I was hanging out to think things over. She gave me a ride to Harrisburg that same night, so please tell Bruce I managed okay.

I'm glad that you found your son. I know that this might sound hard to believe, but I'm not disappointed that you're not my mother. At first, I was, but not now.

Good luck with your travels with *Médecins Sans Frontières.* If you remember me telling you I spend lots of time reading encyclopedias in the library. I read about *MSF* there. I would love to hear how your work with them is going. You have my new return address. As you can see, I moved to Boston. Guess I'll see what I find there.

Your friend,
Sharon

20

Tom Sawyer Whitewashes the Fence

TIM'S BACK IN ILLINOIS. The Fourth of July is coming up, the day his mother said she might return home. "Maybe after your mother comes back, we'll talk again," his father had said. "That's *if* she comes back." Well! Tim is not about to sit by the phone on the Fourth of July and wait for a call from them asking his forgiveness. No, he's going to enjoy himself. He's going to spend that day in Mark Twain's beloved Hannibal, Missouri, as a contestant in the fence-whitewashing contest.

In a parking lot, a few dozen unpainted fence segments wait to be hauled out to the street, five at a time, to be slopped over with whitewash applied by big fat paintbrushes dipped in plastic buckets hauled to the spot by the contestants. Children with splatters of freckles painted across their noses, boys in bare feet, straw hats and lines of fake fish slung over their shoulders, girls in perky dresses and pigtails, swarm the town in hopes of being crowned this year's Tom Sawyer and Becky Thatcher. Tim is all freckled up, too. Like fourteen other oversized Tom Sawyers, he waits in line for the adult division of the whitewashing contest. Oh, he thinks, reflecting on the first time he saw the Mississippi River on the way to the Buddy Holly concert, if Hal Jones could see me now! "Huckleberry Tim," he called me. Aw, to hell with him.

When Tim's turn comes in the contest, he can hardly keep his feet still on the starting line at the far end of the block. At the sound of the whistle, he knees his plastic bucket in his dash to get to his fence first. He is whitewashed with all but a few ounces of the liquid, hardly enough to cover one of the five slats on his fence. That evening while drinking in a local bar in a clean, dry pair of jeans, he sees his red-faced self on the *Six O'Clock News*, badgering the judges, accusing the runners on each side of elbowing his bucket. A replay of the dash to the fences shows they'd done no such thing. When all eyes at the bar turn to him, he departs in a huff.

He drives across the bridge to Illinois, where he has already pitched his tent at the primitive campground directly across the river from Hannibal. The only structures at the campground are a big plastic outhouse with a handicap ramp rising from the parking lot and a kiosk with a payphone. As Tim pulls into the lot, the payphone greets him like a stern father standing at the door with a strap behind his back after curfew. Tim parks, grabs a few things from his trunk, and sneers at the phone as he struts past it. As if grabbed by the collar, he backs up, drops his things on the ground, takes out his long-distance card, and dials his home phone. There is one message: "Tim," Ricardo's voice says, "You are not to set foot in this house as long as Sophia Giovannini's alive, and you are not to call here. Ever. That is her message, word for word. As for me, I'm still your father. Just don't get the idea I think it's okay, what you did. We can meet somewhere once in a while. I'll call you some time."

Tim punches the number 7 to delete the message. Then he hangs up. "So you're still my old man, but Sophia Giovannini is no longer my mother. Now I don't have a mother? Is that it? To hell with her, then! To hell with you, too. You and your message. Hey, I'm doing just fine right here with Old Man River."

Gathering up his belongings, Tim walks past a dozen campsites, all with empty tents and stone fire rings with no fires. Everybody's over there good-timing it in Hannibal. The waters of the Mississippi, rolling along to Tim's right, move in the same direction he's walking. The campground is so quiet that Tim can hear the banjos and fiddles playing in Hannibal. With a sudden bang, the sky erupts with fireworks.

Memories of childhood Fourths burst into Tim's brain. Him and Betsy and lots of friends zooming through the back yard, waving sparklers while the grown-ups sat and laughed and drank. "To hell with family," he says. He goes to the river's edge, takes off his shoes and socks, rolls up his jeans, and slides into the river. The water comes up to his chest. The mud of the marvelous Mississippi

River oozes over his feet, soothing him. What was wrong with Hal Jones that he couldn't see how a kid could love— Love. That is the only word he can think of for how he felt when they came upon the Mississippi River when he was thirteen. And he loved Huckleberry Finn and Jim the slave and Becky Thatcher and Tom Sawyer and Aunt Polly and Muff Potter and—all those marvelous characters Mark Twain brought to life. And he loved the trains that covered the floor in the attic in Mount of Olives, all those tracks and bridges he'd built with his father, smiling as they handed each other pieces. Yet all Hal Jones had to do was sneer at those babyish, those—and he denied them all—the books, the trains, the river. All Hal Jones had to do was hint at no invitation to their family cabin on the Susquehanna River in Pennsylvania if Tim thought the Mississippi was so much better, and Tim took back every wonderful thing he'd said. "Denied the love," he mumbles now. "Even Bum-Knee, for how shitty I always talked to him, tried throwing me a lifeline. I remember. 'You never were invited,' he told me. 'Only you just gave Hal an excuse to say so. The truth ain't gonna get any clearer. Quit makin' an ass outa yourself.'"

Taking in a long breath, Tim springs forward, propelling himself under the water, swimming hard against the current. He flips over on his back and lets the water carry him back to the campground.

"What if I'd listened to Bum-Knee that day? What if I went for the love instead of instead of always going for— How did I end up here, alone? My own mother slamming the door in my face. How?" He pictures Mary Frances McDonald stranded on the corner on the night her brother had forgotten to pick her up after the dance. "What if she was someone a boy loves, not something he gets? What if—" Hoisting himself out of the river, he sits on the muddy bank and pulls his knees up to his chin. He stares dumbly at the life across the water.

CPSIA information can be obtained at www.ICGtesting.com
Printed in the USA
LVOW091211271111

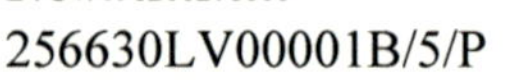

256630LV00001B/5/P

9 780987 756510